Cheyne Curry

THE TROPIC

HUNTER

Bossy Pants Books

*This is or Brenda, who came into my life because of this story
...and stayed.*

ALSO WRITTEN BY CHEYNE CURRY AND
COMING SOON FROM BOSSY PANTS BOOKS:

Clandestine
Renegade
Permission To Recover

THE TROPIC  HUNTER

By:

Cheyne Curry

Bossy Pants Books

This is a work of fiction. All characters, locales and events are either products of the author's imagination or are used fictitiously.

THE TROPIC OF HUNTER

Cover design by Ann Phillips
Back Cover design by Karen D. Badger

A Bossy Pants Book
Published by Bossy Pants Books
Columbus, Ohio 43229
bossypantsbooks@gmail.com

ISBN-10: 1-945124-01-6
ISBN-13: 978-1-945124-01-3

First Edition, April, 2016

Printed in the United States of America and in the United Kingdom

ACKNOWLEDGMENTS

A huge thank you to Karen D. Badger and Badger Bliss Books

http://karendbadger.wix.com/badgerblissbooks

To Day Peterson for keeping me on track.
To Nann Dunn for being Nann.
To Renae Hunt, for just being.
To The Raven, for starting it all.
To Marie Logan for her patience and friendship
To my mom, just because.

Chapter 1

My mother is gone.

The mantra resounded over and over in my mind as I tolerated the flight from Los Angeles to Chicago. Mechanically, I went through the motions of changing planes in O'Hare for my final destination of Albany, New York.

We had taken off late from LAX, which naturally delayed our landing and reduced the time I had to make it from Point A to Point B. To make matters worse, my connecting flight was at the opposite end of Terminal 3 from the gate where my Delta Boeing 737-800 was taxiing in. Typically, with only thirty minutes to traverse a concourse, I would be swearing up a storm and running like a wide receiver going for the touchdown. This time, I didn't even curse. I just didn't care. If I made it, I made it; if I didn't, I didn't.

My mother was gone. There was no hurry for me to get home.

Home. I had lived away from Otter Falls, Vermont, for sixteen years, returning only once for my Uncle David's funeral, and yet I still called it home. I had lost track of all my old friends, declined the invitation to attend my tenth high school reunion, corresponded only fleetingly with my brothers and other relatives, and I hadn't spoken to my mother in any of those sixteen years. I wouldn't have come back now if she hadn't, for some as yet unknown reason, left me her house, despite having disowned me when I was eighteen.

My mother and I were not friends. We'd had a stormy relationship ever since I was a little girl, butting heads on everything from what I wore to how I styled my hair to, well, pretty much my entire existence. She wanted a dainty, frilly, petite little girl that she could raise to be the perfect lady, the perfect wife, the perfect mother. What she got was a headstrong, rough-and-tumble tomboy who defied her at every turn. It wasn't that I didn't love or respect my mother; it was just that she was always trying to make me into something that I wasn't.

Of her three children, I was the only daughter, and maybe that contributed to our contentious relationship. My two brothers, one older and one younger, couldn't do anything wrong, while I couldn't do anything right. I became resentful and rebellious, and although I never got into any real trouble, I was the epitome of the word "handful."

I decided very early on that the reason my mother was on my case all the time was that I was just like my father, a man she both loved and hated. With their shorter stature, darker skin, and curly black hair, both my brothers took after her side of the family, while I favored my paternal side. I had his silky auburn locks, his fair complexion, his dashing grin, and what he called his "Dodger blue" eyes, which apparently revealed my every thought and emotion. I had his height and his natural athletic grace. I had also inherited his penchant for beautiful women, which was ultimately my undoing with my mother.

Despite her being overly morally conscientious, religious to a fault, and strict, my mother tolerated a lot from me. When I turned thirteen, after several weeks of retribution, she grudgingly forgave me for my refusal to continue going to Sunday worship services, even though I never told her why I didn't want to go anymore. I didn't have much use for a God who, according to the perpetual sermon, condemned me for being born a lesbian, something I knew I was at eleven years old. All my girl friends spoke excitedly about the cute boys in class; I felt the same way they did, only it was for an eighth-grader who just happened to also be female. I knew I was different, and I knew it wasn't a phase. I decided I'd be damned if I would go to a church and praise what appeared to me to be an awfully vindictive, almighty deity.

My brothers dutifully attended every week and stayed on her good side, both of them dating and, eventually, marrying girls they had met at church rather than at high school or through work. I, however, was deemed a lost cause. At some point in my young adulthood, Mom forgave me for dating boys who had no ambition other than to work on their cars and drink. It left me hating myself for feeling the need to date boys at all, but perpetuating the charade helped keep peace in the house.

She forgave me for participating in senior skip day, a lapse in judgment that got me and ninety-six other twelfth graders a week of detention, and she forgave me for nearly getting expelled from school for getting rip-roaring drunk as a result of eating a half dozen vodka-injected oranges at lunch. By fifth period Health class, my best friend, Lesley, and I had passed out at our desks. By seventh period, I was in the girls' room, heaving up what felt like the bottom of my feet and wondering whether I was ever going to live through the experience, all the while knowing that if I did, I might not survive what I was in for when I got home. That little incident got Lesley and me suspended for three days and assigned to detention for two weeks. It also got me grounded for a month and subjected to the silent treatment for almost as long, as well as unending references to me being just like my father... again, a comment which was never meant to convey any speck of pride.

She forgave me for being a "juvenile delinquent," forgave me for continuing to live up to being the black sheep of the family, and she had even started to forgive me for the ultimate sins of not being anything like her and never doing anything up to her standards. But when I was eighteen and she caught me in bed with the wife of the minister of the First Congregational Church, *that* was unforgivable in her eyes. She told me to leave her house that very night and never come back. It was probably the first time in my life that I didn't argue with her. I had never before seen that particular look in her eyes or heard that tone in her voice, and I knew there would be no debating the gravity of this sin. I had finally crossed a line she wouldn't forgive.

Cut loose from my moorings, I went to stay with my father's brother, David, and his family until I saved enough money to leave town, panic-stricken that it would get around that I was gay. I wasn't ashamed of who I was, but I felt being a lesbian in a homogeneous place like Otter Falls would not exactly be conducive to my living a life where I wasn't under a microscope and constantly apologizing for who and what I was.

When I did leave two months later, with twelve hundred dollars in my pocket, it was by Greyhound Bus, which took me across country in four days. Looking back on it now, I'm still amazed I made it through that experience unscathed. I was fortunate enough to immediately find a room to rent and a job tending bar. Although I wasn't legally old enough to drink, I looked and acted twenty-one, and the owner decided to take a chance and overlook my age. After we got to know one another better, he told me that he felt my looks would bring in the male customers, and profit was what it was all about. Ironically, I worked there until I *was* twenty-one and then moved on to something where I felt I could make a career.

I thought maybe my mother would cool off after a year or so had passed, but my attempts to contact her were ignored. One year became three, then three became five, and before I knew it, nine years had passed. When my Uncle David died, I returned to Vermont to pay my respects. Since my mother hadn't attended the services, I went to try to see her while I was in town, but she pretended not to be home. My attempts to contact her by phone also proved fruitless. She had made her decision. I had shown her the ultimate defiance, an unparalleled betrayal; I was as good as dead to her. After that visit, I stopped trying.

And now she was gone.

I got the call from my older brother, Sam, who, even after a decade and a half, never knew what the rift was about. Neither my mother nor I spoke of it to the family, which left friends, neighbors, and nosy strangers frustratingly ignorant of the reason for the irreparable abyss between us. When he said those words, "Hunter, Mom died this morning," I didn't cry; I didn't even react. My tears over losing her had been shed long ago; I had none left.

My mother was gone and so, it seemed, was any chance of ever making things right between us.

I hated flying. Hated it. It had nothing to do with September 11th or the threat of possible terrorism, although that was

4

always in the back of my mind; I hated flying long before any of that. The idea of being several miles above ground with nothing holding me up never set well. You can explain aerodynamics to me until you're blue in the face, and I still will never understand how that monstrous hunk of tin can stay so high in the air for so long. The thought that, at any second, the plane could fall out of the sky for any number of technical reasons and slam into the earth like a lawn dart never quite convinced me that flying was the safest mode of transportation.

When I would express anxiety over an upcoming flight, someone would inevitably say, "When your time's up, it's up." I never liked that saying because what if the pilot's time was up? Why should I have to suffer the consequences of his or her bad luck?

Actually, by the time I was up in the air, I was generally okay. I knew at that point there wasn't a damned thing I could do if anything did happen, so I would try to relax and "enjoy" the flight.

If I concentrated on something other than being crammed in a cigar-shaped tube with about one hundred and seventy other people, forty thousand feet in the air, shooting through the sky at five hundred miles per hour, flying was actually bearable.

Unless I was seated next to someone who wouldn't shut up, regardless of how many polite signals I sent out that I'd rather be left alone. I had brought a word puzzle book to keep me occupied and was halfway through a cryptogram when the young man seated to my left introduced himself as Robert and asked me if he could buy me a drink. I had to blink a few times. I'd never had anyone try to pick me up on an airplane. Talk about a captive audience... I looked up to see a particularly attractive woman moving our way, pushing the refreshment cart. I was torn between telling him that he was definitely barking up the wrong tree and that I'd arm wrestle him for the flight attendant, or if he was going to annoy me the entire flight, he could buy out her cache of Budweiser because I would need it.

Just then the airplane started to rumble and shake, and the seatbelt sign lit up. To a seasoned traveler, it was a minor bump in the air current, but to me, any turbulence was an indication of impending doom. I conjured up memories of movies where planes exploded or broke in half, and unsecured passengers were sucked out every hole and crack in the fuselage. Since I didn't hear any further loud noises and nothing that felt like a vacuum was siphoning me in any direction, I opened my eyes and looked around.

No one seemed fazed. In fact, quite a few of the passengers in my field of vision hadn't even bothered to strap in. I never take my seatbelt off while flying anyway, which, in my mind, would give me an advantage over the unbelted passengers should any of the above mentioned scenarios occur. Inwardly, I had reconciled my struggle but outwardly, the color draining from my face must have caught the attention of the older, grandfatherly gentleman seated to my right.

"Don't like flying much, do you?" he asked, his tone and demeanor quite paternal and calm.

"What gave me away?" I gritted out, managing a stiff smile for him as we hit another air pocket.

"You're trying to make permanent handle-grips out of the armrests," he said, and nodded toward my knuckles, which were undeniably white.

"You know, I should enjoy it." I closed my eyes as the plane felt as if it were bucking. "My mother always told me that being on an airplane was the closest to heaven I was ever going to get." We lurched again, then dropped a few hundred feet, leaving my stomach somewhere up near the overhead luggage bin.

He patted my wrist. "Nothing to worry about."

I was just about to ease my death grasp when we shuddered through another large disturbance. The captain's voice came through the tinny speakers, reminding us that he had turned the seatbelt sign on as they'd hit a little "rough air." Rough air, my ass.

Each little vibration sent my life flashing before my eyes.

The flight attendant finally reached our row with the drink cart.

Screw the beer; I asked her for a whiskey and water. But

what I really wanted was for her to crawl into my lap and comfort me. Had I not been slightly terrified, I would have paid more attention and reacted much differently to the subtle touch and flirty little wink when she handed me my drink. Of course, she could just have been feeling sorry for me, as I am sure I looked pathetically vulnerable and unusually small with my nearly six-foot frame folded into that little seat.

Either the flight had returned to being smooth, or after my second whiskey—where I bypassed the water and downed the little bottle of Jack like a shot—I just didn't care anymore. When Robert apparently saw I was a little more relaxed, he regained the use of his voice. Unfortunately.

"You know what Delta stands for, don't you?" he asked from my left. Before I had a chance to answer, he said, "Don't. Even. Leave. The. Airport."

I smiled politely as he repeated it, laughed, and emphasized the acronym by poking his finger in the air to punctuate each word. I was about to tell him I had heard that one before, but it didn't matter. Honestly, any Delta flight I had taken in the past had always been without incident, but I wasn't about to tell him that, either.

"So what's in Albany for you?" he asked.

"A funeral." I knew he was fishing, and I wasn't about to tell him that Albany wasn't my final destination. For some reason, men didn't want to believe that I had no interest in being with them.

First, I would get the "what— you think you're too good for me?" attitude, and then, if I was blunt about my orientation, I would get the cliché, "Obviously you haven't been with the right man yet."

Somehow I knew Robert would not disappoint me if I told him "thanks but no thanks" and why. The fact that I would never see this man again after we landed in Albany prompted me to not reveal any more about myself than necessary.

"Who died?"

"My mother."

"Oh. I'm sorry."

He clearly felt quite awkward, not knowing what else to

say, and I took that opportunity to bury my nose back in my puzzle book. Robert was silent for the rest of the flight.

On our descent into Albany, the plane once again rattled and shook as we cut through clouds. Looking out the window to my right, I grimaced. Flying in clouds always made me nervous, too, because there was no visibility. We were getting ready to land, getting closer to the ground with every second. I wanted the pilots to be able to *see* the airport, *see* the runway, *see* if there were any other planes in our vicinity, and *see* just how close the ground was.

"So, Ms. Legs-That-Start-At-Her-Shoulders, how tall are you, anyway?" The man to my right with the kind eyes was trying to distract me from thinking about what the plane was doing.

"Five-foot-twelve," I answered. It was my standard reply, as it somehow made people feel less intimidated than my saying six feet.

I was, in reality, a hair under the six-foot mark, but not enough below it to truthfully claim five-eleven. By the time I was sixteen, I was only two inches shorter than I am now. Thankfully, I was good at basketball, because I was the team's center whether I wanted to be or not.

"That must keep some men at bay."

"You have no idea." The plane shook hard as we slipped below the cloud cover and then smoothed out as land, trees, houses, and roads came into view. I heard and felt the wheels being lowered, and I couldn't wait to get on solid ground.

"Do you know how to tell who lands the plane?"

I looked at him quizzically. "I certainly hope the pilot lands the plane."

"Not always. Sometimes the copilot does."

This piqued my interest. "Okay... how can you tell?"

"When we land, if you feel the right wheel touch the ground first, the copilot is at the controls, if the left wheel touches first, the pilot's landing the plane."

I found that utterly fascinating, as I never really paid attention and thought both wheels hit the ground at the same time. When I knew that we were about to connect with Mother

Earth again, I focused intently and felt the right wheel touch the ground a half-second before the left one did. I looked up at my seat companion, feeling like a little kid in school about to raise her hand with the correct answer. "The copilot, right?"

He nodded, laughing at my enthusiasm. Of course, I had no idea if it was true, but the concept enthralled me. I wouldn't have minded talking to him instead of Robert during the flight, as he didn't appear to be after anything other than pleasant conversation.

As we taxied up to the terminal, I felt as though I had somehow lost out on something important by not getting acquainted with this distinguished-looking gentleman.

As I disembarked the plane, my drink-serving flight attendant said goodbye to me with another smile and wink that under different circumstances would have caused me to wait around inside for her.

But it was after five o'clock in the afternoon, and I still had a two-hour drive ahead of me—fifty miles of it on a two-lane country highway. So I didn't try to get her phone number, just collected my luggage and went to get my rental car.

I wasn't exactly sure what awaited me when I got to Otter Falls, but I did know that my life would never be the same again.

Chapter 2

The sun was beginning to set as I drove through the outskirts of Otter Falls. The "Welcome To" sign proclaimed that the population was now a little over seventeen thousand. Since the town had always seemed so resistant to change, the small city had grown more than I'd ever expected it to. The need to boost the economy must have overcome the desire to stay quaint, I thought, as I passed a Super Wal-Mart, three chain drugstores in a row, a Home Depot, and several fast food restaurants that were now situated on the main drag leading into downtown.

Before I found myself in a snarl of traffic, if downtown was anything like I remembered it at dinnertime on a week night, I pulled over and called Sam to get directions to his new house. Otter Falls hadn't changed so much that I couldn't have remembered how to get to his old address, but he was now living in a recently built housing development on the north side of town, and I was too anxious to be at the end of my journey to try to find it on my own.

My rental didn't have a built-in navigator, and GPS was not an application I wanted to pay to upload onto my phone.

I really would have preferred to stop somewhere for a beer or two and relax a little before facing the family. It was a persistent temptation, as there appeared to be some kind of bar or eating establishment that also served alcohol on every corner. Some things never changed.

Regardless of the businesses that had cropped up over the last decade, the newer establishments had evidently not deterred the average townsfolk from their favorite pastime of drinking. There was really nothing much else to do here unless you skied, which a majority of the citizens of Otter Falls didn't. They couldn't stand the attitude and crush of flatlanders, who swept into the resorts at the first sign of snow, taking over the mountain. The locals preferred to stay away from the ski lodges and bars that littered the access road.

They kept the city taverns in business by patronizing them instead.

Frequently. Otter Falls once made the record books for having more bars per capita than any city in the USA, and there was a reason for that.

I decided to wait until I got to Sam's to have a beer. Unless he had changed completely, I knew he would at least have a six-pack of something on hand. I smiled at thinking about my older brother because, despite his grief over losing Mom, he sounded excited that I was finally coming back. When I spoke with him, I felt the familiar warmth I always used to feel around Sam when we were growing up.

My older brother was a good guy. All those years ago, he had recognized that my being forced to live in his shadow and suffer from unfair comparisons was not the fault of either of us. It wasn't because he was so perfect and I was so imperfect, it was that he followed all the rules and did everything that was expected of him, and I did not. Sam knew that regardless of how hard I tried to please my mother, it was never good enough, and I finally just gave up trying. Every time Mom and I had a fight and I got sent to my room, Sam always tried to console me, even if he never actually spoke up and said anything to her about her blatant bias. I understood the position he was in, and even though I'm sure his punishment for rebuking her wouldn't have been very severe, our mother had a volcanic temper. Deliberately provoking her wrath wasn't wise, as I was sure he learned from my example.

My other brother, Dane, was a different story altogether. He was three years younger than I and spoiled rotten, well, as spoiled as my mother would allow. Dane was sneaky and conniving and calculated his moves wisely. He was smart enough to never go after Sam because he knew Sam was the golden boy, but he had no problem taking advantage of our mother's dislike for me, and he set me up every chance he got. He was always successful at making himself look good by making me look bad. He contributed to my life at home being a living hell, something in which he seemed to take great joy and pride.

The only time I ever got even with him was when I tied him up, gagged him, and shaved all those curly locks off his head before his freshman dance with his dream girl. As vain as he was about his appearance, especially about his hair, it made the statement I had intended, even if he did go whining to Mother afterwards. It was worth it. By that time I was seventeen and had a part-time job after school and on the weekends, so grounding me didn't have the impact it had in the past.

From what I understood, Dane hadn't changed much. He was still behaving like a pampered child, only now he was doing it in adult situations. I didn't often contact my younger brother via phone calls or emails. We weren't close, and any communication between us usually ended on a sour note. I really think the only reason he got in touch with me at all was to see if he could weasel out of me why Mom and I hadn't spoken to each other since my hasty departure.

Sam had advised me that Dane was less than thrilled that Mom's house hadn't been left to him, and that I should expect trouble from him. I didn't say anything to Sam, but the house had no sentimental value for me; it held a lot of bad memories, and although I could have used the money from the sale, I didn't really want the hassle. I lived too far away to deal with the legalities and the time it would take to get rid of it. If Dane really wanted it, I wasn't above signing it over to him.

The three of us grew up being called by our middle names.

Sam was born Gregory Samuel Roberge, Jr., named, of course, after my father. Two Gregs around the house was confusing, so he became Sam, which was my grandfather's first name. I was named Sarah Hunter, Sarah also being my mother's name. So again to avoid confusion, I was called Hunter, which was my mother's maiden name. Three years after me, Jonathan Dane came along. He was named Jonathan after my maternal grandfather, and Dane because my mother loved *The Thorn*

Birds.

My father was a roguish man, loaded with charm he knew how to use. When he met my mother, an absolutely stunning woman who was being pursued by a number of his friends, he knew he had to be the one to get her. He swept her off her feet, seducing her with lies and promises he never intended to keep. My mother was one of the rare few women who actually was saving herself for her wedding night, and I think if she hadn't been, there never would have been a marriage. The only way my father could get her into bed was to marry her. So he did.

In his defense, he tried to behave as a husband should, and according to my Uncle David, my father remained faithful until after I was born. I guess three years was the longest he'd ever been with only one person, and he couldn't stand it any longer. He started cheating shortly after I was brought home from the hospital. My mother became aware of it when one of his many conquests called the house in a fit of rage, complaining that he had dumped her for the next pretty face. Angry, hurt, and mortified, my mother threatened my father with divorce, and it surprised me that he didn't jump at the chance, as it would have meant his freedom. Instead he apologized profusely, swore he would never do it again, and pretended to honor his marriage vows while he continued to sleep around.

After Dane was born, my mother found detailed love letters hidden in a box in the garage. They had been written by three different women. That day, my father came home to find all of his belongings scattered on the front lawn. I remember it like it was yesterday. I had just turned six.

"Daddy, where are you going?" My cry was desperate. I knew he wasn't just leaving for work or going on one of his "trips." This was different. This felt final.

"I have to go away, sweet pea," he said, as he gathered his clothes. He carried them to the car, a bundle at a time. He had filled the trunk and was now tossing things onto the backseat.

"Why?" I bawled as I followed him back and forth like a loyal puppy. "Daddy, don't go! Don't go! Please!" My voice rose with each word until I was screaming.

"Sarah Hunter, you get back up on this porch or I'm going to tan your behind!" My mother's shrill voice cracked like a switch across bare legs, but its sting wasn't enough to prevent me from being with my father. She was holding Dane, and Sam clung to her apron. I ignored her.

Neighbors came out of their houses to watch the spectacle. My mother hissed at me to get in the house, her volume much lower but her tone more threatening. I didn't care. I couldn't let my father leave. I adored him. When he was around, he was fun, and he never yelled at me.

"No, thank you!" I said to my mother. "No" was a word I used often, but I would get punished if I said it without an accompanying "thank you."

"Hunter, you have to do what your mother says," Daddy told me gently. He knelt down, his hands covering my shoulders. "You know you'll be in a lot of trouble if you don't."

"I don't care, Daddy. She can't make you leave." I was whimpering, defeated.

"Yes, she can." This echoed the words swirling around in my head, words I knew to be true. And then he said words I didn't believe. "It's for the best, sweetie."

"Greg, you take your hands off that child or I will call the police, I swear to God," my mother said through clenched teeth.

He sighed and bowed his head. He stood, picked up his last few possessions, threw them in the car, and slammed the passenger door shut.

He held his arms out and beckoned me to him. "C'mere, sweet pea, and give Daddy a big hug."

Looking at my mother, who was forcefully shaking her head at me, I stood there, crying and chewing at my fingers; then I looked at my father and ran to him. He swept me up in his arms, and I hugged him with all my might, never wanting to let go. I was sobbing.

"Hunter, sweetie, you're choking me," he said, his voice raspy.

I kept crying and holding on. He pried my grip loose and kissed my cheek. "Shhh, it's okay. Daddy will see you soon. You better get back to Mommy before you get in any more trouble."

"I love you, Daddy."

"I love you, too, sweet pea." He put me down. "Now go back to Mommy like a good girl."

I stood still, stubbornly not wanting to obey him. When he took a step back, I wrapped my arms around his leg. "Please stay, Daddy."

"Don't make this any harder, sweetie." His voice broke. He rested his hand on my head. "Daddy's got to go. You have to go back to Mommy now. Mommy's going to need you to..."

"No! Mommy doesn't need me!"

I was wrong. My mother needed me to obey her. "Hunter! Get on this porch now! One..."

My father and I locked stares. We both knew what would happen if my mother got to "three."

"Two..."

He nodded toward the porch. Just when I heard my mother take a breath to continue her count, I ran back to the porch, wailing. As I climbed the steps, I saw my mother raise her hand.

"Don't you hit her, Sarah," I heard my father say. "Don't you dare take your anger at me out on her." His voice was commanding, and she responded to it. Her arm fell to her side. "I would like to say goodbye to my sons before I leave."

"Say it from there." Her tone was cold.

"For God's sake, I can't hug them from here!"

"Don't you dare invoke God's name, Greg. You have no right!" Just then she seemed to remember the neighbors were watching. "Children, say goodbye to your father."

I couldn't speak because I was weeping uncontrollably. Sam hid his face in our mother's apron. Dane waved enthusiastically, too young to understand any of it. "Bye bye, Da da."

My father shook his head, got in the car, and left. His blue Chevy disappearing around the corner was forever burned in my memory.

She never spoke to him again. Through his attorney, he agreed to all the conditions of the divorce. On the rare occasion she would allow us to spend the weekend with him, we would meet him out by his car. When I was thirteen, he just stopped showing up. Uncle David told us later that Dad had met a young woman, moved to Florida with her, and had two more children. My brothers and I got a Christmas card from him once. I was fifteen. It was the last time I heard from him.

When Uncle David died suddenly of a heart attack seven years ago, Dad acknowledged his brother's death with an impersonal, generic sympathy card. We all expected my father to show up at the funeral, but he didn't. I was actually disappointed, as I was torn between not wanting to see him and wanting to see him so I could tear into him for being the selfish prick he'd turned out to be. I was firmly convinced that if he had been the faithful husband my mother expected him to be when she married him, my life might have been a little easier. Every time she looked at me, she saw him, and so I reminded her of what she might have had and never did.

I pulled my car into the driveway of an impressive ranch house with a huge, well-manicured lawn. Even though the sun had set and it was dark, the track lighting strategically placed at the walkway and other dominant areas admirably illuminated the landscaping.

There were four other cars parked in front of mine, and I wondered who they belonged to, thinking Sam was lucky to have a long, wide driveway that could hold them all without having the butt end of any sticking out into the road.

I walked to the screened door, knocked twice, and entered. The sound of the voices led me up a small flight of five stairs, and I found myself in an archway in a living room full of people. I recognized the back of Sam's head and reached between two people to poke him. Turning, he pulled me into an embrace and his eyes immediately welled up.

"Hunter."

As I hugged him fiercely, I heard a few muted gasps and all conversation stopped. When my brother released me and we both looked around the living room, all eyes were on us.

"Oh, my God. Hunter." Sam's wife, Trina, took two steps

toward me and enfolded me in her long arms. She had put on a few pounds since the last time I had seen her, and the extra weight looked wonderful on her. She was way too skinny before. "How dare you get more gorgeous than the last time we saw you?"

I believe I was actually blushing. Before I had a chance to respond, I heard the unmistakable, sniveling voice of my younger brother.

"Well, if it isn't the prodigal daughter, returning home to collect her... spoils."

I let go of my sister-in-law and forced a smile as I gave Dane a blatant once-over. He had a glass in his hand, containing what I could only guess was some kind of alcohol. His expression was disdainful, his tone of voice was downright snotty, and his words were slightly slurred.

"Well, well, well, if it isn't my baby brother. You haven't changed. Except..." I deliberately focused on the top of his head.

"Hair's looking a little sparse there. Guess that doesn't want to stay around you any longer than anything else."

She shoots; she scores!

His expression of surprise and frustration indicated that I had landed a direct hit with my first attempt. Did he think sixteen years away from him would provoke amnesia about his sensitivity toward his hair? He was always obsessive about the length, the style, the texture. He constantly checked in the mirror to make sure his hairline wasn't receding or thinning. When I saw him at Uncle David's funeral, he was wearing his hair shorter than I'd ever seen it, but it was also as thick as it had always been. Even now, he had a gorgeous head of hair, but I wasn't about to let him know that.

A preemptive strike was always a good way to start off with him. The ground rules had to be established immediately, and I needed Dane to know that I was neither impressed by his status in the community, nor intimidated by his favored place at our mother's side. A few snickers came from around the room, and Dane's hand immediately went to his head to smooth out his perfectly coiffed style. His eyebrows slanted downward, forming a V, his expression wounded but indignant.

"Well... it's obvious you haven't changed." He brought the glass to his lips and took a big swallow. "You don't belong here, Hunter."

"I'm not here by choice."

"Of course you are. You could easily have chosen to stay in California and complete any of your business through your attorney."

"I don't have an attorney on retainer, Dane. *I* don't need one."

A smirk curled my lips, knowing I'd managed another direct hit, one he most definitely would not dispute in front of an audience.

According to Sam's last report, Dane had been pulled over for DUI on at least three separate occasions just in the past year, and it was only through a well-connected lawyer that he had managed to keep it hushed up and out of the local paper. I had further discovered through other sources that my baby brother was a homophobic elitist who had won a local alderman seat through a very dirty campaign against an openly gay opponent. He preyed on the fears of the town that civil unions and same-sex marriage would be the downfall of western civilization as we knew it, positing that the man he was running against would only further the "homosexual agenda" in the community.

But the real clincher was when he dredged up a supposedly expunged record of his opponent having been arrested for drunk driving at the age of twenty-two. Dane told his adoring public,

"How can we trust his judgment making town council decisions, when he can't even judge when it's too dangerous to get behind the wheel of a car?"

Yes, my little brother was a hypocritical bastard. But then, in my experience, most homophobes were. The fact that he was a politician on top of it only added to his "appeal."

"Okay, that's enough," Trina said good-naturedly. "Time to retreat to your neutral corners." She hooked her arm through mine and addressed the other people gathered in the living room. "For those of you who don't know, this is Sam and Dane's sister, Hunter."

I was then introduced, or reintroduced, to the twelve other people in the room. Eleven of them I had never met before, and that included Dane's disagreeable-looking third wife, Emma. She didn't seem to appreciate it when we shook hands and I offered my sincerest condolences for her being married to my brother.

The one person I did know was someone I would have rather not seen, at least not until I had been in town longer than five minutes. Phil Khaury had taken me to my senior prom. I hadn't wanted to go but got talked into it. My friend Lesley wanted us to share the prom experience, and she convinced me that it would be fun. And it was. Until I got so trashed that I almost let Phil fuck me in the backseat of his car that night. Fortunately, I came to my senses, because if I hadn't put on the brakes, I would have had an evening for which I never would have forgiven myself. Phil had been difficult to cool down at first and got a little aggressive but nothing a knee to the groin didn't take care of.

We didn't exactly part friends that night, and I ended up walking the two miles home in low heels and a floor-length, off-the-shoulder, satin gown, swearing and cursing every step of the way. It was one of the rare times I actually got into a dress, and truth be told, I enjoyed it. It was the first time I realized that I could have a feminine side without betraying my sexuality.

When Phil looked at me, there were clearly several conversations going on behind his eyes, each one as apparent as if it were being broadcast in neon across his forehead like the ticker in Times Square. The first was the most obvious, hound that he still clearly was. His elevator eyes rose hungrily over my body, and when he finally pulled them out of my cleavage, he focused on my annoyed face. The next expression he wore revealed him recollecting the last time we had seen each other. I had ripped him a new asshole for spreading around town that he had nailed me on prom night.

That rumor got back to my mother, and regardless of how much I denied it, I still got grounded and had to listen to a tirade on moral character every night for two weeks. No amount of grief I gave Phil could ever make up for those fourteen unbearable days. If he had anything going for him at all, it was that at least he had told everyone that I was a phenomenal lay.

I crossed my arms. "Hello, Phil."

"God, Hunter, you look… great." He waited, expecting me to return the compliment. I gleefully disappointed him. I couldn't deny that he was a handsome man and that he wore his thirties well, looking more rugged and mature than he had a right to. But my assumption about him being a grownup went right out the window when he gave me that boyish grin, stuck his hands in his pockets and said, "So, are you here with anyone?"

I shook my head in disbelief, although I should not have been surprised. "I'm here in my brother's house, at a gathering that is paying respects to my dead mother, and you're trying to pick me up?"

He immediately looked embarrassed. Taking a step backward, he put his hands up in protest. "No, no, I wasn't, I… you took that wrong."

Why is it that when some people get caught saying or doing something inappropriate, instead of admitting it, apologizing, and moving on, they try to put the blame on their target by saying either "you took it wrong" or "I was only joking. Can't you take a joke?" I knew full well that if his veiled offer had been received positively, he would have taken the ball and run with it.

"Then what were you asking me, so that I can take it right?" I asked.

"Uh… is your husband with you?"

"I'm not married."

"Really?" His eyebrows shot up, and he didn't even try to hide his delight. "How long are you going to be in town?"

I rolled my eyes and walked away from him, shaking my head.

"What? What'd I say?" He actually sounded bewildered.

I joined my brother in the kitchen. "Sam, do you have any beer?" He opened up the refrigerator and handed me a Long Trail Blackbeary Wheat. I handed it back. "A *real* beer?"

He gave me a half-grin and looked in the back on the bottom shelf. "The only other kind I have is a Foster's Lager."

"I'll take it." I removed the cap and tossed it into the basket. I think I drank half the bottle before I set it down on the counter. "I'd love to catch up and get all the details of what I'm in for the next few days, but I think that will have to wait until everyone's gone home, and I'm not sure I can hang out that long."

"Pretty tired?"

"It's been a long day."

"Are you going to stay at the house?" he asked, referring to Mom's.

"I figured I would. I haven't made any other arrangements. That's if Dane doesn't have it booby-trapped." I took another drink from the bottle.

Sam smiled and leaned in close, lowering his voice. "Nothing that little fucker would do would surprise me."

I nearly snorted beer out my nose. Sam took the Foster's from me and pounded me on the back. I waved him away before he broke a rib.

"I'm sorry, did I offend you?" my dear brother asked, sincerely concerned.

"Yes. Watch your fucking mouth next time," I croaked.

Wide-eyed, Sam roared with relieved laughter, and pulled me into a hug. "God, I've missed you."

"I've missed you, too." Up until that point, I had no idea just how much.

He reached into a drawer and pulled out a set of keys, separated them, and held up one in particular. "This is the key to Mom's front door." He then designated the next four keys. "This is the back door key, the key to the door that leads to the garage, the garage door key, and the key to the Wrangler in the garage." He had a distinct twinkle in his eye.

"Wrangler? Are you telling me Mom drove a Jeep, or is there a cowboy in the garage?"

"Mom had a sedan, which is out of commission because it needs a new transmission. The Jeep is Eric's. We're keeping it there while he's at the academy." Eric was his stepson who was away at a military college. Five years older than Sam, Trina had been a widow when they met. They hadn't had any children together, and my brother raised Eric as his own son.

"Where is Eric? Is he coming home for the funeral?"

"No, he can't get away. I told him not to sweat it. Mom knew he loved her. His coming back for the funeral when it's a hassle isn't necessary."

"He won't mind if I drive his car while I'm here?"

"It's just sitting in the garage because he's not allowed to have a car at school his first year. It actually needs to be driven. Hey, we bought him that car, and I'm paying the insurance. And what he doesn't know won't hurt him. Just don't wreck it." He handed me the set of keys. "Oh, by the way, you've also inherited Orion."

I stared at him, blinking his words into comprehension. "Are you kidding me? Really? Orion? Really?"

"Really."

"That cat hates me." I couldn't believe that tough old feline with the attitude of a pit bull on crack was still alive. It must have been the pure nastiness flowing through her veins that kept her going. She was a year old when I was kicked out, and I still had scars from that little bitch attacking me. I also woke up to many unwelcome crawling or slithering "gifts" she had brought inside and dropped in my bed. I swear if she wasn't trying to kill me with a blood infection, she was trying to give me a heart attack. I was sure she would have only become more cunning and ornery in her older years. "Of course Mom left her to me. It makes perfect sense."

Sarcasm saturated my tone. "That's probably why Mom left me the house... so the *Nightmare on Elm Street* cat could finish me off."

When I left Sam's, I decided to go to a bar rather than going directly to the house.

Chapter 3

Despite how progressive Otter Falls had become, there were still no gay bars in town. I knew this because I had checked online before I left Los Angeles. I was disappointed for two reasons, the first being that it would have been nice to be able to have a beer or two in an establishment where I could relax and be myself. The second reason was that I would have loved to see who frequented the bar and whether I recognized them. There were a few people in high school I had no doubt I would have run into there. All male, of course, but it would have been interesting to see whether I had guessed correctly.

Instead, I drove directly into downtown, passing by a few watering holes I had sneaked into when I was a high school senior.

They weren't the classiest joints; the drafts had been watery, and they still looked like dives and even more run-down than I remembered. I decided to bypass them and look for something a little more palatable.

There used to be a running joke: "What do you say to compliment someone from Otter Falls?" and the response was, "Hey, nice tooth." That never seemed truer than for those I saw hanging outside the Main Street Saloon, a bar that used to have an "interesting" atmosphere even sixteen years ago. If the size of the doorman was any indication, "interesting" had turned into "menacing." No doubt I would have recognized a few people in that place, too.

Driving past the First Congregational Church, I felt an unsettling mixture of affection and betrayal. Although it was the coup de grâce to my already fragile relationship with my mother, I could still recall every moment of the day the minister's wife had seduced me.

I had always wondered why my brothers had nicknamed the minister's wife "Mrs. Vixen" until the day she walked into the pizza place where I worked, looking for me. My three male co-workers, all under the age of eighteen, fell all over each other hurrying to wait on her. It was like a scene right out of *Who Framed Roger Rabbit,* with their eyes lust-filled and bulging and their tongues down to the floor. I almost expected to hear horns, bells, and whistles. However, when she asked specifically for me, everything about them went limp, and I'm pretty sure I do mean everything.

I didn't know who she was, but I was definitely intrigued by the sexy vision seated at Table Six, wondering what she could possibly want with me. I wiped my hands on my stained waist apron and approached her, my teenage hormones working overtime. I stood awkwardly at the edge of the table as her incredible light brown eyes started at my boots and slowly, appreciatively, traversed the length of my body until our eyes finally met. I swallowed hard, flustered by her bold, open appraisal, and my brain turned to oatmeal. I finally was able to say, "You wanted to see me?" I knew it had to be wishful thinking that this woman was a lesbian and was going to proposition me, hopefully with something indecent.

"My, you are a tall one."

Her voice was like silk, smooth and refined, and she smiled at me. It was that smile that told me something was going to happen between me and whoever this woman was. Not having had any experience beyond some kissing and fumbling with a girl from a rival basketball team, I don't know how I knew; it was something I just instinctively felt.

"Please sit." She gestured across the table with a well-manicured, short-nailed hand.

"I don't get off for another forty-five minutes." I had no clue how prophetic that statement was. "Can you tell me what this is about?" I studied her intently, as intently as one could when one's lower regions were unexpectedly detonating, making it extremely difficult to focus on anything other than, well, one's lower regions.

She had streaked blonde hair worn in a shoulder-length style that was very becoming. It framed her face in a way that accentuated her slender nose, cheekbones, and full, sensuous lips.

Although I had fantasized about being with a woman, I was still a virgin, and could only imagine what that mouth would feel like on my body. She licked her bottom lip slowly, deliberately, and I had a sudden sense of panic as I wondered whether she could read my x-rated thoughts. My eyes fell to her ample cleavage, unabashedly revealed in a purple tank top covered by a lavender blouse with four buttons undone from the top. When my brain engaged again and I realized I was ogling her breasts, I snapped my attention back to her face, which had absorbed my gawking with a knowing smirk. She extended her hand.

"I'm Jennifer Visson. I was sent here to chat with you."

"Visson?" Then it hit me. "The preacher's wife?" She nodded.

Any and all fantasies should have gone right down the drain, yet that insistent feeling that we were destined to be intimate kept jabbing me in the libido. "Why do you want to chat with me? Who sent you?" I know I must have looked confused, because I was confused.

"Your mother asked me to come and talk you into coming back to church. Your mother met with my husband regarding what she refers to as your 'rebellious behavior' in general and your 'sacrilegious attitude' toward the church in particular. She said you seemed to bond more closely with women and suggested that maybe I could arrange to speak with you."

"Why you and not Reverend Visson?"

"Your mother was unyielding. She said that you would blow him off immediately, regardless of how charming my husband can be."

I blinked at her, torn between being pissed at my mother's unrealistic persistence and thinking that if I got to see Mrs. Visson at least once a week, I might be lured back to church by something other than her husband's sermons. I excused myself to speak to my boss about ending my shift early. Customers had been sparse, and he knew the woman I was talking to had religious business, so he told me to punch out. I did, quickly checking my flour-dusted reflection in the employee room mirror and returning to the table.

I sat opposite her. "I don't want to be disrespectful, Mrs. Vix—

Visson."

Fuck. I couldn't believe I almost called her that. I was mortified. I refused to look at her, in case she was aware of the nickname and it embarrassed her. Then I felt her fingers curl around my wrist, prompting me to glance up at her.

She smiled warmly and said, "Please call me Jennifer." She didn't let go of my wrist.

"Jennifer," I repeated hoarsely. I was so turned on, I actually thought I was going to leave a wet spot on the chair. "I don't know what your husband preaches, but Reverend Riffey preached hate and intolerance. And he, his family, and his flock were all a bunch of hypocrites. The congregation talked horribly about him through the week, then kissed his ass on Sunday, agreeing with every destructive and hateful thing that man said, ready to do his dirty work and further his agenda, whether they agreed with him or not. That's why I stopped going to church. I wasn't interested in being one of the little rats that Pied Piper led around."

She rubbed her thumb over the inside of my wrist. It drove me crazy.

"That certainly is a perfectly valid reason," she said. "My husband has entirely different values."

Her thumb stopped breezing over my wrist, but she increased the pressure of her grasp and I got lost in the beckoning in her eyes.

"As do I. Why don't we go somewhere and talk about bringing you back into the… fold. Maybe to your house?"

I barely remember leaving work and getting in her car. She clearly sensed my nervous anticipation and handled most of the conversation while she drove.

"I've been watching you for a while," Jennifer said. I was

going to give her directions, but I couldn't seem to form a full sentence, so it was a good thing she apparently knew the way. "I found out quite a bit about you."

"Why?" It came out as an asthmatic cheep, which made me sound like a thirteen-year-old boy going through puberty. Could this get any more embarrassing? I prayed the anxiety didn't suddenly thrust my glands into overdrive and turn me into a walking zit.

"I thought I could use the information to personalize how I might persuade you to rejoin the congregation," she said before I had the chance to repeat my performance as a dog's squeaky toy.

"From what your mother has told me and what I have personally observed about your interests, pastimes, and extracurricular activities at school, I'm going to be really direct and guess that you like girls better than you like boys."

"Boys are okay." I was pretty sure where this conversation was going, but on the off chance she was playing with my mind so that she could report everything back to my mother, I decided it would be best for her to make all the moves.

"Sure, boys are okay, but you'd rather date girls." She seemed to sense that I was hesitant to confirm her assessment. She smiled warmly as she reached over and caressed my thigh. I nearly choked on my own saliva. "I like girls, Hunter." I swear her voice dropped an octave and mine raised three.

"But... you're married. To the minister!"

Her hand wandered toward the button fly of my jeans. "I'm bisexual. I like my men, but I love my women."

"Does your husband know?"

"Yes." Her fingers danced lightly over my denim-covered crotch and began to press harder. With every fiber of my being, I knew it was wrong but I didn't want to stop. "He has his little hobbies, and I have mine." Her hand moved against the seam of my pants, rubbing me into an excitement I had never felt before, and my thighs automatically slammed together, trapping her fingers. I envisioned her touching me in a way I had only touched myself. She smiled again, suggestively. "My, aren't we eager?" She maneuvered her hand away from my need and returned it to the steering wheel.

"Are you a virgin, Hunter?"

"Me? No. I've, you know, been around"

"Really?" She didn't sound convinced. "That's too bad, because busting virgins is one of my favorite things."

"In that case, I lied." I was nothing if not accommodating.

"Seriously, I've never been with anyone, um, all the way."

"How far have you gone?"

"Just some kissing. Touching above the waist..." Fumbling, mostly, I should have said.

"Have you ever had an orgasm?"

"Well... yeah. Hasn't everybody?" I was torn between feeling awkward and being turned on. I wanted Jennifer Visson more than anything I could think of, but the conversation was uncomfortable. I wanted to stop talking about orgasms and get to having one that I wouldn't be giving myself.

"Here we are," Jennifer announced unnecessarily as she pulled into my driveway.

"We should probably go someplace else," I said hastily, before Jennifer could turn off the ignition. "My mom could come home, and we'd both be in a world of hurt."

"No, this is perfect. Your mother's helping out at the church. She'll be busy for the next couple of hours. Your older brother will be at work until nine, and your younger brother has debate team tonight. Afterwards, he'll meet your mother at church and they'll drive home together. And your neighbors can tell your mother that I brought you home and went into your house. She will assume I counseled you, just like she asked me to."

"Not exactly like my mom had in mind," I muttered, mostly to myself. I removed my seatbelt. "You really did your homework."

"So what do you say we get right to your counseling?"

We barely made it through the door before she started kissing me. I had about four inches on her in height, so despite her being the aggressor, I felt I was in the dominant position. I had no idea what to do with my hands, and they did a spastic dance at my sides and then behind her head before she finally grabbed one and placed it on her waist. My other hand found a resting place in her hair. My faculties chose that moment to return, and the art of making out started feeling somewhat inherent again. When she broke the kiss, I thought I was going to need oxygen, the sensation had been so sexual. I came back at her like an uncivilized Pepe LePew, and she stopped me and requested that I take a quick shower. She had a point. I smelled like a pepperoni pizza. It could have been worse; I could have smelled like anchovies.

I took the stairs two at a time and hit that stall faster than I'd ever done before, scrubbing only the most important parts. When I returned to my room to comb my hair, Jennifer was in my bed, naked.

Within five minutes, it was over for me. All she did was put her mouth on my nipple and, with one flick of her tongue, an orgasm washed through my body like a small wave. I now knew how a man felt about premature ejaculation. Not deterred, she patiently did things to my body that I had only read about in my father's stash of *Penthouse Forum* that he had left behind in a box in the garage. All that did was cement my orientation. If I had any question before, it was gone. My sexual catechism was thorough, and she left me quivering and greedy for more.

She then deftly guided me in how to make love to her, and I discovered that I liked pleasing her and the reaction she had to my touch almost as much as I liked being pleased. Almost.

By the time she left, I was addicted to her. Later, when I remembered her earlier declaration, it made me wonder who else in town she might have "busted" before me and when she would get tired of me since I was no longer a virgin. Obviously I had something that kept her coming back for more, and I was hoping it wasn't that I fucked like an amateur because I think I conquered that awkward, clumsy stage by her third visit.

We arranged to meet at least four days a week for the next month, until the fateful afternoon when my mother came home early. With us being so heavily into our "unlawful carnal knowledge" of each other, we never heard the downstairs door close. However, we did hear the sharp intake of breath and the "dear sweet Jesus" when she opened my door and saw her precious minister's wife's face buried in my crotch.

Despite the dire consequences at the time, I was grateful to Jennifer for my physical introduction to all things sexual. She awakened my lesbianism into eternal consciousness. I do wish that she, being the savvy adult and the one in control, had selected a classroom other than my mother's empty house. It was convenient, but if I had been anything but a horny teenager, craving this new love like a hummingbird craves nectar, I would have had the sense to suggest another location. As it was, we played with fire, and it ended with my mother consigning us to the burning depths of hell.

The Vissons left town by the end of the month. Jennifer probably implored her husband to leave, no doubt impelled by the same fear I had—being found out for who she really was. I know the only reason my mother didn't publicly crucify Jennifer was that then everyone would have known about her own degenerate daughter.

My mother had no problem crucifying me privately, by banishing me from her life.

Having bypassed some of my old haunts, I decided to stop at an unfamiliar bar, The Night Shift. Inside, I found out that it had been there for eight years, so it was only new to me. It was spacious, with a dark interior and a well-set-up bar, decorated with strings of white Christmas lights that bordered the molding where the walls met the ceiling. It was barely nine o'clock, and the house lights had been dimmed to create a more romantic atmosphere. The two huge televisions on opposite ends of the room with the audio muted, the blaring jukebox music, and the clicking of pool balls thwarted the intended mood. Not that it mattered to me; I was only there for the booze.

The bartender had just served me my second draft beer when I heard a woman call out, "Hunter? Hunter Roberge, is that you?" I was under the impression that my looks had changed over the past sixteen years, but I figured that my height had a lot to do with someone recognizing me. I turned toward the voice, and my gaze met the stunned eyes of my high school best friend, Lesley Riordan.

What were the odds?

I grinned jauntily. "Of all the gin joints, in all the towns, in all the world, you had to walk into mine." I stood up to accept her inevitable embrace.

"God, Hunter, I'm so sorry about your mom," she said, hugging me fiercely.

"Thanks." There was an uncomfortable moment of silence, and then she removed her arms from around my shoulders. She stepped back, and we assessed each other.

She looked good. She had grown taller, which still left her five inches shorter than I was, and she had maintained a trim figure, except somewhere along the way, she had acquired an enormous rack. Whether they were natural or silicone, I had no idea, but they were out of proportion with the rest of her body and clearly made her top heavy. My breasts weren't small, but they were nowhere near as big as hers. My back frequently ached from lugging mine around; I couldn't imagine how her back was managing. If she still jogged, she must have to wear the sports bra from hell. Other than the breasts, she still looked the same, only sixteen years older, with highlighted red hair as opposed to the dishwater blonde color she'd had all through school. On the questionable side, her once pleasant face now had a hardness to it that surprised me. I wondered if never leaving this town and dealing with its "good ol' boy" suppression had done that to her.

"I was wondering if you were going to come back for the service. Last time I saw Dane and asked about you, he said you and your mom still weren't speaking."

"We weren't, but for some reason, she left me the house, so I'm back here to deal with that."

"That's the only reason? God, Hunter, that's kind of cold."

I shrugged, not offended by her faint criticism. It was true.

"You know as well as anyone that my mother and I never got along, never had a traditional relationship. To pretend it was anything else just because she's dead would be dishonest."

She seemed to consider this as she looked around the bar.

"True." She focused back on me, grinning. "The years

certainly have been good to you."

"The years? Jesus, Les, you make me sound ancient. I'm only thirty-four, same as you."

"Well, you look great. Have you seen your brothers yet?"

I sat down on my stool, and she stood next to me. "I just came from Sam's. I had to deal with Dane. That's why I'm here." I held up my beer.

"Dane's not such a bad guy. For a politician."

I gestured at the empty stool next to me. "Join me?"

"Oh, no, I can't. I'm here for a party." She turned and pointed to two long tables pushed together in a corner. Four champagne bottles stuck out of ice buckets, two on each table. "I got here early to set up. Hey… why don't you join us?"

The last thing I wanted was to be sociable to a group of strangers… or a group of old acquaintances. "Who are 'us'?" I felt it was only polite to find out before I refused.

"It's Lisa's thirtieth birthday, so it will be her and my parents and—"

"Wait. Scrawny, bratty, tagalong Lisa? Your kid sister is thirty?"

She laughed. "Well, yeah. She's four years younger than us. Hello."

Now I did feel ancient. Little Lisa, thirty.

"Hey, here they are now."

A group of ten people were walking into The Night Shift, and I recognized her parents immediately—a little plumper, a little grayer, but Mr. and Mrs. Riordan, nonetheless. Lesley waved to them and pointed to their tables as she grabbed my sleeve. "Come on, Hunter.

I know they'd love to see you. It'll be like old times."

"Yeah, old times. Your mom blamed me every *old time* we got into trouble, even though you," I said and poked her stomach, "were the mastermind. What happens if you get drunk tonight? She going to forbid you to see me for two weeks?"

Laughing, she grabbed my finger. "Yeah, she thought you were pretty… um… adventurous."

"When I left here, she thought I was fast and loose, thanks to Phil Khaury's big mouth, even though *I*'—I looked at her pointedly—"was probably the only senior who *didn't* get laid on prom night."

Eyes twinkling, Lesley said, "Your loss." She released my finger. "Listen, no worries. I 'fessed up to her ten years ago that it wasn't you who stole Daddy's bottle of vodka that time, you just supplied the oranges. She figured out the rest on her own. She's forgiven you. And she still occasionally asks if I ever hear from you. But," she added with some sadness, "I told her I guessed that when you gave up on your mom, you gave up on the rest of us, too."

I took a long drink of beer. "It wasn't like that, Les. It had nothing to do with any of you and everything to do with me."

"What does that mean?"

Was this the time? The place? Was I finally going to come out to my childhood friend, someone I'd been away from for as many years as I'd known her? Sure. Why not? I'd kept the secret from this shithole town long enough. I didn't live here; I no longer had to be concerned with my reputation or my mother's, and my brothers could fend for themselves. Sam would cope just fine, and I could only hope it would ruin Dane's higher political aspirations. Maybe no one would even care. Maybe no one would be surprised.

Okay. Deep breath. "Well, what it means is that I'm—"

"Lesley, come on! We want to make the toast!" A young man held up a flute of champagne.

"Okay, I'll be right there," she called and turned back to me.

"Come on, Hunter. Please? At least come over and say hi, even if you don't stay." She pouted and bounced on her heels like a little kid, making her breasts jiggle threateningly.

I moved back slightly, not wanting to risk being beaned by her boobs. "Oh, all right." I rolled my eyes as I picked up my beer mug and stood up. "But if your mother starts counting how many beers I'm having, I'm coming back to the bar."

"She won't." She grabbed my sleeve and pulled me through the crowd over to the table where mostly everyone was seated, each holding a full glass of champagne. "Hey, everybody, look who I found over at the bar."

As I looked around the group, of course the people I had never met were puzzled but the few I recognized, including Lesley's parents, also looked confused. I did a quick scan, trying to figure out which one was Lisa. I pretty much decided it was the mousy little redhead at the end of the first table, looking a tad irritable that the big celebration was being interrupted.

"Oh, come on, isn't it obvious?" Lesley laughed, gesturing at my height. "It's—"

"Hunter Roberge," a voice beside me breathed.

I turned to see who had recognized me. Usually in the movies, when a moment like this happens, the film will go into slow motion to underscore the magic of the occasion. And that's exactly how this felt. I looked down into one of the most naturally beautiful faces I could ever remember seeing, which said a lot, considering that in Los Angeles, pretty faces were a dime a dozen. She had thick, light blonde hair that fell to just below her shoulders, a captivating white smile behind understated red lips, a perfect nose, and mesmerizing green eyes that held me hostage as they attempted to convey a message I was too dazzled to read. There was something about her eyes that did look vaguely familiar, but I couldn't place her. Who was this? And how did she know me?

As I was about to ask, Mr. and Mrs. Riordan were on their feet, smothering me with hugs and condolences. When the formalities were behind us, before I found out who the engaging little temptress was, I figured I'd better say happy birthday to the guest of honor, whose party I was probably ruining by unintentionally becoming the focus of attention. I grabbed Lesley's arm before she could move away from me. "Is that Lisa over there?" I subtly tipped my head toward the obviously perturbed, bespectacled redhead.

"Oh heavens, no. That's Dina, Lisa's secretary."

"Lisa has a secretary? What does she do?"

"Jesus, Hunter, you can ask her directly, she's standing right behind you." Lesley folded her arms, amused.

No. It couldn't be. I spun quickly to see the gorgeous enchantress smirking at me, her arms also folded. "Lisa?"

"Hunter." Just the way she said my name sent a shiver down my spine. I'm sure I looked dumbfounded. She laughed. "What? You thought I'd look the same at thirty as I did at fourteen?"

I guess I did. Thankfully, I had thought wrong. At least now I knew why she looked vaguely familiar. She stepped toward me and pulled me into an embrace I enjoyed entirely too much. It was a full body hug, usually the kind only lesbians knew how to give, but Lisa had always been an affectionate girl so I was probably reading something into nothing. "Happy Birthday," I said, reluctantly releasing her.

"Thank you." Her tone sounded almost intimate. She stepped back and gestured toward the group. "Please join my party. I would love to have you help celebrate my thirtieth birthday."

She didn't have to ask twice. Even if she wasn't gay, she certainly would be easy on the eyes for the next couple of hours, and a party was vastly preferable to going to my mother's house and facing old memories. I grabbed a chair from a nearby empty table and wedged it between Lisa's agitated secretary and Lesley, who poured me a flute of champagne.

"Can we get this toast over with, so I can have my martini?"

Dina called out. At least it told me why she had looked so peeved.

Chapter 4

I was introduced around the table, and although I tried to reply courteously to any conversation thrown my way, I couldn't stop staring at Lisa. She had become a stunning woman, poised and polished, and every time she engaged me with those intense green eyes, she left me breathless. Her transformation had been amazing—from immature little girl to sophisticated adult, from gawky adolescent to absolute knockout. The thing I remembered the most about her was that she'd always followed Lesley and me around, wanting to be included in whatever we did. I wouldn't object to her following me anywhere now.

No husband or boyfriend had been mentioned, and Lisa wasn't wearing an engagement or wedding ring. I was encouraged. Even though I knew I was most likely setting myself up for disappointment, I couldn't help myself. I was incredibly drawn to the former little girl who, wearing an adorable cowboy costume, once told me she would rope the moon for me if I wanted it. She was eight…

The front door swung open, and little Lisa stood in the archway. She instantly grinned, revealing a smile that was missing two front teeth. "Hi, Hunter! Lethley'th not here. Wanna play cowboy with me?"

I was disappointed. Mom and I had just had one of our daily arguments, and I really didn't want to go back home right then.

"Where is she? We were supposed to meet up."

"Thee'th with my mommy at the thtore. They're thuppothed to be back after Lethley geth her thtuff."

"What stuff?" I sounded annoyed. Lisa was used to it.

"You know, the thtuff you're doing for that clath at thcool."

"The stuff for the papier-mâché map? That isn't even due until next week."

"Yeah, but Mom wanth her to thtart it today. Want to come in and wait?"

"Um, sure." I stepped inside and Lisa closed the door.

"Daddy! Hunter'th here!" she screamed, two inches away from me.

"Jesus, Lisa!" I clamped my hand over my left ear. "What is wrong with you?" I wiggled my finger in my ear to try and stop the ringing.

"Lesley isn't home yet, Hunter," Mr. Riordan called from the other room.

"Thee'th going to wait and play cowboy with me!" Lisa grabbed my wrist and led me toward the kitchen.

"That's good, honey, just take it outside," he said. As we passed the living room, he was doing exactly what I pictured him doing—sitting in his recliner in his tank top and pajama bottoms, reading the Sunday paper and smoking a cigarette. "Hi, Hunter," he said without looking up.

"Hi, Mr. Riordan."

When we got to the kitchen, Lisa let go of my wrist and ran to the back door. "Come thee my fort."

"No. I'm not playing cowboy with you, and I'm not going to go 'thee' your fort." I opened the refrigerator door, searching for a can of soda. I snatched a Dr. Pepper and closed the door, then popped the top. As I was about to take a sip, I noticed Lisa at the door, her arms crossed, looking like she was ready to cry. I rolled my eyes. "What's the matter with you?"

"Why are you tho mean?"

"Mean? Me?" I wasn't mean. My mother was mean, and I wasn't anything like her, at least that's what Mom kept pounding into my head. Okay, so I wasn't mean, but I was acting like a jerk. I was twelve; it was a requirement. I looked at Lisa with her geeky little glasses and her long red pigtails hanging down from under her brown felt cowboy hat. She was wearing chaps with white fringe and a matching vest, and a six-shooter cap gun in a plastic holster was strapped to her hip. I reached over and tipped her hat up. "Hey, I'm sorry."

She didn't appear to believe me as she adjusted her hat.

"Seriously, Lisa." I presented my Dr. Pepper as a peace offering.

"You know I'm not allowed to have thoda, and Lethley'th gonna kill you for drinking that."

"Yeah, right." I laughed and took a sip with a loud, obnoxious slurp. "How can Lesley kill me if I have my own personal marshal protecting me?" I tapped the star on her vest.

She looked up at me with a grin so wide, I thought her face would split. All was okay with the world again. "Let'th go to my fort. I'll hide you!"

"You'd do that for me?" She could be a cute kid sometimes.

"I'd rope the moon for you, Hunter, if you wanted it." If I hadn't known better, I would have thought she was swooning.

"Aw, thanks." She could be a sweet kid, too. When she wasn't tagging along all the time. "So is this what you're going to be when you grow up? A cowboy?"

"No, thilly, I'm going to be a thinger." She giggled. I hoped she was joking. She couldn't carry a tune in a bucket.

"Okay, take me to your fort, but when Lesley gets home, I'm hanging with her, okay?"

"Okay." She eagerly yanked me out the door, and we sat in her tree house until her sister got back. I would say we talked, but I couldn't get a word in edgewise. As my mother used to say: Lisa could talk a tin ear off a mule.

I suddenly wished Lisa still had that hero worship. I learned she was an environmental lawyer, which I found most impressive. If she had to be a lawyer, at least she was working for a noble cause. It was an obvious choice of profession for her, as she not only loved to talk, she also loved to argue. At least with Lesley. Mrs. Riordan bragged that Lisa graduated at the top of her class from the Vermont Law School's Environmental Law Center, where she would occasionally give lectures. She also owned her own house, was the proud mommy of two rescued greyhounds, and enjoyed gardening... but the proud mother made no mention of a significant other.

Lesley filled in the conversational lulls with an update of her own life. She was on husband number two, who, at that moment, was home with her twin boys from her first marriage. She said she was glad she'd had boys, because she would never have wanted two girls the same age who were as exasperating as we had been. That was a terrifying thought. Lesley worked temporary jobs eight months out of the year and then really raked in the bucks waiting tables at the bar and restaurant in one of the major resorts during ski season. If I remembered correctly, the hotels didn't pay shit, but the tips were exceptional. One of my cousins put herself through business school on the money she made from waitressing on the mountain.

At length, the conversation returned to my mother. "You know, Hunter," Mrs. Riordan said, "you've had four beers already, not including any that you had before we got here. I guess you've never kicked *that* little habit." Barely taking a breath, she asked, "Had you and your mother spoken to one another before she passed away?"

Before I could respond, she continued, "What exactly was the problem, anyway?"

I turned to Lesley. My raised eyebrow said, *She's forgiven me, eh?*

In a reproving tone, Lisa said, "Mother, that's between Hunter and Mrs. Roberge. It's none of our business."

Mrs. Riordan put a patronizing hand on Lisa's arm and said in a condescending tone, "I just thought Hunter might like to tell us, dear. I mean, Sarah's gone now, what difference could it possibly make?"

It was all coming back to me now: Mary Lynne Riordan, Town Crier. If someone farted on the opposite side of Otter Falls, Mrs. Riordan was on the phone to her sister about it before all the air had been expelled. I should have thanked Lesley for inviting me to join the party, excused myself, and returned to the bar. But when I glanced at Lisa, she was looking at me with an expression of patient understanding, and because

I was melting under her gaze, I chose to stay.

"Mrs. Riordan," I said, forcing restraint, "I wasn't the one who stopped speaking. That was my mother's decision. And because it was something that would invade her privacy for me to discuss, even now, I'm going to respect her memory and leave it in the past, where it belongs." Then I added with saccharine sweetness, "I'm sure you would expect nothing less from your daughters." That elicited a reddening in Mrs. Riordan's cheeks, an embarrassed clearing of Mr. Riordan's throat, and a smile from Lisa that made it all okay.

"So, Hunter." Lesley broke the awkward silence. "What is it that you do out there in California?"

"I'm a chief ranger in the Angeles National Forest." There was a round of the expected "ooohs," and when I glanced at Lisa there was a look of quiet approval in her eyes. I was hoping she was as fascinated with me as I was with her.

"Wow. You're the chief ranger—" Lesley started to say.

"No, I'm *a* chief ranger, not *the* chief ranger. A chief ranger is a supervisor position."

Lesley wasn't deterred by my demotion. "What is it you do as chief ranger?"

I leaned over to Lesley. "You know, this is Lisa's party. She'll only turn thirty once. We can get together and talk about me another time while I'm here." I turned to the guest of honor, who seemed to be studying me with something akin to amusement. "So, back to you."

As if Mrs. Riordan hadn't been following any of the conversation since her embarrassment, she said, "Are you married, Hunter?"

Did I detect a hint of concentrated interest in my answer from the direction of the party girl? "No, Mrs. Riordan, I'm not."

"Not now, or not ever?"

"Not ever."

"What? A beautiful girl like you?" Mr. Riordan piped in.

"What's wrong with all them men out there in the land of fruits and nuts? They all gay?"

"Dad!" The exclamation that came from both Riordan

daughters made me laugh. My best friend's parents hadn't changed.

"What?" He threw his hands in the air, looking sincerely perplexed.

"No, Mr. Riordan. I guess I'm just not the marrying type." I wasn't about to get into my sexuality. I could only imagine their reaction, and I would be damned if I was going to ruin Lisa's special night. But since we were on the subject, and it would bring the focus back to where it belonged, I said, "What about you, Lisa? Married? Engaged? Divorced? Separated? Boyfriend?" *Girlfriend?*

Amidst the sudden dead silence in the room, Lisa leaned forward on her elbows and said, "Actually, I'm single."

I looked around the table and everyone seemed to find interest elsewhere until Lesley, in her best troublemaker tone, said, "What are you talking about? You are so not single."

Lisa opened her mouth to say something, and Mrs. Riordan cut her off, a distinct chill in her voice. "Why don't we leave it at Lisa isn't the marrying type, either."

The expression on Lisa's face showed annoyance, frustration, and amusement. She glanced at me, then cut Lesley a nasty look.

"Actually, I'm—"

"Let's change the subject, shall we?" Mary Lynne Riordan's smile was strained.

"You brought the subject up, Mom," Lisa said.

Well, *this* was interesting. What big Riordan mystery had I stumbled upon? Maybe Lisa had been with someone influential and the relationship was now *almost* over, which was somehow embarrassing to her mother. Maybe she was involved with someone her parents didn't approve of. Surely Lisa and I couldn't be sharing the same secret. Could we? That was too much to hope for.

As the tension at the table became awkward, I realized I would have to be the one to change the subject. I gestured around the room. "This is really a nice place. You all seem comfortable here. Is this a regular family stop?" I looked around the table at each Riordan family member.

"Not a regular stop." Mrs. Riordan sounded scandalized that I would think she hung out in a bar. "We have been here for *occasions*."

"Yeah." Lisa smirked. "The last *occasion* was the celebration of Lesley's boob job. In her honor, for dinner we had a five-and-a-half-pound breast—"

"Lisa!" Mrs. Riordan nearly snorted daiquiri out her nose, and I almost expelled some beer the same way. Lesley's jaw dropped, but she recovered quickly. Grinning like a proud fool, she stood up and pointed to her new additions like Vanna displaying consonants. The table broke into applause, but Mrs. Riordan cringed as Lesley sat back down.

"Oh, Mom, please." Lisa laughed, rubbing her mother's shoulder, "If Vermont allowed billboards, Chesty here would have put her girls out there for the world to see. She's proud of those puppies."

"Well, she wasn't naturally blessed like you were, dear," Mrs.

Riordan mumbled, turning to her husband with an expression that pleaded for rescue.

Doug Riordan did not comply. "Well, hell, Mary Lynne, let her show off the damned things. Wally sure as hell paid enough for 'em. I hope he's getting as much enjoyment out of 'em as she is."

"Douglas!" Mrs. Riordan closed her eyes and hid her face in her hands.

"Dad!" both his daughters chorused.

He threw his hands in the air. "What?"

When Lisa excused herself to use the bathroom, I wanted to follow her, to ravish her up against the wall of one of the stalls. Of course, I remained seated and listened to Mr. Riordan drone on about some local sports competition, Mrs. Riordan looking grateful for the diversion. While her parents were engaged in conversation with others at the table, Lesley leaned over and said in a hushed voice, "Still know how to stir up trouble, I see."

I kept my eyes on my nearly empty beer mug. "I do? How's that?"

"Asking if Lisa's married. That's a sore subject with us all. We try to avoid it. Even though she has no problem telling anybody, which only makes it worse."

"And why is that?" Oh please, oh please.

Lesley's vocal inflection moved from disdain to downright contempt. "My dear, sweet baby sister isn't married because the little perv is a dyke."

My inner, giddy schoolgirl did a happy dance and screamed, *Yes!* As myself fell to her knees and pumped her fist in the air, I couldn't ignore the disgusted way my once best friend had revealed the information to me. Her use of the words "perv" and "dyke" were imbued with a particular revulsion that set my teeth on edge. "Is that so?" I said coolly.

As Lisa came back toward the table, Lesley moved even closer and whispered a warning. "Be careful. She's always had a crush on you."

She, of course, had no idea that I was delighted, not scandalized. I gazed at Lesley and reined in my repugnance for her attitudes, not wanting to cause a scene. "I'll keep that in mind."

Misinterpreting the intent of my response, she sat back with a smug smile. "Yeah. I have no doubt you can kick her ass if she gets out of line."

I wanted to get as far away from my erstwhile friend as possible, so I finished my beer and stood up. "Well," I said, "it's been a long day and the next few days will, no doubt, be even longer. I should get going."

Lesley patted my leg. "Call me about a time to get together. Or do you want me to just stop by?"

Before I could tell her "thanks but no thanks," Lisa was at my side. "Thanks for joining us, Hunter. Seeing you again was an especially nice birthday present." She hugged me and I hugged her back, giving her an extra squeeze. If I was living there and would be around to help take the flak it would cause, I might have taken her in my arms and planted a juicy one on her, just to get a reaction from her family. Okay, not *just* to get a reaction, but that would have been a worthwhile bonus.

Before I released her, I whispered in her ear, "Looks like

you have your hands full with this bunch."

I felt her relax and then in a voice only I could hear, she said,

"Right now I'm concentrating on having my arms full." I know she must have felt my breath catch and my heart start thumping.

When she stepped back and winked at me, suddenly it felt like there was no one else in the room except the two of us. I don't know whether anyone noticed, or felt the sparks flashing between us, and I really didn't care. I couldn't remember ever having felt such desire for anyone in my life. Before I took her in my arms and nailed her with a searing kiss that would have burned holes in her self-righteous family's eyes, I mechanically nodded to everyone and began to back away, inwardly thanking whatever invisible force had arranged events so I was there to join the festivities.

As angry as I was at Lesley's blatant bias against her sister's orientation, I was able to put that out of my mind and concentrate on the fetching surprise that was once the little pest I couldn't wait to get away from. Now all I could think about was finding a way to be around her. It was difficult to reconcile the awkward, androgynous teenager I never gave much thought to, with the "woman-of-my-dreams" status Lisa now held. It was as though I was dealing with two entirely different people, and I was mindful that the fourteen-year-old I remembered was a lifetime away from the thirty-year-old who had just obliterated any common sense I had left. Something that would have been wrong on so many levels sixteen years ago, now felt instantly and indisputably right, and I knew I would have very little, if any, control over my libido if either Ms. Lisa Riordan or I tried to look the other up while I was in town.

As I was driving to my mother's, I thanked the Fates, and whatever other entity guided me to that bar, for pushing me to feel in too much of a hurry to hang around and engage a flirty flight attendant in Albany. At least this trip "home" wouldn't be a total waste of my time.

Chapter 5

I hesitated before I unlocked the front door. Walking inside this house was going to be overwhelming on many levels. I expected the first emotion to hit me would be anger. Anger at what could have been, should have been a loving environment and anger at what was lost all those years ago that could never be regained. I felt anger at my mother for always making me feel so inadequate, and anger at my mother *and* my father for making me so angry.

But what I felt as I stepped over the threshold was sadness.

Sadness for what could have been, should have been a loving environment and sadness for what was lost all those years ago that could never be regained. I felt sadness for my mother for always making me feel so inadequate, and sadness for my mother *and* my father for making me so angry. I not only had some physical housecleaning facing me, I had some psychological housecleaning to do as well.

I immediately detected the faint scent of the cinnamon apple potpourri my mother always had placed throughout the house, and I unexpectedly choked up. Where had that emotion come from? I swallowed the large lump in my throat and turned on the light. As my eyes swept the living room and hallway, I was transported back sixteen years, to the time that a destroyed eighteen-year-old had walked out that very same door for the last time…

Jennifer made a hasty escape after dressing quickly but not before making me feel like crap because we got caught, as though it had been my fault that my mother came home early. I rationalized that Jennifer was upset, humiliated at being found in such a compromising position in the house of one of her husband's most loyal flock.

"Maybe you and I can go somewhere together until things cool down?" I knew immediately that I had made a mistake.

"You can't be that naïve," she whispered harshly. "My family's reputation depends on your mother's discretion." She was in my face, nearly snarling. "What do you think the odds are that she won't say anything?"

"But you said your husband knew."

"Not my husband, Hunter! Everyone else! Christ! I can't believe this happened!" She finished making herself presentable and took a deep breath, preparing to leave the room and face my mother.

"Jen—"

Without saying another word, she opened the door and stepped out into the hallway. "Mrs. Roberge," I heard her say. "Please let me explain—"

"Please leave my house this instant." My mother's voice was deceptively calm.

Self-preservation is a funny thing. I didn't understand that at such a tender age. My world crashed in, and my heart broke into a million pieces when I heard Jennifer say, "Mrs. Roberge, you were right about your daughter. She is indeed depraved. She must have put something in my coffee and I woke up in bed with her. She threatened me with blackmail if I did not... do things to her. I am so sorry."

I flung open my bedroom door and stared at Jennifer in wide-eyed shock. "Mom, she's lying. She seduced me!" I searched Jennifer's face for any sign of the woman who had just been making love to me. There was none. "She told me she loved me."

"Mrs. Roberge, your daughter is also an accomplished liar. You really should get her some help."

As my mother's attention returned to me, Jennifer left the house. I was dazed. "Mom, she's lying. Check the kitchen, we didn't have coffee."

"You think I don't know that you could have washed the dishes? Or you could have had coffee elsewhere before you came back here." Her voice was shaking with anger, and I know she was keeping her arms folded tightly across her chest so that she wouldn't hit me. I should have known she would automatically disbelieve me.

"Did she look like she was being forced to do anything?" I knew the second those words left my mouth, they were not going to help my case.

"You disgust me."

"Mom!"

"No! Enough." Her tone stopped me from arguing. "I am done, Hunter. You are a Godless child. You are a deviant. Your morals are even worse than your father's. I will not have you living under my roof. You are no longer my daughter. You are dead to me, do you understand? I want you to get your things and leave this house immediately, and I never want to see you again. Do you understand?"

"But—"

"Do you understand!"

"Yes."

"You are never to speak of this to anyone. It's bad enough everyone in town still remembers what your father did to me, I will not be further disgraced by your perverted behavior. Tomorrow, I will go to Reverend and Mrs. Visson to ask their forgiveness and beg them not to report you to the authorities."

I realized that whatever I said or did, it would fall on deaf ears. Fueled by years of my being a "bad seed," she had made up her mind.

I packed my only suitcase, throwing in whatever it would hold.

I was numb, embarrassed, pissed off, and ashamed. I also felt used, bewildered, and betrayed.

If only my father had stuck around and pretended that we were important to him. I could have at least gone to his place until I decided what to do. But that was water under a very low bridge.

I hoped my Uncle David wouldn't mind one more child for a while, because I had nowhere else to go.

I stopped at the front door and took one last, lingering look around before I left. I suddenly felt the loneliness of leaving somewhere I was never meant to be, and yet not understanding why things had to be this way. My mother didn't even enter the room to see me off. I closed the door behind me very quietly, so I don't know if she heard me leave. I don't think she cared.

My last thought as I walked away from my home was: why is it that people who demand that you live up to their expectations never care whether or not they live up to yours?

And now I was back. I slowly walked through the first floor rooms and reacquainted myself with my mother's house. Other than updating the curtains and installing a new carpet, she hadn't changed the place since I left. I climbed the stairs and headed for my old room, pretty sure she had turned it into a storage area.

Opening my bedroom door, I was shocked to see that everything was as I had left it… except she had made my bed, and washed the sheets, I'm sure. In fact, when I turned up the dimmed light, it almost looked as if it had been turned into a shrine. As my self-esteem had been pretty shattered when I left, I certainly didn't remember having so many photographs of myself spread out all over the room. There were laminated newspaper articles of my basketball achievements in my junior and senior years, which I know I had never taped to the mirror, and my varsity and junior varsity trophies were all on display on my bureau. I could only think that Sam must have placed all those mementos there, although I couldn't, for the life of me, understand why my mother would have left them there.

I went down the hall and checked out my brothers' bedrooms.

Sam's had been turned into a guest room and Dane's was now a sewing room, which wasn't surprising. Mom had always loved to make clothes. She sewed costumes for two different local dance schools at recital time. Lastly, I walked across the hall to my mother's room.

It smelled like her. Or the flower-scented perfume she always wore—Island Gardenia, I believe it was. It was always a sure-fire, no-fail present. She typically ended up with at least three bottles of it every Christmas morning, that and something to do with her sewing. I sat down on her bed, which was as hard as a rock. She always liked a firm mattress, which translated into her having a completely unyielding slab of concrete. I never understood how that could be beneficial for anyone's back. On her nightstand was a framed photograph of her, my brothers, and me, taken by Phil Khaury on the night of my senior prom. God, I was so young. We all looked so deceptively happy. And I'd forgotten how beautiful she used to be.

Next to the picture lay her reading glasses, open, ready for her to slip them on. I ran my thumb over the frame, choking up. It hadn't had to be like this. I took a deep breath and stood, surveying the walls and floors. Except for a new rug, this room hadn't changed, either.

I went down and got my suitcases, took them upstairs, and put them in the guest room. It had a queen-sized bed, while my room only had a twin. I went down to put a twelve-pack of Guinness in the refrigerator, keeping one out to drink. My thoughts continued to replay a mental film loop of earlier in the evening, of the surprise that had been the mesmerizing Lisa Riordan. It was hard for me to connect the scrawny, smart-alecky, Pippi Longstocking-looking girl with the incredibly hot lesbian who had knocked my socks off. And she knew it, the little brat. She had been quick to recognize that I was a lesbian, too, which impressed me as I was not considered "stereotypic." Usually it took some blatant act on my part to get that message across, even to other gay women. I snickered when I remembered that I had been practically leering at her and salivating.

How much more obvious could I have been?

As I strolled through the living room toward the den, I began to smell something foul. The closer I got, the more overpowering it became. And then I remembered about Orion. Where was she? I didn't particularly like the kamikaze cat, but I didn't want to find her dead, either. When I reached the laundry room, off the den, I discovered the source of the powerful odor. The litter box was piled full with cat poop, like it hadn't been changed in a very long time.

Across the room, Orion's food and water dish both

appeared to be bone dry. I shook my head. Evidently no one had been designated to take care of the cat. Of course, there could be a story behind it, too.

If she was the Orion I knew, someone could have tried to feed her and pulled back a bloody stump.

I emptied and cleaned the litter box and then went to search for Orion, calling her name to no avail. Hoping she wasn't dead from asphyxiation or starvation, I decided to try luring her out of hiding by filling her bowls with fresh water and tuna I had found in the pantry. The smell of fish must have done the trick, as I heard a soft meow from behind me. I turned and spotted the gorgeous, rust-tinged, unusually ill-tempered Abyssinian looking up at me mournfully, her black eyes rimmed in green. Her attack mode eyes.

"Don't you mew at me like a weakling, you little terrorist. I know what you're capable of." I set her food bowl on the floor next to the water, and she trotted over to it, practically inhaling it in one bite. The poor cat was famished.

I picked up the phone in the living room and dialed Sam's number. I knew it was getting late but I had no doubt he was up, probably still entertaining guests. He picked up the phone on the third ring. "Sam. Hunter. Listen, was anyone supposed to be tending to Orion?"

"Yeah. Dane. Why?"

Dane. Of course. "Well, he hasn't been doing it. I thought I was going to have to call a hazmat team and the kitty morgue." I explained what I had found and heard Sam's disgusted sigh.

"He never liked that cat."

"Nobody likes this cat, but that doesn't give him the right to neglect her."

"Sorry, Hunter. I'll speak to him about it."

"No, never mind. I'm sure it wouldn't do any good anyway." I studied Orion as she lapped at the water. "Are you sure Mom wanted me to have her?"

"Yeah. She was very specific."

"Great. Testing me right to the end, I see."

"Come on, Hunter. It's over, okay? Mom's gone."

He was right. I needed to start reining in my bitterness. "So what's up for tomorrow?"

"The wake is at four."

"Open casket?"

"Yes."

"I'll pass."

"Hunter! You have to—"

"I don't have to do anything, okay? Number one, unless Mom changed drastically, she was very private and she would have hated being on display in an open casket, and, two, I choose not to remember our mother the way she looks lying dead in a box. And I will not accept people's condolences to me when obviously everyone in this town knows we hadn't spoken for nearly half my life, and they know saying 'I'm sorry' to me are just empty words."

It had come out sounding more defensive than I intended.

He backed down. "Okay. Got it."

I sighed and pinched the bridge of my nose. "Um... listen... it's been a long day and I'm a little testy. Maybe after a good night's sleep..."

"Yeah. I understand. Really. Get some sleep. You want to come over for coffee in the morning?"

"Let me call you. My body clock is still on a different time zone. I might sleep past coffee time."

"Okay. Call me when you get up?"

"Sure. Sounds like a plan."

"Also, just so you know, Dane's really on the warpath about this house thing, so be prepared for anything. He's pretty tanked up right now. Don't be surprised if he shows up for a showdown."

"Tonight? If he shows up tonight, he just might find himself looking down the barrel of my Smith & Wesson."

"You brought your gun here?"

"No." I snickered. "But Dane doesn't have to know that."

Sam laughed with me. "You're still incorrigible, aren't you?"

"Yep. Goodnight, Sam."

"Goodnight, Hunter. See you tomorrow."

After we hung up, I finished my beer. I hadn't realized it

while I was talking to Sam, but Orion had jumped up and laid down next to me on the couch. She washed her paws, then her face, then her belly. She was actually purring. I took a chance and cautiously scratched her head, then under her chin. She stood up and rubbed up against me. "Don't think you're fooling me for a second. I know you, remember? You'll wait until I think you're asleep from me petting you, and then you'll channel the face hugger from *Alien*. Well, I'm not falling for it." She purred louder and began to head butt my arm. I was tempted, but I didn't fall into her trap.

I took my empty bottle to the kitchen and headed upstairs for a shower before I turned in for the night.

Chapter 6

The shower was a godsend after my long, exhausting day. I had forgotten how different it felt to have hard water beating against my skin. I had become used to a much softer spray that prompted me to occasionally run around in the stall in order to feel rinsed. I stepped out, towel drying my hair and feeling refreshed. Wanting one more beer to help me relax before I tried to get some sleep, I put on a pair of sweat shorts and a sleeveless T-shirt and went downstairs.

I went to the refrigerator, took out an ice-cold beer, and removed the cap. I had just taken a swig when I heard a knock on the door. I looked at the clock. One-twenty. I started to burn. It could only be Dane. Having had too much to drink at Sam's, he now had the liquid courage to confront me on this house issue. Nothing like the little fucker not wasting any time.

I unlocked the door and swung it open, ready to blast my baby brother when, instead of his beady glare and sniveling little pinched up face, I saw the emerald eyes and flawlessly beautiful smile of the woman who had occupied nearly all of my thoughts and a few mini fantasies for the last ninety minutes. "Hi," I managed to get out, surprised but pleased to see her.

"Hi," she responded, searching my eyes in silent interrogation.

I leaned against the door, content to stare back at her. She smiled indulgently. "So... before I go any further and boldly invite myself in, I need to know one thing. Am I wrong?"

I knew she was asking if she was correct in assuming that I was a lesbian. I blinked at her lazily, just drinking her in. "No. You are definitely not wrong." Her grin widened, and I know mine did also.

I stepped back and gestured her inside. "Please come in."

"Why, I'd love to."

She came inside, and I looked out at the street. Only my rental car was parked anywhere near the house. I closed and locked the door. "How did you get here?"

"Since I expected to get pretty buzzed at my party tonight, I arranged not to drive."

"Who dropped you off? Don't tell me Lesley—"

"Not only no, but *hell* no. I took a cab."

That stopped me. "There are cabs in Otter Falls? Since when?"

Her laugh was a delightful sound that caressed my ears. "Oh, since about the same time we got indoor plumbing and moonshine became illegal."

Smart-ass. "Moonshine is illegal? Well, that does it, I can't stay here." I couldn't stop the smile that had a mind of its own every time I looked at her. "Would you like a beer?"

"Hmmm." Alcohol-fueled indecision? "Okay, maybe one." She followed me into the kitchen.

"Are you sure?" I opened the Guinness for her and handed her the bottle. "I wouldn't want to be accused of getting you drunk to take advantage of you."

She stopped drinking mid-sip, grinning, with the bottle still at her lips. "Were you planning to take advantage of me?"

I studied her, excited and yet at ease with her presence. "That *is* why you're here, isn't it?" This was one of the quickest and smoothest seductions I had ever participated in. The scenario was practically writing itself.

She finished her initial sip. "God, I hate being so transparent."

She looked around. "This place looks exactly the same as it did the last time I was here, when I was, what, fourteen?"

"Let's not talk about when you were that age." I couldn't resist her any longer, and I moved to within mere inches of her, looking down into her lovely, revealing eyes.

"Why? Makes you feel kind of dirty, does it?" Her voice was low and breathy, and she returned my gaze of longing. I moved closer as she stepped backward until her back encountered the refrigerator. "You don't waste any time, do you?"

"And if our roles were reversed and I said that to you, what would you say to me?" I asked, closing in on her.

"I would have said that I've been waiting eighteen years for this kiss. I think that's long enough."

"I've been waiting almost two hours for this kiss. That's a record for me." Our lips were nearly touching.

"Dawggie," she whispered breathlessly.

"Woof," I answered hoarsely. And then I was kissing her. And she was kissing me. We were both still holding our bottles. My free hand was in my pocket and hers was bracing herself against the fridge while I leaned into her, deepening the kiss, my body tingling from the contact. It felt oddly familiar and thrillingly new. As the kiss continued, I placed my beer on the counter, removed hers from her hand and set it beside mine. Our arms encircled each other's shoulders and waists and drew us tight against each other; her curves fit very nicely into mine. She made me feel as though I'd always belonged right there, as if I'd come home.

We continued to kiss, content with exploring each other's mouths before we made the decision to move on to something more intimate. Her lips pressed passionately against mine in a fever that revealed her want was as limitless as mine at that moment. My profound desire for her driving me to distraction, I found myself getting aggressive, and we were both panting when I finally broke what felt like an infinite kiss and rested my forehead against hers.

"You need to tell me right now if you don't want to go any further," I told her, feeling like I was ready to implode. I threaded my fingers through her soft hair; her hands ran up and down my back. My body was humming with arousal.

She nodded and drew a deep breath. "That was pretty intense… and everything I'd hoped it would be. But I guess it would be irresponsible of me if I didn't ask you if you really are a hound dog or just joking about that, because… I didn't bring any protection."

I gently lifted her chin, and she blinked up at me. "I've had my days, believe me, but my last, uh, encounter was maybe six months ago with a woman whose history I know very well. My last physical was six weeks ago, and I tested negative for anything that should cause concern, should we, you know, make it upstairs." She absorbed the reassurance with a relieved smile. "You?"

She was hesitant. *Uh-oh.* She lowered her eyes to the floor and said quietly, "I don't have any diseases, but I do have a sort of girlfriend."

"Ah, yes. The 'almost single' situation."

"She's someone I've been seeing for four years. It's difficult to explain."

"Try." I lifted her chin, forcing her to look at me.

"She lives in New Jersey. We get together maybe once a month or so. It's… it's basically more of being in a routine than a relationship. We've talked about calling it quits a couple of times, but because it's so convenient for both of us and neither one of us wants to reenter the meat market of dating, we just haven't. It's really turned into more like occasionally sleeping with a good friend."

Okay. That could qualify as a "sort of" girlfriend. If she was telling the truth. I suppose if she'd wanted to hide the fact that she wasn't available, she would not have brought it up at all. And what did I care? I was only going to be here as long as it took to get the house on the market. Although, if anything could change my mind about hanging around a little longer, it would be the promise of being able to hold this woman in my arms as often as possible. "So why isn't your 'sort of' girlfriend here tonight to celebrate the big three-o with you?"

"Her sister, who lives in Texas, had a baby. She's there, helping out for a week."

"Ah." My hand slid to the back of Lisa's neck, and I brought our lips together for a lasting, torrid kiss that drew moans from both of us. I pushed my knee forward and fit my thigh snugly between her legs, an action that caused her to break our kiss in a gasp. When her lips hungrily latched onto mine, she began to gyrate slightly against me and it drove me to need more. I wasn't sure I could wait until we got upstairs.

I cupped her ass as she grasped my shoulders, and I lifted her so that she was able to wrap her legs around my waist. Never breaking contact, I swung her around and settled her on the kitchen counter. My fingers moved between us, brushing over her left breast, feeling her nipple harden through the fabric of her shirt, lightly rubbing the tip with the palm of my hand. I was about to unbutton her blouse when a voice behind us shattered the spell.

"Well, well, well… isn't this special." I turned quickly to see Dane, barely able to stand, supporting himself against the doorjamb.

Lisa immediately tried to retreat by unhooking her legs, and I felt her palm flat on my chest, keeping me at bay. I knew it was the embarrassment of getting caught in such an intimate moment more than it was shame at doing what we were doing. Before I released her, I planted a brief, reassuring kiss on her forehead, which she didn't avoid.

"What are you doing here, Dane?"

"Catching you with your hands in the cookie jar, or almost in the cookie jar, so it would seem." His words were heavily slurred, and he tried to unsuccessfully focus on Lisa. "Well, hello there, Counselor Cookie."

"How many Lisas am I holding up here?" I asked him, knowing if he answered, he'd probably say "three."

"Funny girl." He belched.

I stepped away from Lisa and rested my fists on my hips. Talk about ruining a moment. "Did you drive here?"

"No. My wife's in the car, waiting for me. Why? Don't tell me you're concerned."

"About you? No. But I would be concerned about whoever was sharing the road with you."

"What would you have done? Taken my keys and driven me home?"

"No. I would have waited until you got in your car and then called the police to report a drunk driver."

"Yeah, you would, too, you bitch."

"Listen, you little prick, this is my house now. You have no right to use your key to walk in whenever you feel like it.

I'm advising you right now that you are trespassing. If you do this again, I'll have you arrested."

"You don't deserve this house!"

"I didn't ask for this house! And this isn't the time to discuss this. Now get your squatty little ass out of here before I do call the police."

"And you can get back to what you were doing, you degenerate. Is this what living in California did to you, or is this why Mom kicked you out all those years ago?"

"Dane, I'm asking you one last time to leave, and if you don't, I'm going to physically throw you out. And you know I can do it."

My tone was even, but there was no mistaking my intent.

He put up a hand in surrender. "Alright, alright, okay. I'm going." He turned around, stumbled, and nearly fell over before regaining his balance. He flipped me off. "But this is not over, Hunter. Or maybe I should start calling you Cunter."

That did it. In three steps I had my hand on the back of his neck and helped him along to the door, opening it with my free hand.

"Don't ever come here again without a direct invitation, you sad, pathetic little freak." I grabbed his collar and his belt and lifted, hopefully giving him the wedgie from hell. Judging by the squeaky voice he was trying to protest with, I think I succeeded. I thrust him outside with such vehemence that he was propelled forward, his arms flailing. After two giant steps, his legs crumpled underneath him and he did a face plant on the front lawn.

"Dane!" his wife yelled, as she hopped out of the car. She glared in my direction, and I thought she might start screaming at me until she started pounding him with her fist. "I told you not to come here, you dumb son of a bitch! I knew you'd make a damned fool of yourself!"

Maybe after tonight, my little brother would be looking at divorce number three.

I shut the door, sensing Lisa in the room, half-expecting that she had called a cab to take her home. When I turned to face her, she was standing in the archway. "I apologize for that."

I could still feel the ghost of her in my arms, still feel her lips on mine, and I very much wanted it again.

"Look, don't apologize for Dane. He was an asshole in school, and his assholery just escalated as he got older. You're not responsible for his behavior, so you shouldn't apologize for it."

"Okay, then I'm sorry for what he interrupted."

That brought a smile to her face, and she glanced down coyly before capturing my eyes with hers. "Me, too." She slowly walked toward me. "Is this going to cause a problem for you? I take it no one knows you're a lesbian."

"To my knowledge, no one *here* knows I'm a lesbian—except you—but everyone where I live knows that I am. I'm very much out. And while we're on that subject, let me say that I find it admirable that you are so out here. That takes guts."

"Not so much guts as patience. It was difficult at first, but now it's a nonissue."

"Not for your family, obviously."

"They love me very much, but they feel my orientation is a private matter and nobody's business, whereas I feel it is as much who I am as my being right-handed, so there's no reason to hide it."

"This town being what it is, I can actually understand your parents' attitude of not wanting you to be so open. I imagine that they think it somehow reflects on them. I don't agree with them, but I understand. But what's up with your sister's attitude?" I know my tone bordered on sounding offended.

Lisa took a step closer, grasping my T-shirt and running her fingers back and forth along the hem. "She married two very controlling men, both deeply opinionated, and their thoughts became her thoughts, or else. You know what I mean?"

"Let me guess—they're also the type that publicly condemn homosexuality but privately get off watching girl-on-girl porn."

"You've got it. So my sister the chameleon says whatever she feels will make her husband proud of her. Whatever ridiculous thought of the day he has, she adopts that viewpoint as her own."

"That surprises me. Lesley always seemed so independent in high school." I really didn't want to be talking about Lesley. I took Lisa's hand and drew her nearer, closing the space between us.

"Yeah, well, she fell into that trap my parents fed her, that her life wouldn't be complete without a husband. She believed it. At least she wanted to." Her hand snaked around my waist.

"How did you avoid that trap?"

She stood on her tiptoes, and her lips hovered over mine. "You."

"Me?" I closed my eyes, put my arms around her, and held her to me. As though Dane had never interrupted us, I was instantly in an advanced state of arousal.

"Yes, you. From the moment I could feel desire, you were always it for me. I never wanted to be with anyone but you. That's when I knew no man could ever generate the longing in me that I felt for you."

"You were fourteen when I left." So clear and strong was my need to make love to her, I was almost panting.

"Yes. Fourteen." She kissed my chin. "And very much aware of my sexuality." She kissed my cheek, lingering there. "You always had such a fire inside you, an energy and a spirit that was so honest and different from everyone else around here. You were the most subtly stunning girl in school, a diamond in the rough. I knew it back then, and I'm very glad to see that I was right." She kissed the tip of my nose. "When you left, I was devastated." She kissed my cheek. "When you came back for your uncle's funeral, I was so obsessed with seeing you that I skipped all my classes at grad school to get here. But you were only here for one day, and I missed you. And—"

I silenced her with a kiss so blazing, the heat alone should have melted us both. I was overwhelmed by Lisa's devotion to me, staggered by the passion she was showing, and a little stunned at the powerful emotions she was bringing out in me. It was as though I had always wanted her as much as she obviously had always wanted me.

The sensation of her lips on mine was at once liberating and conquering. I didn't want it to end, and yet I wanted to move on to whatever would put out this raging inferno in my core. Grinding against each other, we worked that one continuous kiss until I couldn't stand it anymore.

"Lisa, do you want to take this upstairs?" My voice was husky with want.

"No," she said in a throaty response, "I want you to take me right here."

"Oh Jesus." My head fell back as just the idea of that galvanized me.

"But... upstairs would work, too."

I looked down into vibrant green eyes and a confident, sensual smile that inflamed my own desires to even greater heights. "You are still a brat, you know that?"

"So I hear."

I curled my fingers around hers and took her with me around the house as I made sure all the lights were off and everything was locked. As I was pulling her upstairs, my heart was pounding so hard, I thought it might burst before I got her to the bedroom. I guess things had finally come full circle. She had waited all those years for me, and now I could barely wait a few minutes to be with her.

She stood in front of me in the dark bedroom, and I pressed my body against her and slowly backed her up to the bed. When her legs struck the low side frame, she grabbed two fistfuls of my shirt and pulled me down with her as she lost her balance. Laughing, we playfully wrestled for a minute while maneuvering our bodies so that we both fit on the bed. She looked up at me reverently as my face hovered over hers. "You are so beautiful," she whispered.

"Mmm. Thank you. But it's not like you couldn't give whiplash to a monk, you know." Good Lord, she was gorgeous, a perfect medley of, well, *everything*. And there was a sweetness to her sensuality, an extraordinary combination that definitely worked in her favor.

She chuckled and then became serious again. "I can't believe I'm finally here with you."

"If it makes you feel any better, I can't believe I'm here with you, either." I never would have predicted that I would even run into my high school best friend's pesky little sister, much less end up in bed with her, feeling like I was always meant to be there. Stretching out on top of her, fully clothed, was beginning to feel like torture.

"And you still have that deep, smoky voice that's only gotten sexier. When Lesley walked over to the table tonight with you in tow, I thought I was going to faint. I really didn't think you would come back for your mother's service."

"Do you always talk this much when you're about to have the hell fucked out of you?"

That made her really laugh. "First, I don't think that's possible, and second, my, you certainly have an ego, don't you?"

"You don't think I can fuck the hell out of you?"

"No." She put on a Southern belle accent and batted her eyelashes. "But I'd be much obliged if you'd try."

I leaned down and kissed her tenderly, an action much different from what we had already experienced with one another. Her tongue begged entry to my mouth, and I did not deny her. After a few delicious minutes, I lifted my head and rolled off of her. "Why don't you get undressed?" I suggested, my inner voyeur screaming.

In an impossibly seductive voice, she responded, "Why don't you undress me?"

Oh fuck. When did she get to be so hot? Why wouldn't I want to undress her? I positioned myself so that I could get the maximum effect. I unbuttoned her blouse and opened it to find a very full bra that unhooked in the front. I loved those things, so much less fumbling. I'd spent many a morning apologizing for the condition of a bra I'd ended up ripping off my bed partner's body because it was frustratingly impeding the flow of the foreplay.

I ran both hands over her cupped breasts, and then down over her tight, femininely defined stomach. I didn't need to ask if she exercised regularly; it was obvious. I unbuttoned her jeans, and she lifted her behind off the bed so that I could slide them off, then I dropped them on the floor. My eyes devoured the partially-clothed woman on display before me.

She watched my eyes the entire time, getting great pleasure from the way I took in every curve, every inch of her exposed body.

Not being able to wait until she was completely naked, I began at the low-cut waistband of her panties and kissed her warm skin upward until I reached that front clasp. With little effort, the bra was unhooked and I raised up on my arms so that I could see her. I'm not normally a breast snob. Big, small, in between... to me they are all perfect as long as I can hold them and put my mouth on them, but hers were downright exquisite. "Jesus, Lisa." I must have sounded awestruck. Her body was amazing.

"I work out," she admitted shyly.

"So I see." I reached down and pulled her to me by her open blouse, removing that and her bra and then laying her back down. I ran my hand over her panties; she was soaking wet. "These have to come off," I announced as I peeled them off. Scanning her supine form in all its glory, I didn't know where to start.

I ran my hand up her leg, along her thigh, and brushed over her trimmed, reddish-blonde mound. She shivered as I drew my fingers across her abdomen and began circling her breasts. I crawled over her and buried my face into the hollow of her neck, slowly, deliberately, kissed down to her right nipple, and sealed my lips around it. She put her hands into my hair as her breathing hitched and became rapid when my fingers feathered their way south, then stroked their warm, wet goal. When I switched my mouth to her other breast, I must have gone off target, because within seconds her hand was curling around my wrist, repositioning my fingers. When I knew she was getting close, I carefully inched up, trying not to move my hand or lose the rhythm. I wanted to watch her come, to see her expression when she spilled over. I needed to see how she ultimately reacted to my touch.

Her eyes locked onto mine, and she grabbed my wrist again, ensuring I wouldn't lose her when she was so near the precipice.

She was moving against me, fully participating, when her

grip tightened and her breath held for what seemed like a dangerously long moment, and then she exploded with a moan that jolted through me like electricity.

Before she completely recovered her breath, she grabbed my face with both hands and pulled it toward hers, kissing me with a voracity that matched her climax. Still lightly stroking her, I moved my fingers lower, circling her opening, which elicited another groan. She spread her legs and I entered her easily, provoking a gasp of pleasure. For the next fifteen minutes, we kissed feverishly while I pumped my fingers into her and she thrust against each stroke, driving me deeper.

She broke our kiss long enough to tell me she felt like she was almost there. I eased my fingers back, curling them up, feeling for that spot I knew would push her over, and then I increased my rhythm. In less than a minute, she was holding onto me, digging her short nails into my shoulders, panting heavily in my ear while she once again inhaled until she released, bucking and arching, saying my name over and over in a feral growl. I held her until her body settled from its explosive orgasm. I kept my stilled fingers inside her while she breathed heavily against my neck.

"Jesus, Hunter, where did you learn to do that *?*"

"Do what?"

"That… what you just did. I've never felt… that… before."

I raised my head and studied her expression of wonder with astonishment. "You've never had a vaginal orgasm?"

She blinked at me and shook her head. "No. But at least now I know what all the fuss is about."

I grinned, feeling pretty damned proud of myself. "That was really your first?"

"Yes. And hopefully not my last."

"It won't be if I have anything to say about it." I kissed her forehead. What the hell had her "sort of" girlfriend been doing in bed with her for the past four years?

"Are you eventually going to take off your clothes?" Her smile was salacious.

"Eventually. Just not yet." I winked at her, kissed her, and slid down her body.

"Oh my God," she half-laughed, half-wailed. "I don't know if my body can take this."

"Only one way to find out." I parted her folds, then cleaned up the residual of my earlier handiwork. She tasted amazing, and I immediately knew I was never going to get enough of this. I stayed nuzzling in my furry nook for another extended orgasm, until she begged me to stop. I slithered back up her magnificently fit body, collapsed beside her, and pulled her over on top of me.

"You're going to have to give me a minute here."

"Take all the time you need," I told her, feeling very content, a little cocky, and suddenly very tired.

"Okay. I'll just lay here like this then."

"Fine with me." I yawned.

"You're yawning?" She pretended to be insulted. "Do I bore you?"

I smirked at her. "You wore me out."

"*I* wore *you* out?" That made her laugh, and she rested her head on my chest, squeezing me tightly, basking in the afterglow.

And that's the last thing I remembered until morning.

Chapter 7

I awoke, sensing I was not alone but too fuzzy to connect the dots right away. As the recollection of the previous night filtered into my jet-lagged brain, I slowly opened my eyes to see a blonde head on my shoulder and a warm, naked body snuggled against me.

I smiled as the vivid images of making sweet love to this special woman filled me, and I squeezed her shoulder with more affection than I thought I had in me.

"You snore." Her sleep-soaked voice vibrated against my breastbone.

"You drool," I countered, seeing a small puddle on my T-shirt by her mouth.

"Well, that's attractive," she mumbled. "Thanks for pointing that out, Ms. Buzzsaw."

I chuckled and kissed the top of her head. "Did I keep you awake?"

She lifted her face to look at me, grinning impishly. "Not by snoring."

Kissing her forehead, I said, "Did I ravish you in my sleep?"

"Mmm, no. You didn't need to. What you did before you fell asleep was enough to keep me awake."

"You sound awfully sleep groggy for someone who's been awake all night."

"Exhaustion tagged me about two hours ago. Despite your snoring." She kissed my chin and nestled her head against my right breast.

"Was it that bad?"

"No. It was kind of cute, actually." I could hear the grin in her voice as the hand under my T-shirt lazily brushed back and forth over my nipple. As tired as I still was, she was starting to fire me up. "You never even got undressed."

"I was waiting for you to undress me," I whispered into her hair. She pinched my nipple hard. I laughed, my hand covering hers.

"Ow! What was that for?"

"Undress you? Do you realize how out you were? I'm not into necrophilia. I like my lover to be conscious, thank you."

Lover. I liked the sound of that word in connection to her.

"Sorry I crashed on you."

"It's okay. I could see at the bar last night that you were tired. I was being very selfish by coming over uninvited, I know." She raised up on one elbow, looking at me. "But I wanted to give myself the ultimate birthday present. I only got half my wish, though."

"What was the other half?"

"To make you feel as good as you made me feel."

I know I should have gotten up and brushed my teeth before I kissed her again, but I couldn't resist. She didn't seem to mind as she stretched out over me and prolonged the kiss, an action that began to liquefy my body. She freed her lips from mine and sat up, straddling my hips, giving me an opportunity to feast my eyes on her magnificent body. Her wetness on my lower belly made me want to flip her over and fuck her senseless. I reached up and cupped her breasts, then drew my hands down her sides until they rested on her thighs.

She slowly lifted my T-shirt, revealing a little bit of skin at a time until she got the shirt over my head and off my arms, then tossed it over her shoulder onto the floor. Her eyes and hands roamed over my chest in appreciative investigation, and she slowly, softly touched my breasts and then my nipples, which couldn't have gotten any harder if they had been encased in cement. She had a way of looking at me that took my breath away. "Very nice," she said after several minutes of exploration. "Very, very nice."

"Glad you approve." I wondered what she was going to do

next. I didn't have to wait long. She swung her leg off me and stripped off my boxer shorts, dropped them on top of my T-shirt, and laid down on her side. Facing me, she scanned my nakedness, paying particular attention to the parts she hadn't seen before.

Leaning over, she kissed me passionately and then trailed more kisses down the length of my torso until she got to the volcano pulsing in my center. She was going for the gold her first shot. I loved being stroked and I loved being entered and driven to orgasm, but nothing gets me off more fully and completely than a well-placed, skilled tongue.

"Mmm… I feel like I should say grace." She nuzzled me before settling in with her torturously sweet assault, tempering her pace.

Thoroughly enjoying her catering to my overwhelming need at the moment, listening to and feeling her attentions, I shut my eyes as she continued her "mmms." I maneuvered a pillow under my ass to give her better access, and she wrapped her arms around my thighs, never missing a beat. I felt the sensation start to build and began to rock against her mouth. I tried to keep my movement to a minimum, because she was exactly where I needed her to be and I didn't want her to lose her place.

She stimulated me right to the verge, and then, when I crested, she prolonged the stimulation, drawing my climax out, making me come twice in a row. With her mouth still on me, she pushed deep into me with two fingers, just their penetration provoking a third orgasm from me almost instantly. I was stunned. I had never been multi-orgasmic. Interesting. We had both given each other something new.

"Jesus, you're good at this." It was a thought that was said out loud.

I felt her smile against me, and when her tongue started moving again, I had to stop her; I was a tad tender. And I was impressed that she had been down there for as long as she had and never seemed to come up for air… not that I had really been paying attention until now. "So, can you teach me how to breathe through my ears like that?" She laughed as she rested her head on my thigh.

"Sure. As soon as you teach me this little trick." She wriggled her fingers before she slowly withdrew them and crept up my body, roosting on top of me, tracing my lips with the fingers that had just been inside me.

"Don't put those in my mouth," I warned her good-naturedly.

She took that as a challenge, attempting to force them past my clenched teeth. I grabbed her hand and moved it away, but she was a strong little shit and she swung them back to my mouth. "You don't want to taste yourself?"

"Not particularly."

She was coltish and persistent, giggling while we scuffled playfully. I finally rolled her over, trapping her beneath me, and I pushed her fingers into her own mouth, where she slowly, deliberately fellated them. "Mmm. Lisa like."

I found her actions erotic and her friskiness endearing, and I just had to kiss her. She poked her tongue inside, making sure it hit every section of my mouth until I captured it and lightly sucked on it.

Separating her face from mine, she said, "Guess you got to taste yourself after all."

She was, indeed, a brat. I gave her a few quick pecks as I held her. "Do you have to be at work or anything?"

"No. I wasn't sure how I would be feeling the morning after my birthday, so I arranged to be out of the office today."

"So, you don't have to be anywhere at any specific time?"

"My parents wanted me to come over for lunch, but I can blow them off."

"Jesus, don't tell your mother you were with me all night. She'll ground you until your AARP kicks in." She gave me a half-hearted swat. "It's true. She finds out you've been with me, she'll probably blame me for you being gay."

"Well, it kind of is your fault," she teased. She brought her lips to mine for another kiss. "If you hadn't been so damned beautiful and sexy and strong and commanding…"

"I'd say flattery will get you everywhere, but that's a cliché and I avoid clichés like the plague." My feeble joke made her chuckle again. "Tell you what… I *really* like cuddling with you, so why don't we try to get a couple more hours sleep and then decide on the rest of our day from there?"

"God, I would love that," she admitted honestly. We snuggled in, getting comfortable, me on my back and Lisa burrowed against my side with an arm around my waist and a leg hooked over mine.

"Hunter?"

"Yes?"

"Welcome home."

Two things hit me immediately when I woke up – the phone was ringing, and I was alone. The phone could wait.

I sat up and searched the room for Lisa, hoping she hadn't called a cab and gone home. The thought instantly made me miss her. I couldn't imagine her leaving without waking me, though, and I rubbed the sleep out of my eyes and tried to get my bearings.

I looked at the clock and groaned, seeing that half the day was gone already and I still needed to make an appearance at Sam's at some point. Better I go to his house than he show up here. One brother catching me with my pants practically down before I had a chance to come out to them was bad enough. I wanted to tell Sam myself rather than having the news come from Dane's warped perspective.

After stretching as I got out of bed, I put on the same clothes I'd worn after my shower the night before. It was then I noticed that Lisa's clothes were still on the floor, which coaxed a warm smile out of me. She was somewhere in the house… naked.

My first order of business, though, had to be relief for my bladder.

On my way back from the bathroom, I passed my old room and saw that the door was half open. Knowing I had closed it the night before, I peeked in and saw Lisa leaning close to the vanity, reading one of the newspaper clippings from so long ago. Wearing my old bathrobe, which was way too big for her, she looked adorable.

I knew she knew I was up because you could hear that toilet flush three states away. "Finding anything interesting?"

Not turning, she addressed my reflection in the mirror. "I remember these basketball games like they were yesterday. You took us to sectionals and then to the state championships." She pivoted and walked over to me. "I went to every one of your games."

I stopped and thought about that. "Oh my God... you did, didn't you?" I took her face in my hands and kissed her tenderly, then wrapped my arms around her. "And I was so rotten to you sometimes. How could you have been so loyal?"

"You weren't really rotten, per se, you were just obviously annoyed. Come on, I *was* a little pest." She laughed.

"You had your moments," I agreed. "I always thought you shadowed us all the time because you wanted to be like your sister or just didn't want to be left out."

"Me? Want to be like Lesley? Uh... no." She shook her head emphatically. "I never wanted to be like Lesley."

I took Lisa's hand in mine and led her downstairs to the kitchen. As she filled the automatic coffee maker with water, I went in search of the coffee. I swung open a cupboard door and, instead of what I was looking for, I found three cans of cat food, which reminded me that I needed to feed Orion. I plucked out a can and held it in my hand while continuing to look for coffee.

Lisa took the cat food from my grasp. "Mmm, liver, bacon and cheese bits... Never had this particular brew, but as long as it has caffeine..."

"Very funny. It's for Orion."

"That monster is still alive?" Her incredulity was clear in her voice.

As if on cue, Orion slunk into the kitchen, meowing, homing in on my bare leg and making a beeline for it. I froze as I prepared for the assault of teeth and claws, but it never came. Instead, she circled my calf, rubbing up against me and purring loudly. "She hasn't attacked me yet. Either she's changed, or she's saving it up for one horrendous assault." I suddenly remembered that my mother used to keep her coffee in the freezer. And that's where I found it. "Aha."

Lisa made coffee while I fed the cat and returned to the kitchen to accept a full mug and a quick kiss before we sat down opposite each other at the table. "So, Hunter, do you think Dane is going to cause trouble for you?"

"In general, or because of last night?"

"Both, I guess." She rested her chin on her palm and gazed at me.

Feeling the urge to grab her and take her right back upstairs, I reluctantly behaved myself. "I think he'll give me trouble in general.

He's probably waited the last sixteen years for this chance, and I'm sure he thinks last night will give him some leverage. I think Sam might be the only one he'll tell, because the last thing Dane is going to want is for people to know that he has a lesbian sister, especially since he's upping his political stakes by running for Congress."

"Say, that's right." With sudden realization, she said,

"Actually, you kind of have him over a barrel, don't you? You could publicly come out to, say, the local paper and really bury him."

"And don't think that isn't tempting. I guess I'll wait and see how dirty he wants to fight."

"Oh, by the way, Sam called and left a message on the machine, wondering if you were up yet."

My mother still had an answering machine instead of voicemail. I shouldn't have been surprised. After all, she was a prominent member of a city that had always hated change. "I was wondering who called."

We sat and chatted through another cup of coffee and went back upstairs to shower, something we did together, which ended up with more than just hot water steaming up the bathroom. I couldn't get enough of her. I couldn't get enough of touching her, of looking at her, and especially not of hearing her voice moaning my name.

When we were finally clean and dry, we dressed and discussed what we were going to do that afternoon.

"Although I would much prefer to spend the day with you, I think I'm going to go to Mom and Dad's for a late lunch after all,"

Lisa said, as she dressed in the clothes she had worn the night before, except for her underwear.

"And I would love to spend the rest of the day with you, but I have a few things I need to do and I wouldn't be able to devote the time to you that I would like to."

"I have to go to my parents' house to pick up my dogs. They've been visiting 'grandma' and 'grandpa' for a week while I had new tile installed in my kitchen. I suppose I could have just blocked off the work area, but I think they would have been too tempted to find out what was going on. I'm sure you don't want to visit my folks again so soon, and I don't want you sitting out in the car…"

"No, no, go and pick up your kids and relax and have a bite with your parents. We can get together later, if you'd like."

"Oh yeah, I'd like." Her smile was unabashedly wanton. It made my mouth go dry.

I cleared my throat and tried to work up some moisture. She grinned, knowing the effect she had on me. I needed to get my head back into the present and away from thoughts more lascivious.

"Could you help me return the car before I take you home?"

She drove my rental car, and I followed her in my nephew's Jeep, loving the way the rugged vehicle handled. It was a five-speed manual transmission, and the stick shift moved easily from gear to gear. I missed driving a stick. At home in L.A., with the constant stop and go of rush hour traffic, it was easier on the car, and my temper, to have an automatic, but I preferred driving a shift any day.

As it was unusually warm for October, I had removed the ragtop and let the sun beat down on me the seven miles from my mother's house to the south end of town. After returning the car at the rental office and getting the paperwork squared away, I drove Lisa to her house so she could change her clothes.

"It wouldn't do for me to show up at my parents' house wearing the same outfit I had on last night," she said with a grin. "Especially since we don't want my mother to ground me." She gestured toward the house. "Would you like to come in?"

"I'd love to, but I think I'd better not." I shrugged at her immediate pout. "You know I can't trust myself to keep my hands off you, and then neither of us would accomplish anything this afternoon. Well... anything *productive*."

She leaned over, as if to kiss me, and I drew back a little and glanced around at the surrounding houses. "What if your neighbors are watching?"

"It's a small town, Hunter. People know my romantic inclinations, remember?"

She kissed me then, and I watched her get out of the car and walk to her front door, a smile on my face. She turned and gave me a little wave before she disappeared inside, and I drove away, grinning like a fool, feeling like a schoolgirl in love.

Welcome home, indeed.

Chapter 8

In Sam's driveway, I pulled up behind what I assumed was his car. I knew it wasn't Dane's, or at least it wasn't the car he had ridden in the night before. I wondered if he had already outed me to Sam, which was why I had decided to just show up as opposed to calling. I didn't want to get into the subject of my orientation over the phone. Mom's wake wasn't scheduled to start until four o'clock, so we had a couple of hours to get things out in the open.

I knocked on the frame of the screen door and waited this time instead of just walking in. Last night had been different, when he had obviously been expecting guests. With the chatter in the living room, he would not have heard me knock. Someone descended the steps inside, and Trina was at the door, pushing it open.

"For heaven's sake, Hunter, you don't have to knock, you're family." She gave me a playful swat on the shoulder as I slid past her. "Sleep off your jet lag, did you?" she asked, as she followed me upstairs to the kitchen. I thought I caught a hint of teasing in her tone.

"Sort of. That always takes a few days."

"Especially if you've been up all night," she said, with a raised eyebrow and amused expression. She held up a mug. "Coffee?"

They knew. "Sure. Got anything to put in it?"

"Baileys?"

I seriously thought about it and then I shook my head. "Black is fine. So, when did Dane call you?"

She filled the mug and handed it to me. "About two hours ago. And, oh, the names he was calling you."

I took a sip and looked at her over the rim of the cup. She didn't appear to be put off in the least. "I'm surprised he can speak at all, considering the condition he was in last night."

"Unfortunately, that's normal for him when he's at an event where there's alcohol of any kind. He's working on his fourth DUI, which is why Emma drives after parties or functions."

"Lovely. And the town keeps voting him into office? How can he keep that kind of behavior quiet? A politician's life is an open book, and there's always somebody who can't be bribed to shut them up, no matter what kind of lawyer he has."

"Yep. But, don't worry, the longer he's in office, the more enemies he's making. If he gets voted into Congress, I'll be surprised. And... speaking of lawyers..." There was that look of amusement again.

"What exactly did Dane tell you?"

"He told Sam, who told me, that he caught you having sex with Lisa Riordan in the kitchen."

"We weren't having sex." I took another sip of coffee as she folded her arms and waited patiently. "We were making out when Dane walked in. We had sex later."

She shook her head, laughing. "Well, I have to tell you, Hunter, you've got excellent taste. Lisa Riordan is very well-respected around here. She's gone after some pretty big businesses for violating state eco-laws, and she's won. Not to mention she's classy and quite beautiful."

"That she is." I studied my sister-in-law. "You don't seem surprised or shocked... about either Lisa or me."

"Just because we live in East Bumfuck doesn't mean we automatically have to think and act like rubes, you know. We *do* have connections to the outside world. Sam and I guessed a long time ago that you were probably gay, and we've known about Lisa for a while."

"You guessed about me?" Why is it when we make the decision to finally come out to family and loved ones, we're stunned that no one is surprised?

"Well, yeah. Come on, Hunter. You were the ultimate jock in high school, you told Sam all those boys you went out with were really just buddies, and then you nearly kicked Phil Khaury's ass for telling people that he did something with you he didn't, so that Sam wouldn't go kick his ass—"

"Sam? Kick somebody's ass?" I smirked at the visual. Phil would have annihilated Sam, and then I would have had to beat the ever-loving shit out of Phil, which would have humiliated my older brother *and* Phil. But I didn't care about Phil's reputation.

"He was mad enough to," she said defensively. "Anyway, you're thirty-four-years old, you're not married, never have been, never even come close, never talked about a boyfriend, not even dating anybody and... Shit, Hunter, you're gorgeous, you're obviously in great shape, and you're not too intolerable to be around," she added with a smile. "I agree, it would take a very confident, strong man to be with you, but you can't tell me that out where you live, you haven't met at least a few. So, we figured you were a lesbian and you'd tell us when you wanted us to know."

Wow. Why hadn't I thought that they would be able to put the pieces together? "Sam is okay with this?"

"Sam loves you. He just wants you to be happy. He doesn't care who you sleep with, your sex life is none of our business. He—no, *we* would like you back in our lives on a regular basis."

I nodded in acceptance. "And you? What do you think about it?"

"Hell, I think it's hot. Not that I want to try it myself, but you and Lisa Riordan? Very hot." The look on her face was actually making me blush. "You certainly didn't waste any time last night, did you?"

"She came after me." I supplied an edited recounting of the evening before, right up until Dane's intrusion. "I called Pucinski's Safety and Security before I left the house today. They're coming out to change the locks about three this afternoon." I was about to ask where Sam was when I heard a door open and close down the hall. He entered the kitchen, looking like he was freshly out of the shower.

"Well, well, well... if it isn't my sister, the stud." He put his arm around my shoulder. "The kitchen counter, huh? And with Lisa Riordan, no less."

"Oh, God." My chin touched my chest. So much for privacy and discretion. My cheeks were burning. "I'm going to kill Dane."

"Stand in line." Sam chuckled. He took a bottle of water out of the fridge, opened it, and took a long swig. "So are you sure you're not going to come to Mom's wake?"

"Yes, I'm sure. But thanks for asking." I tried to make light of it. I was grateful that after he made his little comment, he immediately moved on to something else.

"How'd the house look to you after all this time?"

"Smaller. It was weird. I can still feel her presence, though."

Suddenly I wished that Trina had added some Baileys Irish Cream to my coffee.

"I don't think she ever stopped loving you."

"Well, she had a funny way of showing it."

"You know how she was. Once she got something in her head, her pride would never let her change her mind, even if she knew she was wrong. She was too stubborn to ever admit her mistakes."

"I tried to see her when I was here for Uncle David's funeral. She'd had nine years to swallow her pride and at least talk to me. That's all I wanted, just for her to talk to me. She made her point. I got it. She not only rubbed my nose in it, she stomped my head into the ground. I don't see how you can classify that as love," I said, getting angry all over again.

He nodded, acknowledging my frustration. "I can't explain it. I just know she was never the same after you left."

"She kicked me out and shut me out of her life. I think that would change anyone with a conscience. How do you justify treating your child like shit her whole life and then acting like she doesn't exist? Mom was supposed to be such a religious woman. Doesn't the Bible teach about forgiveness? Hate the sin, not the sinner, and all that crap? I mean… did she ever even ask about me?"

"No. She didn't have to. Any time you would send an email or when you and I would talk on the phone, I would always just happen to mention it to her. She would always pretend she wasn't listening, but she never asked me to not talk about you." He took another swallow of water. "So, what was it that caused such a rift, anyway?"

Now that they knew I was a lesbian, holding onto "The Secret" any longer didn't make any sense. I sighed and held my mug out to Trina. "Now you can put some Baileys in here." She took the mug and did as I requested. "You haven't guessed?"

"She knew you were gay?" That assumption came from Trina, who handed the mug back to me.

I nodded. "Yeah. But not until she came home unexpectedly and caught me in bed with someone."

Sam nearly dropped his water bottle. "Mom caught you in the act?" He exchanged shocked glances with Trina. "Oh, my God... she... you... oh, my God."

"Yeah. And it was right *in* the act, too." The memory of that act and the look on Mom's face as she stood in my doorway conjured up a plethora of emotions, all of which caused my face to flush.

"Who did she catch you in bed with? Don't tell me it was Lisa Riordan."

"Lisa? For God's sake, Sam, Lisa was only fourteen when I left. Jesus! Give me some credit here."

"Hey, it was just a wild guess. You guys did hook up awfully fast last night. And finding you in bed with a fourteen-year-old girl could certainly be grounds for expulsion from the house."

"No, it wasn't Lisa Riordan. Although, Mom may have preferred it be Lisa."

"Who was it?"

I thought about not revealing the identity of my very first lover.

It was sixteen years later, but I had held it all inside me for so long, protecting her, that not saying her name was second nature now. I knew she was most likely far, far away, the event long forgotten shortly after, when she moved on to her next conquest. Why was I sheltering her? She not only sold me out to try and save her own ass, she never took any responsibility for the incident or even tried to find out if I was okay afterwards. I know she had heard about my banishment, the whole town knew about it; and yet she did nothing to try and make it right, or easier. I took a deep breath. "It was Jennifer Visson." I waited for the reaction, which was understandably delayed as the name registered and then the impact hit.

"*The minister's wife?*" Trina said finally.

"That's the only Jennifer Visson I knew."

Sam was stunned. "You had sex with Mrs. Vixen? And Mom caught you?" I nodded to both questions. And then, ever the practical one, he said, "What the hell were you doing fucking her in the house? You *deserved* to get caught."

"Sam! I was eighteen, it was my first affair. I didn't care *where* we had sex, as long as we had it. She kept assuring me we wouldn't get caught, and I believed her."

"Is that why they left town so quickly?" Trina asked. "Nobody bought the excuse that her parents were ill. She could have gone, tended to them, and come back. Uprooting the whole family didn't make sense."

"I think she was afraid Mom would expose her and bring scandal to her family and the church, so they left before there was any backlash."

"But she was married… had kids," Trina said in confusion.

"That doesn't matter. I know a lot of closeted gay people who are married and have families. I know a lot of married-with-kids gay people who have come out after they've discovered they don't have to live that lie anymore."

"Did Reverend Visson know about her, uh, inclinations?" Sam asked.

"Yes. And back then? I didn't care that she had a family. Her husband and her children were her concern, not mine." I shrugged. "I was so hooked on her, nothing mattered except when we were next going to get together. I was eighteen and having sex for the first time in my life with the hottest woman in town. If her husband was okay with it, who was I to be the moral compass of their marriage?"

There was dead silence. Sam and Trina again exchanged looks of disbelief. Sam shook his head. "The minister's wife.

80

God, she was such a fox, the unobtainable fantasy of many a boy in the congregation, I'll tell you. Jesus, Hunter, when you do things, you do them big."

Sam, Trina, and I talked about the rift in more detail; it was a relief to finally get it all out. It felt like I had cleansed my soul, and I wished I hadn't kept it inside for so long. Maybe if I had outed myself sooner to my brother and others in Otter Falls, it would have forced my mother to face some truths and realities rather than perpetuating the shadow of shame and evil she'd created around the whole thing. Perhaps if Sam and Trina had found out the reason for my exile sixteen years earlier, they might have reacted differently, but their attitude now was one of acceptance and sadness for the time lost and wasted. I thought back to the time I spent with Uncle David.

After I told them that Mom had kicked me out, Uncle David and Aunt Cissy took me in and never asked why. The only comment my aunt made was that she knew it was just a matter of time before Mom relented. I assured them I would only stay as long as it took for me to earn enough money to leave town. I was grateful for their generosity, bunking down in the basement guest room they normally used for teenage slumber parties. Even after I had been there for three weeks, and despite the persistence of my four nosy cousins, I hadn't really spoken to anyone. I went to work, begged for extra shifts, and rarely slept.

I clocked out from work, threw my soiled apron into the dirty clothes bin, and walked to my locker. I was still a zombie, reeling from feeling like the life had been slapped out of my soul and wondering if I was ever going to stop smelling like pepperoni.

It was dark when I walked outside and right into Sam. We stared at each other for a moment until he broke the silence.

"What happened?"

"What do you care?" I snapped. "I've been out of the house for almost a month, and you haven't even bothered to try and talk to me, to see if I was okay." It stung worse when I heard the words out loud. "I would expect that from Dane, but not from you."

"You know my work schedule is the total opposite of yours, and I'm working just as many hours as you are. Besides, I knew you were at Uncle David's. He called and told Mom."

"Wow, I'm so glad he did. I'm sure she was so worried," I said, my voice dripping with sarcasm.

"They had a big fight on the phone, and she told him she had no daughter anymore and not to call her again."

"What else did you hear her say to him?" I asked cautiously.

"Nothing about why you two aren't speaking, if that's what you're wondering." We walked slowly toward the bus stop. "Come on, Hunter, what happened?"

"Why do you want to know? What difference does it make?" I was suddenly angry, and I turned and punched him in the arm, hard.

"Ow!" He rubbed his bicep. "Shit, I didn't kick you out. Why are you pissed at me?"

"Because you have no balls! You never stand up to her. You never tell her what she's doing is wrong. You just go along with her."

"But I've told you I know what she does is wrong."

"And how has that ever helped me?" My anger was turning to frustration, and I could feel the tears threatening. I took a few deep breaths to hold them back.

"Well," he said, "I have to look out for myself, you know? If I sided with you, she'd get mad at me, maybe even kick me out. I'm trying to save enough money so that when Trina and I get married, I can afford a house. I can't do that if I have to pay for an apartment and utilities and all that other stuff."

"She'll never get that mad at you, Sam. She needs you. You're all she ever wanted you to be. You make her proud because you're nothing like him. How many times have we heard that you look exactly like pictures of Grandpa Jon when he was your age, that you take after her side of the family—like that's the biggest accomplishment in the world. And then she looks at me with disdain and tells me what a pity I had to take after the Roberge side, with Grandpa Sam being such an

82

irresponsible drunk and Grandma Viv being such a slob."

Sam winced at the words. He'd heard them as many times as I had.

I smiled ruefully. "You can't tell me you're not relieved that you look like the Hunter side of the family. It doesn't matter that you have no control over it."

"Is that what the fight was about? Again? Why would this time be so much worse?"

He just didn't get it. "Shouldn't the first time have been one time too many? She's my mother, she should love me no matter who or what I look like." We stopped at the bus stop. "But, no, that's not what this fight was about. This fight was a wake-up call for me. I'm never going to get anywhere in Otter Falls. Mom has never made me feel like I really belong to this family, and before she poisons the rest of town about me, I need to go."

"Go? Go where?"

"I don't know yet. I'm thinking maybe California."

"California? Are you nuts? You don't know anyone in California."

"That's why I want to go there. If no one knows me or anything about me, they won't have any expectations, and I won't be disappointing people all the time." My bus pulled up to the stop.

"Can I give you a ride to Uncle David's?"

"No, thanks. I've got to start relying on myself, or I'm never going to make it." I stepped onto the bus. "Maybe you should start thinking about doing that, too, before it's too late."

"Aw, Hunter, you're talking crazy. Give her a couple more weeks, she'll cool off and—"

"No, she won't. Not this time. I'm not going to be her punching bag anymore. I'm not going to take the brunt of her unfinished business with Dad anymore. You and Dane are on your own, because I'm done, Sam."

The bus doors had closed and that was the last time I saw Sam until Uncle David's funeral.

"Sam, do you have any idea why Mom, who seemed to hate me so much, would leave me her house?" It was something I couldn't figure out with the limited information I had.

"Not a clue."

So, though he was the executor of her will, Sam was also at a loss for an explanation that made sense. All he knew was that in her will, she was very specific about leaving me the house and anything that was in it, including Orion. And although Vermont had no state inheritance tax, her modest estate had provided enough to pay for an inspector to evaluate the condition of the structure as well as the electrical and plumbing systems. Since the estate value wasn't anywhere in the vicinity of the allowable $3.5 million, there was no federal inheritance tax, either.

"I do know that she stipulated which real estate agency you should use because the company has a good track record and they have a reputation for getting fair market value for the houses they sell," Sam said.

I laughed and shook my head. She was still trying to control me from the grave. "When is the official reading of the will? Shouldn't that happen before I do anything about putting the house on the market?"

He smiled. "That only happens in the movies and on television.

There's no legal requirement to gather the family together to ceremoniously read a will."

"Well, that's good. The last thing I want right now is to be shut into a room with Dane... where there are any witnesses."

"Mom's attorney's main responsibility is to ensure that the will is filed with the county clerk's office and to provide counsel before anything is done with the equity in the house. The will is likely to go through probate, and the lawyer will supervise the payment of mandatory taxes and bills, the collection of assets, and the distribution of wealth. As for the infamous reading? The reading will be done after all of the heirs have received the copy of the will which was mailed to them. In fact," Sam said, "you most likely have an official letter waiting for you back at your home address in California."

A sad yet oddly anxious tone colored Sam's next words. "I'm taking an educated guess here and thinking that you're probably going to sell the house."

"There's really no reason for me to keep it. I'm certainly not going to move back into it, and renting it is out of the question because I'm not here to make sure Dane doesn't do something to make the place uninhabitable. Do you want it? I have no problem signing it over to you... or whatever I would have to do to transfer ownership."

"Look, Hunter, Mom was very precise. You can't give it away, you have to either sell it or keep it. I'd love to have the house, but we can't afford to buy you out and Trina doesn't want to sell this place. Even if you could give it to me, I'd be torn. We could use the money from the sale, but then, we all grew up in that house, so it also has sentimental value for me."

"Which means you really wish I wouldn't sell it." When he didn't answer, I said, "Well, whatever I decide, I guarantee it will not go to Dane."

Sam looked at his watch. "We need to get ready for the wake. Are you sure you—"

"I'm positive. Even if Mom and I had been speaking, I wouldn't attend her wake. I think it's morbid. She's dead. That's not her lying in that box. It's a badly made-up shell. Why would I, or anyone else, want that to be my last memory of her?"

"Reverend Massey insisted on a wake, and Dane agreed. He's a deacon, you know."

I rolled my eyes in disgust. "Why am I not surprised? What about what you wanted?"

"I wanted what she wanted, and she wanted things done in accordance with the precepts of the church."

I nodded. "The church." My voice was not without hostility. "Hasn't that church already done enough to divide this family?"

Chapter 9

After I left Sam's, I drove to the nearby supermarket and picked up some groceries and necessities for the house. There was plenty of canned and frozen food there, but not much that I ate in my normal diet or that appealed to me. Once I got back to Mom's, I would take a really good look around and see what needed to be done. I supposed I should start going through everything and deciding what I would ship back to California and what I would sell.

Four bags full and a hundred dollars later, I pulled into Mom's driveway. Mom's. It was my place now. Regardless of legal ownership, I could never think of it as such. It never felt like my home even when I lived there.

I settled in the living room to see if the TV satellite was still connected. I figured it would be paid for until the end of the month.

I knew I should be more productive, but I just wanted to relax. I sat on the couch, swilling an energy drink, flipping through basic cable channels and wondering what Lisa was doing. So I called her cell phone.

It was ringing for the sixth time when she picked up. When she said "Hi," the smile in her voice matched my own.

"Hi, yourself. Just thought I'd see what you were up to."

Without warning, the memory of her writhing in my arms threatened to overload my sexual circuitry.

"I'm at your mother's wake." Her voice was hushed. "Well, actually, I stepped outside to answer your call."

"What are you doing there?"

"My parents insisted. I tried to tell them that other than running into her occasionally around town, I really hadn't seen your mother since high school, and that I had planned on going to the funeral, but, well, you know my mother."

"Yes. I'm sure she had something to say about me not being there with my brothers."

"She had a few comments. The most interesting was, after she viewed the body, she turned to me and said that you're the spitting image of your mother."

"Your mother is saying I look like a sixty-year-old dead woman?"

"Hunter!" Lisa laughed in spite of herself. I loved the sound of her laugh.

"First, your mom needs to get her eyes checked. Second, if my mother ever heard anyone say I looked like her, she'd be rolling over *before* she hit her grave. In fact, if many people said that, you could probably start calling her Pinwheel Sarah."

"Hunter, stop! I can't believe you're saying these things," she said, stifling a chuckle.

"Alright, fine. How did Dane act toward you?"

"He gave me a few glares, but nothing I haven't seen a hundred times magnified in a courtroom, so I gave him my sweetest smile and moved on past the receiving line." There was silence between us, and then she said, "Did you call for anything in particular, or just to get people to give me dirty looks for not remembering to turn my cell phone off?"

"I was wondering what you might be doing for dinner."

"Oh. Sorry. I have a date."

My heart sank to my feet, and all the blood in my body went with it. Of course, she could have a date. She had a long distance, sort of girlfriend she rarely saw, and she certainly hadn't been expecting me to show up in town. It was entirely possible that she had made previous plans. "You do?" It came out weaker than I intended.

"Yeah. She hasn't actually asked me yet, but I know she's going to, so I'm waiting."

Aha. The little stinker was talking about me. "Well, she should hurry up and ask you then, huh? If she doesn't, somebody better might come along and beat her to the punch."

Lisa played along. "Well, there is nobody better, so I don't think that will be an issue."

I was taking great pleasure in this. "So where is she taking you?"

"Let's see… I think it should be Atomic Seltzer's for drinks and Lariat's for dinner."

I had never heard of Atomic Seltzer's, but Lariat's I knew well. A steak house decorated in western motif, it had been around for years. The food was great, the prices were reasonable, and the dress code was casual. "And after dinner?"

"I think a nightcap will definitely be in order."

"Mmm. Absolutely. And, uh, when is she picking you up?"

"I think she should be picking me up at six-thirty. At my house."

"I'll call her and tell her not to be late, because if she is, I'll be there to take her place."

"Sorry, no one can take her place."

"Huh. Guess I'll have to keep trying then. Enjoy the rest of the wake."

"Oh yeah. I will," she said dryly, "because, you know, it's such a festive occasion."

Before I went to pick up Lisa for dinner, I started sorting through my mother's clothes and had most of the contents of her closet laid out on her bed. Orion acted as my helper, so after I kept finding items on the floor that I had placed on the nightstand, I put anything "bat-able" out of her reach. She then switched to supervising from a curled up position on one of my mother's cashmere sweaters. I still felt she was entrapping me by making me think she had mellowed, so I stayed alert around her.

I considered what I should do with Mom's clothes. My mother had excellent taste and always dressed very stylishly. She took care of her wardrobe, expertly repairing what needed it and discarding what couldn't be saved, unlike me, who wore an article of clothing until it was nothing but threads held together by willpower. Just one more thing we'd butted heads on. I divided the clothes into categories of dressy, casual, and whatever came between. I would save my final decision until tomorrow, but I was leaning toward donating everything to the local shelter for battered women.

As I pulled into Lisa's driveway, I thought she might meet me outside when she heard the Jeep. When she didn't, I went up to the entry and was about to knock when the door swung open.

"Hi." Clearly happy to see me, she grinned as she pulled me inside.

"Hey." I looked her over appreciatively. "You look great." She was wearing form-fitting, faded jeans that hung low on her hips, and a lightweight, V-neck pullover that revealed a hint of cleavage, with a hem that didn't quite make it down to her belt and showed off a bit of luscious skin.

She stepped up and greeted me with a kiss that warmed me to the bone. It wasn't quick, but she didn't linger, either. She took a handful of my jersey and led me through a long hallway to her kitchen. "Let me introduce you to the boys, and then I'll show you around." She opened a sliding glass door and whistled, and within seconds, two greyhounds were bounding into the room, whimpering and barking, tails and rear ends wagging, looking as though they were trying to turn themselves inside out. "Hey, hey... come on, settle. Settle," she ordered in a voice that was commanding but not harsh. It took them a couple of minutes, but they finally calmed down. She touched the head of the brindle-colored dog. "This is Azizi, which is Egyptian for precious. And this is Sadiki, which is Egyptian for faithful. But around here, they're just plain Oz and Deke." She scratched behind the ears of the fawn-colored Deke.

"You can pet them. They're very gentle and friendly."

I reached down, the gesture alone prompting both dogs to approach, Deke rubbing up against me like a cat and Oz leaning against my leg. Oz happily licked my hand, and Deke put his mouth around my wrist, gently grasping but not biting. "Why Egyptian names?" I petted the dogs affectionately.

"The Egyptians worshiped greyhounds as gods. From what I understand, they are descendants of a breed that goes back to ancient Egyptian times. Besides, I didn't name them. I did nickname them, though." She grinned. "So, would you like me to show you around?"

"Sure. But I'm not so sure we're going to make it past the bedroom, so maybe we should go out first."

"Horny devil, aren't ya?" She reached up and pinched my cheek. I grabbed her hand and pulled her into my arms, which made her gasp. The dogs started to fidget and whimper, bounding around us.

"Just being honest," I told her, our lips almost touching.

Never taking her eyes off me, she snapped her fingers at the dogs, who stopped bouncing. "Well, it's not like I'm starving or anything." She lifted an eyebrow.

Not kissing her at that point was just not an option. When the kiss ended, I tapped her gently on the nose. "I want to take you out to dinner. Knowing what is going to happen after dinner is going to make it that much more… appetizing."

She took my face in her hands and kissed me again. "Then let's skip Atomic Seltzer's and go directly to Lariat's. We can have drinks there. And then let's come back here so that you can have… the *grand* tour."

Walking into Lariat's was like stepping into a time warp. It hadn't changed since the last time I had been there for Sam's graduation dinner when I was fifteen. The exterior facade made it look like a saloon from the late eighteen hundreds, and the spacious interior tried to give the customer the same feel, with wood-finish, Old West-style décor. The dim lighting helped create a moderately romantic atmosphere. Sawdust and peanut shells were scattered on the floor, which added to the ambiance, and the walls were decorated with knotted ropes, lassos, and old-fashioned sepia photographs. Lariat's was known for modestly priced steaks that were cooked on an oak-fired grill and for their multi-counter salad bar.

We were shown to a booth with high backs, and Lisa ordered us a bottle of wine. I kept sneaking peeks at her over the top of my menu, still not quite absorbing how beautiful she had become and that we had spent such a remarkable night and morning together.

After our orders were taken and our wine was poured, Lisa

proposed a toast. I raised my glass to touch hers, and she said, "To dreams coming true." As we drank to that, it was also hard for me to believe that she had harbored these feelings for me for so long. It was flattering but also scary. The last thing I wanted to do was disappoint her with the real me replacing her fantasy of me.

We were almost finished with our extremely comfortable and enjoyable dinner when a voice we both recognized burst our private little bubble. That was the other thing about Lariat's—it was the premier meeting place in Otter Falls, especially on a Friday night.

"Hey! What are you two doing here?" As Lesley approached our table, her breasts reached us five seconds before she did. Her head snapped back and forth between us like she was watching a tennis match.

"Eating." Lisa gestured at the plate in front of her with a "duh" tone in her voice.

Lesley shot her sister a nasty glare, then focused on me. "I thought you were going to call me."

"Gee, Les, I don't remember saying that," I said amiably. "I've only been here a day, and I've been kind of busy."

"Not too busy for my sister to get her claws into you."

"Well, I do have to eat," I said, hoping she'd go away.

"What are you doing here, anyway?" Lisa asked her sister. "Shouldn't you be at home with the family?"

"We got our babysitter to come watch the boys so Wally and I could have a nice evening out."

"Well, enjoy," Lisa said dismissively.

"Yeah, I know why you're trying to get rid of me," Lesley said to Lisa, shaking her head. She glanced at the bottle of wine, then at Lisa. "If I didn't know any better, I'd say this looks like I interrupted a romantic dinner. What's Sharyn going to say if it gets back to her that you're sniffing around another woman, regardless of how useless your pursuit might be?" Before Lisa could respond to that, Lesley turned her attention to me. "You'd better be careful, Hunter. People are going to think you two are together."

"We are together," I told her frankly.

"No, I know you're together, here in the restaurant, dining, but they're going to think you're *together*. You know what I mean."

I looked her dead in the eyes and reached across the table, taking Lisa's hand in mine. "We are *together*, Lesley," I said, putting the same emphasis on the word as she had. I realized this wasn't the time or the place or how I wanted to get into this with her, but I couldn't tolerate her thinking that I would, in any way, agree with her assessment that homosexuality was wrong and disgusting. Lisa squeezed my hand. Lesley was shocked.

"Wait. What? You mean…" She stared at our joined hands, then at her sister and then at me. She got very quiet. Her voice hushed, she said, "Oh, I see. So I really did interrupt a romantic dinner."

"No. This is just dinner. The romance will be later." Lisa smiled.

"That's… that's really repulsive." Lesley was glaring daggers at me.

"You weren't invited over, Les. If you don't like it, then by all means, go back to your own table," I said. "And, just for the record, what's really repulsive is your attitude and behavior."

"Is that so?" she said coolly. "Well, I'm not the carpet muncher here, am I?"

"Lesley, for Christ's sake," Lisa began to say.

I let go of Lisa's hand and studied my former best friend. "Tell me something—when's the last time you gave your husband a blow job?"

Staring at me, appalled, she hissed, "That's none of your business!"

"You're right. So why do you feel my sex life is any of yours?" I let that sink in. "Now if you'll excuse us, we'd like to finish our wine, pay our check, and get out of here."

"No wonder your mother disowned you," she spat out before turning on her heel and walking away.

"That went well."

Lisa was concentrating on her wineglass. When she looked up at me, she was flushed, trying to control her anger and embarrassment. "I'm sorry about that."

I took her hand in mine. "You have no more reason to apologize for your sister than I do to apologize for my brother. Let it go, okay?" Hearing someone politely clear their throat, I looked up to see our server with our check.

She saw our entwined fingers, and a tiny smile curled the corner of her mouth as she set our bill down. "I'll take that whenever you're ready."

"You can take it now." I released Lisa's hand and we both reached for a credit card at the same time. I handed mine to the young woman first, and she walked away. Before Lisa could protest, I said, "I asked you, remember?"

"Not really."

"Whatever." I grinned at her. "Let's just get out of here. I have some serious plans for you."

Chapter 10

I had never had the experience of two dogs intently watching me have sex. There was something perverse about it, especially since they seemed so focused and interested. I finally asked Lisa if she minded shutting them out of the bedroom... at least until we were ready to go to sleep.

It probably would have been wiser to go back to my mother's, as I still didn't trust that Dane wouldn't somehow get in and destroy the place. But unless he'd had me followed, which I wouldn't have put past him, he wouldn't know whether or not I was home without actually entering the house. Hopefully I had intimidated him away from that idea. Regardless, I wanted to be with Lisa more than anything, and she wanted us to christen her house.

Making love with her was a revelation. With the women in my past, including Jennifer Visson, sex had always been a physical release and nothing more, regardless of how initially exciting. But with Lisa, sex actually meant something. I felt alive in a way I never had before. She elicited sensations and emotions within me that were new yet familiar, as if I was always meant to be with her.

After leading the greyhounds into the hallway and closing the door behind them, Lisa ran to the bed and jumped into the empty space next to me. I grabbed her and pulled her to me to keep her from bouncing right over me and onto the floor. Laughing, I rolled over on top of her and kissed her with abandon, as she manipulated her fingers inside me and proceeded to fuck me into oblivion. We traded orgasms into the night before we were both lulled to sleep by the rhythm of rain beating against the roof. The time I was spending with her, in

94

bed and out, was heady and stirring and inspiring, and I never wanted to let her go.

While we were in bed, Lisa's mother called and left several messages, warning Lisa away from me. I wasn't quite sure what was so bad about me. I thought I had done pretty well with my life so far, especially for someone who grew up being told she would never amount to anything. And it certainly wasn't me that turned her daughter into a lesbian. Well... not really.

Just before we fell asleep, her cell phone rang again. When she finally listened to that voice mail, her expression changed from surprise to sadness, and then to annoyed frustration. "That was Sharyn. Lesley called her and told her that I was sleeping with someone else and she thought Sharyn should know." She slapped the phone down on the bedside table with a sigh.

I guessed that Sharyn wasn't a fan of Lesley's either, and wanted Lisa to call her, but I wasn't going to ask.

Before we got up in the morning, three more calls came in from Mrs. Riordan. We listened to them after we were up and dressed.

The least accusatory said, "Lisa, I don't know what is wrong with you. Why do you feel the need to flaunt your personal life in public? Maybe you are okay with... with... what you are, but it's embarrassing to the rest of the family."

Seeing the look on Lisa's face, I shook my head. "I bet they don't think twice about Lesley flaunting *her* personal life in public. That double standard always pisses me off. What was 'flaunting' about having dinner in a restaurant?"

"I love my mother, but she drives me crazy," Lisa said, pouring me a cup of coffee. "I keep hoping that someday she'll change."

"And I keep hoping that I'll be reincarnated as Angelina Jolie's thong. Somehow I don't think either has a chance of happening."

We were sitting at her table working on our second pot of coffee and splitting a toasted bagel, when her cell phone rang again.

It was Sharyn. Lisa hesitated a long moment before she

connected the call. I knew the only reason she didn't want to take the call was that she didn't want to hurt her sort of girlfriend, but she knew she had to tell her the truth. I didn't want to listen, but Lisa stayed at the table when she answered the phone. When I pushed back my chair to leave and give her some privacy, Lisa's fingers gently curled around my forearm, indicating she wanted me to stay.

"Hi." Her voice was subdued. "No, I was home last night." She closed her eyes. "No, I wasn't asleep." She listened for a few seconds, and her hand tightened on my arm. "No, Sharyn. Lesley was telling you the truth." Her head dropped. "Yes. I'm sorry." My hand covered hers and patted it reassuringly. "Hunter Roberge. ... Yes, *that* Hunter Roberge." She listened some more. "Look, honey, we've known this has been coming for a long time. I'm just sorry it had to be like this. ... No, I had no idea she was going to be here. ... Yes, of course I would have told you."

More listening. I could tell by her face that she was taking heat from a woman who may not have considered herself as "sort of" as Lisa did. "Yes, she's still here." She closed her eyes. "No, Sharyn, don't come back early. There's no need—Well, I would have preferred it had happened differently, too. ... I'm sorry. I don't know what to say to you that will make it hurt any less." She flashed her eyes at me, biting her lip. "Well, that won't happen. I—" She closed the phone and set it on the table. "She hung up. Do you know how much I hate my sister right now?"

"I have a pretty good idea."

"I would have told Sharyn about you, but I would have done it in person. She didn't deserve to find out from a third party."

I brought her fingers to my lips and kissed every one of them. "Lisa, maybe you should have taken a little time to think about breaking up with her. You do realize I'm not staying here, right?"

Saying that caused my insides to roil, as it meant leaving her.

"I know. But as far as my relationship with Sharyn goes,

that doesn't make a difference. Whether you're here or three thousand miles away, my heart belongs to you, Hunter. It's always belonged to you."

We studied each other meaningfully, then I rested my forehead on the back of her hand. "I know this sounds insane, but I wish I could take you with me when I go. I don't want to be without you. I know I don't have the right to ask you to give up everything you've worked for here, but I also know I can't live here."

"No, it doesn't sound insane. What probably sounds more insane is that I believe this—you and me—was always meant to be. Nothing has ever felt more right."

I nodded. I knew what she meant because I felt it, too. I realized we had only been together two nights, but I had known her since I was eight years old, even though I had never paid much attention to her before now. It was like we were pieces of a puzzle that fit perfectly together. I stood and pulled her up into a very tight embrace.

"There are forests and parks here, too, you know. You wouldn't have to live right in Otter Falls," she said into my neck.

I kissed the top of her head. "I can't see myself coming back here to live."

"Looks like we have a dilemma then, huh?"

When I got back to my mother's, I was actually relieved to see that the house was still intact. I fed the cat, changed her litter, and went up to Mom's room to continue sorting her clothes.

Everything was happening so fast, my head was spinning. I didn't want to move back to Vermont. There were too many bad memories here, too many restrictions that I no longer had to live by, too many closed minds, too much repression. And yet, I was already visualizing us sharing my mother's house or Lisa's house. I had never before thought in terms of living with someone, of sharing that kind of space or time with anyone, but it was almost painful to think of not going to sleep and waking up every morning with her.

How was that possible with someone I had just become reacquainted with two days ago? Was I crazy? I certainly couldn't blame it on overwrought emotions due to my mother's death, because I honestly didn't feel much of anything about that. All I knew was that something hit me like a hammer to an anvil when I saw Lisa at her party, and it wasn't going away. She seemed to have a place in my every waking second, and in a rare moment of possessiveness, the thought of her not being with me and ending up with someone else was unbearable. I had to swallow a sense of panic, the intensity of which I had never experienced.

I sat down on a chair next to my mother's bed, somewhat dazed and feeling like the wind had been knocked out of me. What was going on?

Before I could get too introspective, I heard the doorbell ring. I didn't care who it was, it was a needed distraction. I went downstairs and opened the door to reveal a nice-looking, well-dressed, middle-aged man who was holding a clipboard.

"Can I help you?"

"I hope so." He smiled. "My name is Bill DeMartino, and I'm running against Dane Roberge for Congress. I'm gathering signatures for a petition to open an investigation into Alderman Roberge's transference of funds between various departments while he's been in off—"

"Where do I sign?" I enthusiastically grabbed the pen attached to the clipboard and scribbled my name on the line where he tapped his finger. It didn't matter to me what they were investigating, just knowing that they found Dane's ethics questionable confirmed my feelings of constant disappointment in his conduct. I was sure that whatever they thought he had done, it had actually been worse.

I knew my signature wouldn't mean shit, as I was not a registered voter in Otter Falls, but I wanted my name in big letters on any petition that might finally take my brother down at least one peg and make him take responsibility for his actions. I finished writing my name as legibly as I could.

"Thank you." He looked down at the petition in his hand, "Mrs.—"

"Ms."

"Ms.… Roberge." He looked up at me, his eyes wide with surprise.

"I'm his sister." I grinned. "And good luck," I told him sincerely, pumping his hand vigorously. I closed the door. Now *that* made my day. And probably Mr. Bill DeMartino's day, as well.

I was torn as to whether or not I should make an appearance at my mother's funeral. At the last minute, I held my ground and decided not to go. I knew that would make Sam feel bad, but my attendance would be dishonest, not to mention that the stir it would cause would take the focus away from the real reason people were there—to pay their respects to my mother—Saint Sarah, the martyr.

By the middle of the afternoon, I had her room pretty much cleaned out and organized. My mother's clothes were packed in large green garbage bags, which were lined up in the downstairs hallway, ready for me to load into the Jeep and take away. Next, I needed to go into the sewing room to see what projects were unfinished, which were completed, and which still needed to be distributed to whoever had ordered and paid for the clothing and costumes. I would tackle that tomorrow. There was nothing to clean out of the guest room closet, but there was still a full wardrobe of clothes in my old room. I added that to the list of tasks I would get to tomorrow.

I went downstairs and grabbed a beer out of the fridge and had just taken my first swallow, when I heard a persistent pounding on the door. It was too early for it to be Lisa, who had agreed to come over after the funeral and the little soirée at the church afterward. I swung the door open and saw a very pissed-off Lesley standing there, reeking of whiskey. Before I could say anything, she pushed past me and into the house.

"Why don't you come in?" I said as I shut the door and turned to face her. She stood there with her hands on her hips.

"I just need to know one thing, Hunter. Were you like this before? In school?"

I wasn't going to make it easy for her. "Like what?"

"You know like what. A dyke. Were you a dyke in high school?"

"Yes."

"God damn it. Why didn't you tell me?" Her words slurred, and she wobbled slightly.

"Why would I tell you? Especially if this is the way you would have behaved." And I couldn't trust that she wouldn't have outed me to the world.

"I was your best friend. Best friends are supposed to tell each other everything. How could you have kept something like this from me? You owed it to me to let me know."

"I didn't owe you a damn thing, Les. My orientation had nothing to do with you."

"People might have thought I was one, too."

"Well, they didn't. Hooray for my team." She totally missed my slam.

"You know, I wondered why you kept staring at my tits that first night. Now I know why." After two tries, she finally crossed her arms over her ample chest.

"Well, first, you nearly poked my eyes out with them, so it was pretty hard to miss them. Second, the Pope would find it difficult to tear his eyes away from those things! They're like freaking pontoons!"

"My husband likes them just fine!" She spat the words.

"He must be overcompensating for not being breastfed as a baby," I shot back.

"You're just jealous that it's his mouth that's on them and not yours!"

"Jesus, Lesley, he must have a piehole like a large mouth bass. No, thank you, your husband can have them. You sister's are just fine for me." I closed my eyes. I hadn't wanted to open that particular can of worms. Too late.

She stopped dead and cocked her head, squinting at me suspiciously. "Did you turn my sister? Is that why you left town? Is that why she's a dyke? Is that why she never stopped crushing on you?"

I was really beginning to resent this implication. "I never touched your sister. She was fucking *fourteen years old* when I left."

"Well, isn't that the best time to recruit them? When they're young and vulnerable like that?"

I was aghast. "What planet do you live on? That is such backward thinking, I honestly shouldn't dignify that with a reply. *Recruit them?* Get your ignorant ass online or go to the library and educate yourself. Your sister was born a lesbian, as was I. Fortunately, she openly acknowledged her sexuality a lot sooner than I did and caused herself a lot less grief."

"So you were really like this in high school? I mean... I used to get undressed in front of you in the locker rooms. We spent the night at each other's houses..."

"Oh Christ. And nothing happened, did it? No advances were ever made toward you, were they? You were never touched in an inappropriate manner, were you?"

"No." And then, after a beat, she added, "Why? What's wrong with me?"

"What?" She was giving me a headache.

"Aren't I attractive? Why wouldn't you come on to me? What's wrong with me?"

I was speechless. Then I managed to say, "What *is* wrong with you? You weren't like this in high school. You were the one who told all the snobby cheerleaders and jocks to shut the fuck up when they picked on Joey Lassiter and called him gayboy and fruitcup and JoeHo and fagsicle. You had them toeing the line. What happened to that girl?"

"She smartened up," she declared indignantly.

"Really? Are you sure? Because spewing hate isn't smart. And it's really unattractive on you. And it's made you very hard-looking."

Her hand immediately went to her face. "That really wasn't nice."

"Oh, and your remarks and comments have been?" I took another swallow of beer. "Come on, Lesley, I don't buy that you really believe all the crap you say now. It sounds to me like you're the mouthpiece for bigoted views you feel compelled to repeat out of some misguided love and loyalty. What do you think would happen if you didn't agree with your husband or your parents? I guarantee the world wouldn't stop turning."

She took a defiant step toward me. "I *do* believe what I say."

"Well, then"—I went back over to the door and opened it—"we have nothing more to discuss. You go back to your little Stepford Wife existence. But keep your husband's opinions to yourself when you're around me. Come back and talk to me when you get a mind of your own." I motioned her outside.

"Fuck you, Hunter."

"She'd be the best lay you ever had." Lisa breezed by her sister in the doorway.

"That's disgusting." Lesley glared at her. "I thought you were at church."

"I saw you leave. I had a good idea you were going to come here." Lisa's tone was not amused.

"This your new home now? You two going to set up house?"

"What is this really about, Lesley?" Lisa asked, putting her arms around me and kissing me on the cheek while Lesley's mouth dropped open. "Are you really repulsed, or are you jealous of me?"

"You're both sick!" She staggered by us and out the door.

We watched her try not to teeter as she navigated the front walk. "She's drunk," I said.

"She's always drunk. She's too miserable to be sober."

"That's sad."

"That's an understatement." Lisa relieved me of my Guinness and took a drink.

"You're nothing like your family. Where did you come from?"

She shrugged. "I don't know. Obviously the same cabbage patch you did."

I lifted her chin with my thumb and forefinger. "I don't care where you came from, I'm just glad you're here." I kissed her and hugged her tightly.

"I'm glad I'm here, too."

I looked back at Lesley, standing on the sidewalk as though she couldn't decide which way to go. "Did she walk from the church?"

"More like she staggered from the church, actually."

"We can't let her walk down the street like that."

"Yeah." She sighed. "Somebody might step on her hands."

I chuckled and kissed her forehead. "How about you go round her up, and I'll get the Jeep. We'll toss her in the back and get her home."

"Oh boy, this should be fun," Lisa said without any enthusiasm.

Chapter 11

Arms flailing, Lesley protested wildly before she finally wound down and agreed to allow us to take her home. She initially wanted to go back to the church, where she had been with her parents, but Lisa talked her out of it. "You know that if you go back to the church in this condition, Mom will rip you up one side and down the other." She turned to me and said softly, "Not that Lesley doesn't deserve to have her ass chewed after all the problems her big mouth has caused the last twenty-four hours."

Lesley lived in Teabury, a town fifteen miles northeast of Otter Falls, where most of the houses were only accessible by unpaved roads. I hadn't been up in this area since Lesley and I attended a graduation party when we were both eighteen, but it hadn't changed much. It was still mostly dense woods, dirt streets, and log cabins.

Five hundred thousand dollar log cabins. Lesley had always dreamed of living in this small, elite community. I wondered whether she had married her current husband just to make that wish come true.

The day was unseasonably warm, so I removed the canvas top from the Jeep, not really thinking or concerned about how the wind would be assaulting Lesley in the backseat. She wasn't pleased, but I figured the fresh air would do her good. Unfortunately, the gusts didn't shut her up, and, between taking regular hits from a flask in her purse, she accused us of doing every evil thing she could think of, except being on the grassy knoll in 1963. We were twisted; we were going to hell; we were the devil's spawn; we should have to register as sex offenders wherever we lived; we shouldn't be allowed around children;

our lifestyle was going to tear a hole in the universe... Okay, she didn't actually say that last one, but she might as well have. I was getting fed up with listening to her channel Reverend Fred Phelps.

She didn't respond to Lisa's requests to knock it off, and like a four-year-old throwing a tantrum, she began kicking the back of my seat with her high-heeled shoes.

"Lesley! Stop it!" Lisa and I hollered at the same time.

"Aw, isn't that sweet? You two even yell in perfect harmony. It's a match made in purgatory," she commented loudly enough for us to hear, a sour look distorting her already nasty expression. She folded her arms across her chest.

I had had it. I spotted a huge mud puddle ahead in the road, jammed my foot on the gas, and sped through it. A wave of thick, brown water crested over the windshield, missing Lisa and me and drenching Lesley with a resounding slap. Seeing her in the rearview mirror nearly caused me to drive off the road. Lisa looked into the backseat and put her hand over her mouth, trying not to laugh. She couldn't stop herself.

Lesley was speechless for the first time in twenty minutes. It would have been difficult to talk with a mouthful of wet, slimy dirt.

She looked like one of those women who had just climbed out of a spa mud bath, except she didn't have cucumber slices over her eyes and she was attired in more than a towel. I hoped her dress wasn't too expensive.

"Ou bith!" she screamed, spitting out water.

"Bith?" Lisa repeated, giggling uncontrollably. "What's a bith?"

"I don't know." I shrugged. "But apparently I am one."

"Thop thith cah ite nah!" Lesley was wiping her eyes and mouth with a filthy sleeve.

So I stopped the car, assuming that was what she requested, put the Jeep in neutral, and set the emergency brake. I turned to look at her. "Oops. Didn't see that puddle until it was too late."

"Bullshit! Fuck you, Hunter. You're going to pay for cleaning this dress!"

"Okay," I agreed willingly. "It was worth it."

She inspected herself then shook her head, which seemed to make her dizzy. She looked up at me. "Great. Now I have to pee."

"How much farther to your house?"

"Maybe ten more minutes," Lisa said.

"I can't make it," Lesley announced, pouting. She removed her seatbelt.

I looked around, "You're going to go here?"

"I could pee in the Jeep." Her expression told me she might just do it.

With the amount of mud and water that decorated the backseat, it might not have made a difference. I was probably going to have to have it thoroughly cleaned anyway, but I didn't want to have that memory of my high school best friend squatting and relieving herself, regardless of how damaged our friendship now was. "No. Go do what you have to do."

"Just watch out for nature's toilet paper with the three pointy leaves!" Lisa called after her sister, who stumbled over to an area with a low rock wall. She stepped over the wall, fell, swore up a storm, helped herself back up, and dropped her drawers right there.

"She's a gem, ain't she?" Lisa asked rhetorically, shaking her head.

We both turned around to give Lesley a modicum of privacy, whether she wanted it or not. Out of the blue, Lisa swatted me and started to laugh. "I can't believe you did that."

"You loved it." I reached over and patted her thigh.

She grinned. "Yeah. I did."

"She's pretty trashed. She's really like this all the time?"

"Usually not this bad. And never when she's got the boys with her... at least I don't think so. God, I hope not. I think finding out about you being gay may have triggered this particular binge."

"I'm shocked that she's so hateful. How have you put up with this all these years?"

"I ignore her. I'm used to it, so—"

"Hey. Heeey." We turned in the direction of the voice. "Can somebody help me here?"

All we saw were two legs ending in high heels sticking straight up in the air in the shape of a V behind the stone wall.

We both rolled our eyes as I backed the Jeep, parked it, and went to the wall to help Lesley into an upright position. "What happened?"

Once she was on her feet, she shook us both off. "I was climbing back over and I sat down to readjust my shoe. And then I was on my back."

Right where she relieved herself, I noted silently as I helped her up. I was going to have to boil my hands for an hour when I got back to my mother's. We walked behind her as she started to climb back into the Jeep, and then she stopped and shook her head.

"Oh no. No, no, no." Lesley turned around, wagged her finger at me, and pointed to the puddle. "I'm not falling for that again. I'll walk around it, and you can meet me on the other side."

"Lesley, Jesus," Lisa said, but I put my hand on her arm.

"If she feels more comfortable walking around, let her go."

"That's the smartest thing you've said all day," Lesley mumbled as she moved away from us. Her heels punctured the soft ground with every step, making her even less steady on her feet. It was quite comical.

I nodded my head toward the Jeep and we got in. I released the brake, wiggled the stick shift into neutral, and waited. When I saw that Lesley was halfway around the puddle, I stepped on the gas pedal, barely hitting first gear.

Lisa's eyes got wide. "Oh, no, you're not."

Oh yes, I was. I sailed through the puddle at a different angle this time. Very little mud went into the backseat. Instead the dark wave crowned to my left and soaked Lesley again. Whatever parts of her weren't already wet, weren't so lucky this time. When I got to the other side of the puddle, I threw the Jeep into park and looked back at Lesley. She stood frozen in place, eyes still closed, mud dripping off her nose and chin.

"Hunter, you are so bad," Lisa snorted in a hushed tone.

I knew it was immature of me, but I wasn't a turn-the-other-cheek sort of person anymore. All I learned from that parable was that I ended up with both sides of my face slapped. "Okay. I'll behave now," I told Lisa. "Hey, Lesley, come on. We haven't got all day, you know." I tried to sound annoyed, but I couldn't help smirking.

She refused to get back into the Jeep or to speak to either one of us, walking the rest of the way home as we followed behind her, an endeavor that took forty-five minutes instead of ten. By the time she reached her front porch, she had her shoes in her hands, her stockings were torn on her feet, and she was limping and hobbling.

She crawled up the three steps to the door and turned to look at us scornfully. "Heh. I made it. Guess I showed you two."

"Yep, you sure did." Lisa admirably kept a straight face.

After Lesley slammed the door behind her, I put the Jeep in gear and pulled out of the driveway. "Well, that was fun. Want to go back to my place and order pizza?"

"Do you really think she's jealous of you?" I asked, as we parked in the driveway of my mother's house.

"Yeah. Not in a sexual way, of course. I think she's jealous that now I have a bigger piece of you than she does, a piece that she can never compete with me to get."

We exited the Jeep, and she followed me to the side of the house. I turned the faucet on, picked up the hose, and dragged it to the driveway. I began rinsing the caked-on mud out of the interior of the Jeep.

"Think you can get it clean?" The animated look on Lisa's face made me think she was reminiscing about the earlier bath we gave her sister.

"No. But at least I can get it to the point where Sam doesn't have a heart attack when he sees it." I would do whatever I had to do to leave it in as good condition as it was when my brother loaned it to me.

Lisa took my keys and entered the garage through the side door. She returned a few minutes later with a pail and sponges.

Together we washed the Jeep until it practically shone. The seats would have to dry out before I could assess what else needed to be done to them, but whatever I would have to pay to fix it was worth what I had done to get them that way.

After we were finished, I saturated Lisa with water from the hose and she doused me with the contents of the pail while chasing me around the Jeep. When she caught me, we fell against the spare tire mounted on the back and I held her against me, kissing her.

I'm sure my mother's neighbors were scandalized. At least I hoped they were.

Inside the house, Lisa accompanied me upstairs and we took a hot shower together. The evening temperatures had started to set in, and we were both a little chilled from being waterlogged. We spent more time making love than warming up and getting clean. Not that either one of us complained.

Afterwards, Lisa suggested that we do something to get our minds off the frustration Lesley had generated. I would have thought the sex would have relieved any frustration, and it did some, but not enough. She rummaged in my old bedroom for a T-shirt and a pair of light sweatpants to wear and helped me divide the finished projects in the sewing room from the unfinished. We also placed swatches of material and sewing accessories into separate piles. I had planned to wait until tomorrow, but I was glad the task was done.

We were in the living room, watching television and snuggling, waiting on a pizza we had ordered, when another knock came at the door. I looked at Lisa and rolled my eyes. If it was either Dane or Lesley—which I doubted, as I didn't think Lesley was going to be on her feet too much for the next couple of days—I was really going to lose my temper.

I swung the door open with vigor, ready to take the head off of whoever was standing there. I calmed down when I saw Sam's soft brown eyes. "Come on in. Where's Trina?"

"She's home. Why didn't you show up? I know you said you weren't going to attend the wake, but this was the funeral. You really should have been there." He followed me into the living room. "Hey, Lisa."

"Hey, Sam. It was a nice service."

"Thanks. And thanks for being there." He glared at me.

"Why weren't you there with her?"

I shrugged. "It didn't feel right. I thought my presence would cause too much of a stir, and the service should have been about Mom, not speculation and gossip about me."

He thought about that. "Okay. That point's fair." He slipped his tie off and undid the top button of his shirt. "By the way, the garage door is open. You might want to close it before you settle in for the night. Hey, I saw that you washed the Jeep. That was nice of you, but unless you get it, you know, really funky, don't worry about it, okay?"

"Sure." I sneaked a guilty glance at Lisa.

"And you might want to put the top up next time," he suggested. "Good thing it's all-weather upholstery."

"Yeah. Sorry. I got a little carried away."

He nodded, apparently not bothered by the wet interior of the Jeep. "Lisa, I saw you leave right in the middle of Dane's eulogy."

"Yeah. Sorry, Sam. Was that too rude?" She blinked up at him.

"Hell, no. I was envious." He looked at the beer in my hand.

"Got any more of those?"

"I bet if you look in the refrigerator, you might find a couple."

Sam returned to the living room with a bottle in hand. He pointed to the garbage bags. "What are those? Did you clean out your old room?"

"No. I've been leaving that until last. Those are Mom's clothes. That's not a problem, is it? I figured it would be easier for me to go through them, as I had the least attachment."

"Do you really not feel anything at all about her being gone?"

"Sam, come on, face it—we were dead to each other years ago."

"That's not what I asked you."

I glanced over at Lisa, who looked like she wanted to be in a different room, then I returned my attention to my brother. "I spent the last sixteen years conditioning myself not to feel anything. I did it to protect myself. It became easier for me to be the hard-ass and convince myself that I didn't care, instead of having to come to terms with the fact that my mother didn't care about me. For nine years, I held on to the hope that she would see me and all would be okay. After that didn't happen, I closed my heart to keep it from getting broken by her again. So, to answer your question, I really do not feel anything about her being gone."

There was dead silence. He turned to Lisa as he took a long drink, not knowing what to say.

"Hey, how 'bout them Red Sox, huh?" she said, breaking the tension.

"Listen." He put a hand up in surrender. "I'm not judging you, Hunter. I'm just trying to get a handle on the way you're thinking, that's all."

I put my hand on his shoulder and squeezed. "Just don't presume to think you know everything about me. I'm not the same scared, broken teenager who left here all those years ago."

"Okay. I get it. Not one of us is the same anymore. I won't bring it up again."

I knew he probably would, but I would give him the benefit of the doubt. "Thank you."

"You want to stay for some pizza, Sam?" Lisa asked, as she aimed the remote at the TV, flipping channels.

"I'd love to, but I should get home to my wife and the dinner she's cooking for me. You know what? You two should come to dinner one night while you're still here, Hunter."

I looked over at Lisa, who nodded enthusiastically. "Okay. Set it up with Trina, and it's a plan."

"I will. She'll love it." He regarded Lisa curiously. "Hey, I'm wondering about something. How does Lesley feel about this whole thing going on between you two?"

Lisa and I exchanged smirks as we both sighed at almost the same moment. "If I told you that Lesley and Dane would be a great match, would that answer your question?"

He looked heavenward and took a long drink from his bottle of Guinness. "Oy."

Sam left minutes later, and Lisa settled on a rerun of an old

80s TV cop drama as acceptable background noise while we waited for the pizza. "Do you ever hear from your dad?" she asked out of the blue.

"No. Don't know if my brothers ever do. I've never asked. And really? I don't care." It shouldn't, but it still stung that my father had allowed my mother to drive him away from the children he'd produced with her. It stung that he chose to stay away. His behavior made my mother bitter, and then he blamed her for the vitriol that surged through her veins. It stung that he created me in his image and then left me to take the brunt of the punishment for his misdeeds, never offering me an outlet to ease the constant onslaught of venom directed at me because of him.

Lisa seemed to sense her question had provoked thoughts that brought dormant anger to the surface. She reached over and took my hand. "Sorry."

I blinked back the old wounds of betrayal and focused on her eyes, then leaned over and kissed her. "Don't be. Thinking about him is a waste of time and emotion." I smiled to let her know I was okay. "Honestly, I don't even know if he's still alive. He probably is, but I have no idea if we would ever be contacted if something did happen to him."

"Do you think anyone let him know that your mom died?"

"I doubt it. I mean, why would they? He demonstrated a long time ago that he didn't care. He has a different family, he doesn't want to acknowledge us. His choice."

Lisa lifted my hand to her lips and kissed it. "His loss."

"Thank you, but you might be a tad biased." I grinned and turned my attention to the television. But my mind went back to my childhood...

I climbed up on my father's lap as he sat in the recliner. I rubbed my eyes and felt grumpy.

He positioned me so that I could snuggle against him. "Hey, what are you doing up? It's way past your bedtime." I knew it was late because *Hill Street Blues* was on TV and that was even past Sam's bedtime.

"You and Mommy yelling. It waked me up." I lifted my

head from his chest and looked around. "Where's Mommy? Did you send her to bed for saying bad words?"

He chuckled and kissed the top of my head. "No, sweet pea. Daddy was bad. Mommy was right to yell at me."

"What did you do, Daddy?" I looked up at him with a five-year-old's wide-eyed innocence.

"I forgot to be home for dinner, and I forgot to call and tell Mommy I was going to be late."

"Oh. Yup. She was mad." I nodded vigorously. I played with a button on his shirt. "She got mad at me, too."

"Why was she mad at you?"

I shrugged. The memory of her screaming at me brought tears to my eyes. "She doesn't want me to be like you. She said I'm gonna be just like you." I looked up into my father's eyes. "Why doesn't Mommy love us, Daddy?"

My father wore an expression of suppressed anger. He drew a deep breath and let it out. "She loves you, sweet pea. It's just... well, when she gets mad at me and I'm not here to yell at, she yells at you because you look so much like me."

I made a face. "But... you're bigger than me, and you're a boy."

"I know you don't understand. It's a grown-up thing." He hugged me closer to him. "Now let's get you back to bed before you get in any more trouble." He stood up, taking me with him.

"But, Daddy, I not sleepy no more. Can I stay up and watch TV with you?"

He held me out in front of him, pressed his face closer to mine, and rubbed noses with me. "No." He carried me upstairs and into my bedroom, laid me down on the bed, and tucked me in. "Just remember, sweet pea, your daddy loves you enough for both him and Mommy. And Daddy will always love you, no matter what."

I had believed him. I believed him until I was leaving on that bus to Los Angeles when I was nineteen. By the time Uncle David died, I no longer believed him, but I still had hope that I might be mistaken. After the detached condolences he sent to Aunt Cissy and the kids, a woman he'd known practically his whole life about a brother he always claimed to be close to, I had to let him go as just another disappointment in my life.

But as much as I tried to deny it, it still hurt. As much as I tried to act indifferent, I had no idea how I would react if he walked through the front door at that very moment. My brain would demand I act apathetic, but my heart might be a traitor.

Chapter 12

After I locked up the house and garage, we went back to Lisa's for the night because of the dogs. She didn't spend a lot of time away from them unless it was absolutely necessary, and when she had to leave them for any length of time, she always made arrangements for them not to be alone. She did have a pet door, and they had a safely enclosed dog run and weight-activated food and water dispensers, in case something came up and she couldn't get home to them. She loved them very much, and they worshipped her.

I didn't blame them.

There was never any question that we would spend the night together, regardless of where. It was a given that it would happen, as if we'd been sharing a bed for years. Each time we made love seemed to bring out a different level of passion that was electrifying and intoxicating. I wanted to fuse myself to her so we could be together all the time. I would fall asleep sated, exhausted, and yet emotionally energized by sensations I'd never felt before.

I began to have no doubt that I was meant to be with Lisa Riordan, that what was developing between us was genuine and inevitable. I had never been a big believer in Fate, but being with Lisa was whittling away at my skepticism. She had told me she felt our reuniting was predestined, and every moment I spent with her was proving that prediction to be true.

When we fell asleep that night, I spooned her, securing her naked form to me, absorbing her warmth and her spirit, knowing if I held her any closer, she would be inside me. She settled back into my embrace, her arm covering mine, our fingers intertwined, our legs tangled, and our hearts beating in the same rhythm. My mother had been wrong about me being in an airplane: *this* was as close to heaven as I was ever going to get.

We woke up at four in the morning to the sound of one of the dogs throwing up. I wonder why no one ever invented a clock where the alarm was the sound of an animal puking. Nothing seemed to wake someone and get them out of bed faster than that particular noise. It's not a sound you hear and just roll over and go back to sleep.

Eyes flying open, fully alert, Lisa raced out of bed to locate the poor dog and whatever pile or piles he had deposited on the floor.

That way she could do a spot analysis of what may have caused the greyhound's upset stomach and clean up the mess before either she or I got up and unexpectedly stepped in it. A few minutes later, she climbed back into bed and snuggled up to me.

"Who got sick?" I asked her, yawning.

"Oz. Looks like he ate part of one of my plants again, but he seems fine now."

"Good." We resettled into our former positions, and very shortly we were both asleep.

Three hours later, we were awakened by a ringing telephone.

The sun was shining; possibly it was time to get up. Lisa reached over me and fumbled with the cordless receiver before finally getting it to her mouth.

"Hello?" Her voice was filled with sleep. "Morning, Mother."

She resumed her former position, snuggled up to my back. She gave my shoulder blade a few kisses while she listened to her mother drone on. "Well, she's lying." I guessed they were talking about Lesley. "We did not make her walk home, she chose to walk those last few miles. ... I'm sorry she can't walk today, but it's not my fault. ... No, it isn't Hunter's fault either."

I visualized Lesley covered in mud, and I laughed silently. Lisa responded to my body shaking with a light slap.

"She was drunk, that's why we didn't bring her back to the church. ... Yes, she was, Mom, she was drunk, *again*, and you can't tell me you didn't notice. We were doing her a favor by bringing her home. ...Yes, actually she's right here. ... Yes, Mother, she spent the night." Lisa sighed in annoyance. "Why is it that Lesley being falling-down-drunk in public is more acceptable to you than my spending time with Hunter?" Her voice was getting clearer and angrier as the phone call progressed. "Mom. Mom? Mother! I'm not having this conversation with you. I'm tired of it. Keep pushing me on this issue, and maybe you'll push me right out of here and to California with her!"

My eyes snapped open, and I know I stopped breathing. Did she say that just to get a rise out of her mother, or did she mean it? I turned in place and looked at her, my eyes searching her face for a clue. I could tell she was pissed off by the tone of her voice, but there was a softness in her eyes when they engaged mine. I reached over and cupped the side of her face, my thumb lightly rubbing her cheek.

"Yeah, Mom, I *would* do that." She smiled at me. "She would be worth giving up everything for." I leaned over and gave her a soft kiss on the cheek. "Well, it's my life, so it's ultimately my decision, isn't it?" Green eyes blinked up at me lovingly. "I don't consider it throwing my life away. I'm in love with her. I always have been."

I laid down as she sat up. I could hear her mother ranting, even though I couldn't understand what she was saying.

"Mom? We're done talking about this. ... Tonight? Nope, I have plans." I ran my fingers gently up and down her back. "Okay. I'll give Aunt Bethany a call. Bye." She pressed the Off button and tossed the phone down to the bottom of the bed. "She drives me fucking nuts sometimes!" Lisa vented, then she went back to cuddling against me

"So... uh... what you were saying to her... about going to California with me and giving up everything you have here... were you serious?"

Lisa tightened her grip on my waist as her head snuggled on my shoulder. "I'm serious about being with you. Just how we're going to accomplish that is something we're going to have to discuss."

"Did you say that stuff to her just to get her going?"

"Initially. Funny, though, the minute it left my mouth, it didn't sound like such a bad idea."

I put both my arms around her and squeezed. "Do you really think you're *in* love with me?"

"I know I am." She said it with such finality, it made my heart lurch in my chest.

I wanted to stay on this subject, but it was almost too overwhelming. I kissed the top of her head. "Why doesn't your mother like me?"

The segue didn't seem to faze her. "I don't know. I guess because Lesley always lied about your responsibility in the antics you two got involved in back in high school."

"The night of your party, Lesley told me she 'fessed up to all that."

"Lesley lies. She lies a lot. She never let our mother believe anything other than that you were the troublemaker who got Lesley detention, and suspended, and drunk. Whatever bad thing Les got caught doing in high school, she'd blame you. And I would always defend you, and that would make Mom angry, too. I think she recognized even way back then that my feelings for you were more than what she thought they should have been." She kissed the base of my throat. "When you left and it got around that your mother kicked you out and basically disowned you, that's all she needed to confirm her suspicions that you really were, in her words, a wicked child."

"This is one of the big reasons I can't stay here, Lisa. A majority of the people here aren't like you and Sam and Trina, they're like Dane and Lesley and your parents and my mother."

"I know it wouldn't be easy. Trust me, it hasn't been easy, but—"

I rolled over on her and quieted her with a kiss. "Can we talk about this later?"

"Sure." Her eyes held a vulnerability I hadn't seen before. "As long as we *do* talk about it."

After we ate the very nice breakfast Lisa cooked for us, she made a phone call to her Aunt Bethany while I played fetch with Oz and Deke in the backyard. They were cool dogs, very fast and eager to please. They took to me immediately, and I felt like their Alpha figure, until Lisa walked out into the yard and I no longer existed.

"It's a beautiful day." She squinted and shielded her eyes from the sun. "Why don't we take the boys over to Evergreen Ridge and go for a hike?"

"You know…" I reached for her hand, and she took it. "I would love to go anywhere with you, but spending time in a forest is like a busman's holiday for me."

She grinned. "I know. I just thought you might like to look over the 'office' you could be working in."

I tapped her nose a few times. "Or, when we get to L.A., you can do all the hiking you want with a personal escort."

She put her arms around me. "Okay, what do you want to do this afternoon?"

"Watch football?"

She perked up. "You like football?"

"I love football."

"Who's your team?"

"Not the Patriots." I laughed, wondering if that would upset her. Most New Englanders were diehard Patriot fans, almost to the point of rabid loyalty.

"Why not the Patriots?" She didn't sound indignant, which indicated they weren't her team either.

"I had a falling out with a friend once who ate, drank, slept, and breathed the Patriots. She was obnoxious about it, especially after the falling out. So now, I don't care who plays, as long as the Patriots lose."

"Then I would suggest you don't go watch any games at any of the bars from here to Maine."

"Well, that's good, because I don't want to watch football at a bar. I want to stay home and watch it with you."

She kissed the cleavage between my breasts and looked up at me. "I like that—calling wherever we are together 'home.'"

We walked hand in hand to her back door. "I need to go over to my aunt's tonight for about an hour or so. Ever since their store got broken into last year, even though they have an alarm system now, they don't leave the place unoccupied. Usually my cousin is there, but he has something going on and my aunt and uncle also have to go somewhere."

"So you have to babysit the place for an hour?"

"I told her I would. I know they're paranoid, but it gives them peace of mind. Besides, it's only an hour. It won't interrupt our evening. Do you want to go with me?"

"Sure."

I couldn't believe her father's sister and brother-in-law still owned that little general store. It was a corner Mom and Pop shop that served a lower-middle-class neighborhood. Lesley and I used to get our beer there. We'd visit her cousin Tommy, and when the store was closed in the evenings and her aunt and uncle were busy watching TV or napping in their chairs, we'd sneak downstairs into the store and grab a six-pack or two. With Tommy as the referee, we'd play this silly little game where one of us would sit in the shopping cart and pull items off the shelves and into the cart on top of us, as the other would push the cart as fast as possible through the aisles. Then we would put everything back and switch. The object was to see who could get the most in the cart and pile it the highest.

I really missed that person who used to be my best friend.

Regardless of whom she blamed for our escapades. I remembered a particular day...

We walked into the store and looked around for Tommy, who was supposed to be driving Lesley and me to the football game.

When I didn't see him, I checked my watch. We were fifteen minutes early, so we strolled over to the beer cooler to see if he was in that aisle. Tommy usually brought the beer, and I wanted my choice this time so I started looking over the selection while Lesley scoped out the snack aisle. I thought it was nice that he was so loyal to the local breweries, but those beers never did it for me. Lesley didn't care one way or the other, as long as the beer was free and plentiful. After spending five minutes in the cooler row, I still hadn't made up my mind. I figured Tommy wouldn't listen to me anyway, so I went around to the front of the store to see if he had shown up. Lesley was going outside to look for his truck.

"Hi, Mrs. Cioffi," I said to Tommy's grandmother.

She smiled at me and gave me a quick wave. "Ciao, Hunter."

"Dove è Tommy?" I asked in my limited Italian, hoping she would answer me in a language I understood.

"Da boy no here." She always called him 'da boy' and I never learned why. I don't think even Tommy knew.

Tommy's paternal grandmother was a colorful woman who emigrated directly from Sicily. She settled with her husband and four young children in the unlikely town of Otter Falls, Vermont.

One of those children, Gino, grew up and married Bethany Riordan and bought a little corner market in a neighborhood that was always a risky place to live.

Mrs. Cioffi would sometimes run the cash register when no one else was available. They only left her alone in the store when it was absolutely necessary, because she was a petite, frail-looking woman whose grasp of the English language was sketchy, at best, someone they assumed was a crime victim waiting to happen.

Apparently a local hood was under the same misconception. I was about to tell her I would wait for Tommy outside when a gangbanger wannabe entered the store, wielding a knife. Before I could react, he shoved me out of the way and approached Mrs. Cioffi. "This is a stick-up!" he said, waving his knife in her direction.

Without hesitation, Tommy's fiery grandmother grabbed the broom kept by the register and beat him with it all the way out the door while screaming, "Stick-a this uppa you ass!"

I thought I would pee my pants.

The would-be robber never came back, and there was no retaliation. Unfortunately, I couldn't help the police who came to take a report because it all happened so fast, the only things I could remember were his filthy white sneakers and pumping elbows as he fled up the street.

After that, there were no further instances of any problems in the store.

Lisa told me that last year, a week after Tommy's grandmother died, the store was burglarized. The perpetrator was still at large, but the first person I probably would have interviewed as a suspect would have been the punk who had been humiliated all those years ago.

It would be interesting to see the store again, and the massive three-story apartment that was over it. Tommy Cioffi threw some hellacious parties on that third floor, which was a huge recreation room. It would be good to see Aunt Bethany and Uncle Gino, too.

Hopefully Mrs. Riordan hadn't already poisoned them against me.

Lisa wanted to take the dogs for a leisurely walk before we left them alone the rest of the day, so we put them each in their different colored nylon harness, hooked them up to their retractable leashes, and made our way up the street. She was being led by Deke, and I had the pleasure of being walked by Oz. They seemed very excited to be out of the confines of their home and yard, sniffing every tree, bush, and blade of grass along the sidewalk, peeing indiscriminately on pretty much anything stationary and upright, searching for the perfect place to poop or the perfect pile of shit to roll in. A trip around the block, which should have taken twenty minutes, took at least forty.

Despite the frequent stops, it was a pleasant way to spend an hour. Lisa's interaction with her "boys" was just one more thing I found endearing about my new girlfriend. Their mutual devotion to each other was clear, but her gentleness with them was not without its firm edge resulting in them minding well, unless they were severely distracted.

While we were walked, Lisa updated me on renovations that had taken place on the town square over the past years. I was so enthralled by the enthusiasm and melodic tone in her voice when she animatedly described the changes, I didn't notice that Oz had slowly pulled away from me until I felt a slight tug on the handle, indicating that his leash was extended as far as it could go. Both Lisa and I looked up just in time to see the brindle-colored greyhound shove his narrow nose into the crack of a woman's ass and lift her a couple inches off the ground.

"Oz!" I yanked the leash back while pressing the retractor button; Lisa hurried to the victim, with Deke tightly heeled.

The young woman was dressed in black leather pants, which looked to be held up by a belt made from pairs of handcuffs linked together. Real handcuffs, not decorative ones that might have been purchased at Hot Topic. She wore a spiked dog collar and had the BDSM Rights emblem shaved into the back of her closely cropped blonde hair, which was tinted with black, blue, and white stripes, and the red and white Triskelion. That should have been red flag number one. When we reached the woman, she had turned around, looking less startled and actually beginning to smile at the puzzled dog who had so vigorously goosed her. That should have been red flag number two.

"I'm so sorry," Lisa apologized, mortified by Oz's action. "He's never done anything like that before. He's normally very well behaved."

"Oh no." She flicked her wrist, dismissing the apology. "He's fine. He must smell my Great Dane."

Lisa opened her mouth to reply, but closed it when there just didn't seem to be any diplomatic response to that statement. As the woman waved and strolled away from us toward town, Lisa and I looked at each other. "What did she mean?" she asked, though I don't think she wanted an answer.

"I don't know," I said. "I can only hope that means she's sleeping with Connie Nielsen."

"Connie Nielsen?"

"The Danish actress. Some call her the Great Dane."

Comprehension dawned—"Oh. Yeah. Right."—followed by a snicker.

We both eyed the woman, who was waiting to cross the

street.

Seeing someone dressed like that, so unabashedly displaying her bondage proclivities, would never have raised an eyebrow had I been in Los Angeles. But here in Otter Falls, she was quite the sight to behold. "Where do you think she's going dressed like that, first thing in the morning?"

"Church?"

I stared at Lisa. "Where? Our Lady of the Dungeons?"

"As long as it's not the animal shelter, she can worship wherever she likes."

"My, Otter Falls sure has changed." I honestly had nothing against anyone who practiced any of the Bs, Ds, S's or Ms, and I would have been lying if I'd said I hadn't dabbled in a bit of the domination and restraint playing myself. It was mind-boggling, though, to think someone in this little town would be either so courageously or ignorantly blatant about such a misunderstood fetish.

I reached over and took Lisa's hand in mine. I thought she might balk, being that we were in public and in her neighborhood. Even though she was fully out, there were still some lines that needed to be stepped over carefully for safety reasons, but without hesitation, she squeezed my fingers.

I figured that if someone about half my age had the guts to be who she really was, regardless of what that meant, why should I let outdated protocol stop me from engaging in a simple ritual that even the most basic teenager was allowed to do—hold my girlfriend's hand.

We strolled the rest of the way back to Lisa's with our fingers entwined, talking about how we were going to teach the dogs not to poke their noses where they didn't belong.

When we got back to my mom's, we went through the house and made a list of what needed to be done. My initial plan was to contact my mother's chosen real estate agent in the morning and discuss my options. I could tell Lisa was disappointed with that decision, but she remained silent. I couldn't stay indefinitely; I needed to move forward with whatever I was going to do with the house and the property.

And yet, I couldn't reconcile the sense of panic I felt at the thought of us not being together. Lisa had put a spell on me that I never wanted her to remove.

The in-depth checklist and surface inventory took us over two hours, and when we were done, I was satisfied with the game plan. I think Lisa believed that just because I was more than likely going to sell this place, it didn't mean I couldn't settle down with her at her house if she didn't end up in California with me.

We grabbed a couple of beers and some munchies and planted ourselves in front of the television to watch the Minnesota Vikings play the Detroit Lions. I took the Vikings and she took Detroit, and we made a friendly little sexual wager, the winner, of course, being rewarded with a night of fantasies fulfilled. Which was really no different than any other night we had spent together.

During halftime, Sam called and we set up a dinner date for Tuesday night and decided on an acceptable menu for all. Our contribution would be the wine and dessert. I was fine with buying something, but Lisa insisted on baking a pie of some sort. I didn't want to tell her that I rarely ate pie, except maybe a slice of pumpkin at Thanksgiving, and then only with whipped cream, or that I almost never ate dessert, but then I remembered that it wouldn't be for me, it was actually a gesture of appreciation for being included and so readily accepted.

I also realized that Dane was being abnormally quiet for someone who seemed to thrive on causing trouble. I was sure something was brewing, that he had something up his sleeve, and I would just have to wait to find out what it was. As long as it didn't involve harming Lisa in any way, I knew I could handle it. If he had any brains at all, he would have already figured out that Lisa would be a weakness of mine. Although I thought he would also have to realize that any manner of attack on her might send me into a homicidal frenzy. He should also bear in mind how the privileged information I had could result in his political downfall. It was definitely his move, but he needed to be at his most calculating to pull anything off successfully without it backfiring and ruining him instead.

My Aunt Cissy, Uncle David's widow, also called and asked when she and the kids were going to see me. We spoke briefly of Mom, and thankfully, she wasn't overly solicitous, but then, she knew firsthand the results of my mother's actions and behavior toward me. I told her I would call her back sometime tomorrow to make definite plans with her. My aunt was a kind woman, and I now wished I had been better at keeping in touch with her and my cousins. Maybe I could make amends.

After the game, where Detroit spanked Minnesota, we returned to Lisa's and made sure the dogs were fed, watered, exercised, and given tons of attention. We went to dinner at Applebee's, and didn't run into anyone I knew personally or we knew together. Lisa was greeted by several acquaintances, and I was introduced as her *friend*.

It was said with such intimacy in her voice that only the densest individual would have failed to interpret that as meaning something much more. But then, I was in Otter Falls, where people only heard what they wanted to, what didn't invade their personal comfort zones.

I couldn't understand how Lisa could be happy here.

Chapter 13

Bethany and Gino Cioffi seemed happy to see me. They extended their condolences about my mother, and we reminisced briefly before they left for their evening out.

"You know," Aunt Bethany said, a humorous lilt in her voice, "I always hoped Tommy would find a *spirited* girl just like you to marry. With one obvious difference, of course." She chuckled and shook her head. "If he'd had someone like you, maybe he wouldn't be divorced and back living with us until he gets back on his feet."

Maybe if I had been straight, I would have gone after him. He was quite the handsome heartthrob in high school, but as I admired the gorgeous blonde by my side, I was glad I was destined to be with innies and not outies.

Uncle Gino winked at Lisa. "At least *somebody* in the family ended up with Hunter." His comment made us both blush and provoked a jab in the side from his wife.

After Lisa's aunt and uncle left, she took me on a tour of the huge, refurbished apartment, and then we ventured down into the closed store. We left the lights off, but the streetlights outside provided enough brightness for me to see that nothing had changed in the quaint interior. Lisa deactivated the alarm system, and we walked around, sharing memories of separate and collective good times there. We had a little over an hour to kill in the store before Tommy was coming to relieve us. It would be good to see him.

"You know," Lisa said, a hint of impishness in her tone, "I always wanted to play that game that you and Lesley used to play with the shopping cart."

I laughed. "We were lucky we didn't break anything in the

store or injure ourselves. And Lesley always used to accuse Tommy of cheating in my favor because she claimed he was hot for me."

"He was. It made me insanely jealous, thinking you might actually end up with him."

I studied her briefly. "Really? You had no idea about me back then?"

"Only what was wishful thinking. I thought if you were a lesbian, Lesley would know and that would have been the end of your friendship."

"But… she didn't act like that back then. The only reason I didn't say anything to her was that I didn't think she could keep it to herself."

"She wouldn't have, believe me. And the only reason she seemed to act so differently in high school was that she went through a phase where she knew going against the grain would get her noticed."

"So her defense of Joey Lassiter that one day where she stood up to everybody was bullshit?"

"Remember all the kids that made fun of Joey? Remember the guy she really liked at the time, Ryan Machain?"

"Yeah." I wondered what one had to do with the other.

"Ryan was all into political correctness. He actually was heading a student committee against high school bullying."

"Ah, so she did it just to get his attention." Why hadn't I known that about her?

"Yep, but they only went out once. Ryan found out what a liar and a phony she was."

"She told me she didn't go out with him again because he was dull. Jesus, did I really know her at all?"

"Probably as well as anyone. You knew exactly what she wanted you to know."

I was really jarred. Had I been so wrapped up in my own world of secrets and hurt that I never saw Lesley for who she actually was? Or was I just as guilty as everyone else of seeing only what I wanted to see? Lisa tugging on my sleeve nudged me out of my self-scrutiny, and I looked at her. Her eyes sparkled in the darkness, reflecting the limited light that was filtering into the store. She took my breath away.

"Kiss me."

She didn't have to say it twice. I pulled her to me more quickly than she expected me to, startling her, and I hungrily covered her mouth with mine. She unleashed the animal inside me; I wanted to devour her right there in front of the huge, wall-length, clear-glass window that faced the street. We probably stayed lip-locked longer than we should have, on display for anyone walking by that might look in and see. I didn't care. I could have stood there kissing her all night. As it was, she had to gently push me away to break the kiss.

"God, Hunter," she gasped. "I can't believe how weak in the knees your kisses make me."

"Yeah? Just wait until later."

She grinned, slowly backing away from me. "Braggart."

"Yep, I am. And you know I can make good on it, too." I moved toward her. "How much time do we have before Tommy gets here?"

"About a half-hour." An expectant, sensuous grin played on her lips. "Just what do you have in mind?"

"This." I grabbed her around the waist, lifted her and dumped her in a shopping cart, butt first, so that just her arms, legs, shoulders and head stuck out over the top. She was laughing so hard after her initial struggle, she couldn't have stopped me if she tried.

"Ready?"

She nodded, and I made a speedy trial run up and down each aisle, getting the feel of pushing the cart with the balanced weight.

"Okay, we do it for real this time. I'll bring you close to the shelves and you have to put as much as you can into the cart and on top of you. We'll go through once, and then turn around and hit the other side of the aisle on the way back. Then I bring you up to the cash register, which is the finish line. Then it's my turn. Since Tommy's not here to ref, we'll have to judge, honestly, who has the most.

Anything knocked on the floor and not in the cart doesn't count."

She was still giggling. "I can't believe you guys used to do this all the time."

"It was fun. Putting everything back on the shelves sucked, but it was worth the once-a-month competition. Ready?" I stood still, pushing the cart out then pulling it back to me, as if revving the engine.

She put her hand up and pointed forward. "Let's do it."

I raced her around the store as she swept anything and everything within reach into the cart and onto her midsection. By the second time around the store, the cart was getting a lot heavier than I remembered from the past. I needed to start working out my arms and legs more. She had cans and other items piled pretty high on her by the time we reached the cash register.

"God, I can't move! This was so much fun. I didn't realize—"

We both stopped dead when we saw the spotlight of the patrol car shine in the window, directly on Lisa. "Uh-oh," was all I could manage. We watched the officer exit her car, put her baton in its belt loop, and key the mic clipped to her epaulet. I guessed she was calling in her location. Her approach to the front door of the store was neither aggressive nor threatening, her hand nowhere near her holster.

"It's Kim Fredette. Shit!" Lisa's voice was hushed and a little panicked.

I scrunched down behind the cart as the officer switched on her Maglite. "You know her?"

"Yes. She's always asking me out. You know her, too. She used to play center for St. James."

"Kim Ligouri?" She was the girl I used to make out with in a deserted part of the school after basketball games. I didn't want to see her again, not even after all these years...

"I kicked your ass on that court, Ligouri." I was purposely being obnoxious to continue the façade of animosity between us as we walked off toward the locker rooms.

"Bullshit, Roberge. If the ref hadn't been working for your side, you wouldn't have had half of those free throws," she shot back.

"It wasn't the ref, Kim," another player on her own team shouted. "You just can't keep your hands off her, and the ref sees that as fouling, not fondling."

A group of girls laughed and others "oohed" ominously, eyes watching us to gauge our reactions to the remark. Everybody suspected Kim of being a lesbian, but to my knowledge, no one had a clue about me. Except Kim.

"Okay, ladies, that will be quite enough," Coach Costa from St. James High School announced. No one had noticed her close in behind us. "Everybody hit the showers. Jaguars, you have forty-five minutes to get your butts back on the bus."

Kim and I were usually the first two in line for the shower. It had become a ritual for us whenever our schools got together for competitions. Neither Kim nor I had a car, so we had to take our opportunities whenever they were available. Usually that meant whenever a bus took one of us to the other school as either a player or a spectator for some kind of sporting event.

We originally kissed on a "Truth or Dare" sort of bet. Her androgyny fascinated me, and I shamelessly flirted with her while playing against her. We were both centers, so we covered each other defensively. I think I flustered her, so she finally bet me that if she outscored me, she would win a kiss. At first I was surprised that she thought I would agree to her terms, but I honestly believed she wouldn't outscore me so it wouldn't be an issue. So I laughed and said, "Sure."

She played her best game ever and scored forty-four points to my thirty. We found a discreet nook and made out until it was time to get on the bus. That was the first of our rendezvous.

"We have a half-hour," Kim said, meeting me under a dark basement stairwell after our showers. "Let's make the most of it."

She pulled me to her, roughly covered my lips with hers, and shoved her tongue halfway down my throat. She had been my first and only experience with kissing a woman, and although it was opening doors for me psychologically, her technique left a lot to be desired. She was impatient and aggressive, and while making out was enough for me at this point, it wasn't enough for her. Kim was attractive in a boyishly cute sort of way. She had a great, confident smile, and she was willing to indulge my experimentation. I was pretty sure I didn't want Kim to have my virginity, but I didn't want to stop these little sessions, either.

After fifteen minutes of kissing and groping, Kim released me, panting and frustrated.

"Hunter, you're driving me crazy. We've been doing this for three months now. We need to kick it up a notch or two." She sounded desperate.

I knew what she was saying, and I should have known that what we were doing was coming to this. I wasn't sure I was ready to "go all the way." At least not with Kim. I had heard that how people kissed was an indication of how they fucked, and I was looking for a little more patience for my first time. "Like what?"

She rubbed my nipple through my sweater until it was painfully erect. "Like fucking you. I want to fuck you, Hunter." She pressed up against me and began to ride my thigh. "Wouldn't that feel good?" She stroked the crotch of my jeans.

Something inside me was starting to stir, and it scared me. I knew enough about myself to know that I might give in because I loved feeling good. And, according to my guy friends, nothing you could do to yourself felt as good as actual sex with another person.

I was getting lost in the sensation of her touch and the sound of her moaning, and it was obvious the friction being caused by her own movement was quite stimulating. I realized if I didn't stop her, this was going to reach a point of no return right here and now. I reached down and seized her wrist, slowly but firmly removing her hand from between my legs, and I adjusted my stance so that she could no longer dry hump me. She slumped against me, groaning.

"Kim, you need to get going or your coach is going to come looking for you."

"Hunter." Her tone was exasperated. "I mean it. I can't keep doing just this."

"All right, okay." I was trying to calm my overheated body.

132

"What's the plan?"

She grinned wickedly. "How about next Friday? The boys teams play each other. You can ride over on the bus, and I'll meet you outside the gym. My sister lives a block from school, and she'll be working. She'll let me use her place." She looked at me expectantly, and when I didn't answer her right away, she prodded,

"Sound good?"

"Uh, yeah, next Friday. I'll see if I can get the night off."

"Call in sick if you have to." She kissed me again, her tongue pursuing my tonsils. She ended the kiss and said, "I have to go."

"Yeah, okay." I released her and felt a confusing mixture of emptiness and relief.

Kim patted my ass. "Can't wait 'til next week." She took a couple of steps away, pointed at me, and said, "I can't wait to be inside you, Hunter. It's going to be so good."

"Looking forward to it," I lied. I was intrigued; I was petrified.

I was intriguingly petrified. I leaned back against the wall and watched her leave. Playing around with a willing participant was one thing; it was another to go all the way with someone I didn't really want that particular history with. On the one hand, Kim lived thirty miles away, so it wasn't like we had to see each other all the time after "it" happened. On the other hand, with Kim living thirty miles away and not having easy access to transportation, I didn't have to see Kim at all if I chose not to.

I chose not to.

Now a police officer, Kim flashed her light through the glass door, illuminated Lisa, and obviously recognized her. Kim knocked on the metal frame with her flashlight.

"Hunter, let her in," Lisa said, her voice still quiet.

Let her in? I didn't even want her to see me, which is why I stayed hidden behind the cart. I hoped Kim would acknowledge that one of the town's most prominent lawyers was trapped in a shopping cart, in front of a cash register in a fully stocked, dark store, after hours, with probably a hundred dollars' worth of groceries piled high on top of her, and then leave.

Kim knocked again. "Lisa? What's going on?"

"I'm okay, Kim," Lisa hollered out to the woman in uniform.

"Hunter, let her in," Lisa said in an urgent whisper.

I remained frozen in place. No, no, no, no, why me? Why Kim? Fuck, fuck, fuck!

"Hunter!" That was a bark. "I said let her in!" That was a hiss.

Kim's knocking turned to pounding, and Lisa reached her hand behind the cart and grabbed a fistful of my hair. "Ow, owowowow *ow*, all right!" I slowly stood, an action that made Kim take a step back as her hand hovered above the butt of her 9mm.

"It's okay, Kim. Hunter's going to let you in."

I put my hands up level with my shoulders and walked to the door. I had been hoping that maybe I would let her in, Lisa would have a friendly little chat with Kim, and she'd let us both off the hook without even finding out my name. But Lisa had shot that in the ass. There weren't that many women in the world named Hunter, and I knew that when Kim saw my face and height and put that together with my name, I'd have some 'splainin' to do about ancient history.

It didn't matter that it was seventeen years ago and we were just horny teenagers. Lesbians had it all over elephants when it came to never forgetting.

She raised her Maglite and shined it in my face as I unlocked the door. Once the green and purple spots disappeared, I could see her smirk. "Well, well, well… if it isn't Hunter Roberge. That is still your last name, isn't it?"

"Yep. Hi, Kim." I closed the door behind her.

She gave me a shameless once-over and turned to Lisa.

"Counselor," she said.

"Sergeant." Lisa returned the titled courtesy, embarrassed to the point of almost glowing in the dark.

I noticed the three chevrons on Kim's sleeve as she returned her full attention to me. "Sorry to hear about your mother," she said, practically leering.

"Thanks."

"Is that what brought you back to town?" She hadn't changed much. She was still as tall as I was, still thin, still androgynous, still had piercing hazel eyes and a way that she curled her lip on one side that I found quite sexy when I used to get all hot and sweaty with her on and off the basketball court. I wondered if her kisses were still forceful and sloppy.

"Yes, it is." I would only share more information under duress and maybe not even then.

"How long are you staying?" Her tone and demeanor indicated that she was still very interested.

Obviously realizing we had some kind of history, Lisa cleared her throat to get our attention. "Uh... does someone want to help me out of this cart?"

Kim turned back to her, and I walked over and started removing the items from the cart and placing them on the counter.

"Would either of you like to tell me what's going on here?" Kim asked.

"Any way of getting out of it?" As Lisa clasped my arm and pulled herself to her feet, I held the cart so it wouldn't tip. It was a few minutes before she could fully straighten up.

"You're good at that, aren't you, Hunter? Getting out of things." There was an acerbity in her words.

I loaded all of the groceries back into the cart as Lisa approached Kim and smiled. "We're watching my aunt's store until my cousin gets here, and we were just having a little fun. We're authorized to be in here, so you don't have to file a report... right?"

Her tone was amiable but professional. It was more urging than asking.

"Well, that depends."

"On?" Lisa tilted her head, waiting for the blackmail.

I slowly moved behind Lisa and put my arm over her shoulder and across her chest, my hand coming to rest on her bicep in a gesture that could have been interpreted as territorial. Okay, so it was blatantly territorial, and Kim's eyes widened, especially when Lisa's fingers curled around my forearm. She got the message.

There was a challenging look in my eyes, and Kim raised a hand in concession, smiling.

She shook her head. "Figures." She keyed her mic. "Lincoln eight to base, code four at this location." When she received a "ten-four" in response, she studied us both, still smirking. "I got a call that someone reported suspicious activity at this location. Must have been whatever the hell you were doing in that cart." When Lisa opened her mouth to explain, Kim put her hand up again. "I don't want to know. I figured whoever was in here belonged, because the alarm didn't go off. Then I get here and find the cutest couple in town doing... something. Anyway, as long as I don't get any complaints from the Cioffis, I'll log this as a security check."

"Thank you, Kim," Lisa said sincerely. When I was silent, she subtly elbowed me.

"Oof. Thanks, Kim," I added.

"If I was a different type of person, I could threaten to report this as a 10-59 and then hold it over your heads until you bartered with me. Even though you've turned me down several times, Counselor," she said to Lisa, "and you owe me, Hunter, I'm not the kind of person who abuses her authority like that."

"Thank you, Kim," Lisa repeated sweetly.

I was a little incredulous. "I owe you? Jesus, Kim, that was a lifetime ago, and you would actually call this malicious mischief? By what stretch of the imagination? It's certainly mischief, but there's nothing malicious about—" Another poke to the ribs. "Oof. Thank you, Kim."

"I don't forget people who back out on agreements, Hunter. Not when they look like you, anyway. It doesn't matter when it happened, just that it did happen. And how do you know what a 10-59 is? Don't tell me you're a cop, too."

"I'm a park ranger."

She nodded. "Nice. Okay. I need to get back on patrol. Ladies, it was good seeing you again. Wish I were meeting both of you under different and separate circumstances, but them's the breaks, huh? Stay out of trouble." She stepped to the door and opened it, then turned back to me. "If... uh... things don't work out with you two, give me a call."

"Thank you, Kim," I recited, a fake smile plastered on my face, and I immediately locked the door once she was outside. When I turned, I came face-to-face with amused, questioning eyes.

Lisa's arms were folded across her chest. "Something you'd like to share with the class?"

"Hey, Lisa! You down there?" Saved by Tommy. "Hey, Hunter, you with her?"

"Yeah, we're both here," I answered.

We heard every step as he come bounding down the stairs.

"Where's the girl who launched thousands of my wet dreams?"

"Charming." Lisa laughed and shook her head. She glanced pointedly out at Kim, who sat in her patrol car, entering the call on her log. "Seems like you launched quite a few wet dreams back then."

I was really going to have some 'splainin' to do when we got back to my mother's.

Chapter 14

Tommy had changed. He was balding, and a beer gut and love handles hung over his belt, giving him that "muffin top" look. He had gone from resembling his mother to being a clone of his father, right down to the bushy mustache. He still had eyes that smiled and a grin that charmed and a hug that crushed. He was one of the few people who could actually lift me off the ground when he hugged me.

After he gave Lisa's shoulder a quick squeeze and gushed about how good he thought I looked, he noticed the cans in the shopping cart. "Oh, man! You guys played shelf sweep without me? You couldn't have waited?"

"It was kind of spontaneous," Lisa said.

"Want to play again?" he asked enthusiastically, bouncing up and down on his heels like a little kid.

"Uh… no," I said, looking out the window as Kim's squad car made a U-turn in front of the store and sped toward downtown.

He helped us return everything to the shelves, and we went back upstairs to catch up on each other's lives. Thanks to Lisa's parents, he was aware of my orientation and other than his "what a loss" comment, he seemed fine with it. He also said that if his beautiful cousin had to be a lesbian, he would be happy if she'd end up with someone like me. I hadn't realized his family genuinely liked me as much as they did. It warmed my heart.

There were some good people in this town. It was unfortunate they had to be so few and far between.

"You used to make out with Kim Fredette!"

We were on our way back to my mother's. Lisa was

driving, and I had just explained Kim's earlier cryptic statements. "She was Kim Ligouri back then, and yes. She was safe. She was obvious. She didn't live in town." Lisa was silent, absorbing the new information. "Would it help if I said she was a lousy kisser?"

"So why did you keep meeting up with her?"

I shrugged. "Practice?"

She laughed, slapping at my arm. "That's terrible."

"It's true. Why is her last name Fredette now? She couldn't have gotten married."

"Actually, she did."

"To a man?" I stared at Lisa in surprise.

"Yes. To a man. And they had a kid. They were divorced the year after her daughter was born." She glanced at my face, which must have looked totally blank because I was dumbfounded. Kim Ligouri? Had sex with a man? And had a baby? I was expecting the sky to start falling at any minute. Lisa returned her attention to the road. "Don't ask me. I'm not close enough to her to know all the dirty little details of her life." She glanced at me again, smirking.

"Obviously."

"Hey, we just kissed and felt around a little bit, that's all."

"She wasn't your first?"

"No. That's why she's still pissed. I told her I would, and then I... didn't."

"Why didn't you?"

I sighed. "I got scared."

"You? I didn't think you were afraid of anything."

"We're all afraid of something." I glanced out the window. "I didn't want her to be my first."

"So, she wasn't your first. Who was? Anyone I know?"

I snickered. She'd never believe it. "Maybe. Who was your first? Anyone I know?"

"I wanted it to be you." She pulled into the driveway and shut off the engine. "Besides, I asked you first."

I unhooked my seatbelt and waved her off. "You probably don't remember her. She left Otter Falls not too long before I did.

She was older. Thirty."

"And you were eighteen?"

"Yeah. Late bloomer, I know. You?"

"My first was older, too. She was thirty-three, I was seventeen. It happened at a retreat my parents insisted I go to up near Plattsburg. Actually, she used to live in Otter Falls, but I didn't personally know her then. She was very alluring, very persuasive. She was married, though, and that always bothered me." There was a melancholy tone to her voice I found puzzling.

"Mine was married, too."

"So, come on, who was it?"

I rested my hand on her shoulder. "It was the minister's wife. From the First Congregational Church. Jennifer—" I stopped at Lisa's sharp intake of breath.

"Visson?"

I didn't like the look in her eyes. "Yes. Why?"

She looked stunned. "I don't believe this."

"Oh, no. You're kidding me. She was your first?" I was whirling in a kaleidoscope of emotions, the strongest of which seemed to be anger.

"Yeah, she was," she said quietly.

Jennifer Visson was a predator. I realized that after I had gotten older and looked back on the experience. Although I enjoyed the time I spent with her in bed and was appreciative of her personal instruction, she had proven she was not a nice person, showing the nasty side of her the night we got caught. To find out that she had also "busted" Lisa... A silent storm began raging inside me. It was a surprising link, but a sexual connection I wished we didn't share. I knew how Jennifer was with virgins. I could visualize exactly what they had done that first time, and picturing Lisa in her clutches was almost too much for me.

"Huh." I swallowed my outrage. I didn't want Lisa to think I was in any way angry with her. "Why don't we go inside and talk about this."

Lisa and I sat on the couch, my arm around her holding her tight against her side while we discussed Jennifer Visson and our first times. I could not seem to reconcile my feelings about this development. I had foolishly hoped that Jennifer had learned her lesson by getting caught with me and barely escaping scandal and ruined reputations. Apparently not.

"What happened? How did she find you?" I was trying to be calm, but I'm sure Lisa could feel me vibrating with anger. She reached up and clasped my fingers.

"It's not like she specifically targeted me, Hunter. I never even would have met her if I hadn't gone to the camp," she said.

"What camp?"

She hesitated and blew out a deep breath. "I guess when the Vissons left here, they relocated to a suburb outside of Plattsburg."

"New York?" When she nodded, I added, "I thought they would have moved farther away." On the other hand, Plattsburg was not the kind of destination citizens of Otter Falls would consider visiting unless they had specific business, so maybe it was just far enough for the Vissons to get away from the consequences without being too much of a move. "Why were you in Plattsburg?"

"There was a Christian retreat near Saranac Lake, and she—Jennifer—volunteered there."

"What were you doing at a Christian retreat? You weren't at a gay conversion therapy place, were you?" I nearly surged to my feet at the thought, but Lisa tightened her grip and held me back.

"Settle down there, terminator. I was seventeen, and I never hid my orientation from my family or, eventually, from anyone else. My parents—okay, my mother—thought they would never survive the disgrace of me being gay. She asked around and was directed to Abiding Horizons, a Christian-based camp, and she and my dad arranged for me to go."

"If it wasn't for reparative therapy, why did they send you there?"

"I was told that I needed to examine my spiritual priorities and deepen my relationship with God. The camp was only a week. I figured that it was easiest for me to just go to shut them up. When I got there, I realized that Abiding Horizons was a religious haven not for gays, but for women. If there were lesbians there besides me, they stayed closeted. The retreat focused on reawakening the faith of the 'lost.'"

"Lost women? I don't understand."

"Most of the women were housewives, sent there by their husbands to find their way back to knuckling under to the 'obey' part of their marriage vows."

"How Stepford Wife." The thought that such places even existed made me shudder.

"No kidding. It only took me a half-day of orientation to realize I didn't belong there. I kept thinking that if I was really vocal about being a lesbian and showed them that I was not about to conform to any of their regulations, they'd send me home. But all that got me was a room by myself, because no one wanted to bunk in with a dyke. Except for one lecherous maintenance man, who was convinced he could change me." Lisa chuckled.

"Where does Jennifer come in?"

"She was the Activities Director. Aptly titled," she said with a rueful grimace. "When word of my declaration reached her, she took me aside to give me *personal* guidance. To be fair, I was very attracted to her. She was a charismatic, strong woman. I was flattered by her interest but unnerved by her aggressive pursuit. I avoided being alone with her because even though she made my heart pound with excitement, she was almost too anxious, and that honestly felt a little creepy. On the last night at the retreat, while everyone was celebrating their 'reconditioning,' I went back to my room and found her naked, in my bed."

"Seems she has a routine," I said, mostly to myself. "She took your virginity."

"Yes." There was no pride in her voice. "I couldn't… okay, I didn't want to resist her."

"I'm a little confused, then. Vaginal orgasms are Jennifer's specialty. If she was your first, why didn't you experience one?"

"Although we did pretty much everything, when she entered me, it was with a dildo and not her fingers. It was big, and I'm small down there. It's not that I wasn't ready, but the dildo was as big as a freaking thermos and it was uncomfortable. It was too much. I bled, and I panicked. It kind of put an end to everything. Jennifer got impatient with me and annoyed, and she left in a huff. I cried myself to sleep after she left. I felt used and... sordid."

I really wanted to find Jennifer and make her pay, not just for avoiding any responsibility for my situation, but for preying on virgins. Her having to be their very first was an unhealthy obsession that left casualties in its wake. She was a seductive package, and she knew it, knew that no curious and willing girl in her right mind would turn down an offer from an experienced, sexy woman to "show her the ropes." The problem seemed to be that Jennifer had moved on to not caring whether or not the girl was willing. She would wear her victim down to get what she wanted. And her victims had started to get younger.

It didn't matter that it was thirteen years after the fact, my heart broke for Lisa. She deserved a better first time. I squeezed her close to me then eased my grip. "I'm so sorry, sweetie."

"Thankfully, my experiences since then have been very pleasant and mutually satisfying. Not to say my experience with Jennifer wasn't enlightening or stimulating, because until the penetration part, it was."

After sharing my own Jennifer Visson story, we went upstairs and crawled into bed. Initially, we just held each other. I was still too disturbed to think about anything other than tracking Jennifer down and calling her to account for her actions.

"Penny for your thoughts?" Lisa's soft voice broke through my preoccupation as her warm handmade gentle circles on my ribcage.

Her head was on my chest, and my arm was around her shoulder.

When I didn't answer right away, she said, "A person's heart rate speeds up when they're thinking angry thoughts. Yours is pounding like a trip-hammer."

"You know, I used to think it was pretty cool to tell people I had been seduced by a minister's wife, leaving out, of course, what resulted from us getting caught together."

"But?"

"But finding out that she nailed you, too, puts an entirely different spin on it." I turned on my side and faced her. "The bigger picture isn't so cool. Maybe if my mother had actually said something to someone, anyone, maybe the threat of negative publicity for the Vissons and the church might have prompted counseling, or sanctions of some sort."

"You know what a scandal like that would have done," Lisa said. "Jennifer would have just stuck to her story of being your victim, and because she is married—to a minister, no less—and has children, who do you think would have been believed? If I had ever said anything to my parents about what happened that last night at the camp, it would have somehow been my fault."

"I know," I said, frustrated. "And, in my case, even though she blamed me in order to save herself, I didn't want anything bad to happen to her. I was too broken to think clearly. I just wish now that I had been able to do something that had resulted in Jennifer having no future opportunities to indulge her overactive libido. Or, at least, have forced her to associate humiliatingly harsh consequences with her selfish lascivious choices." I sighed. "How old would she be now?"

"Forty-six, I believe."

"I wonder if she's still on the prowl, and what lines she might have crossed in the thirteen years since she was with you."

"Your heart is still racing."

"I can't stop thinking about Jennifer and how I wish I had her in front of me right now."

"Right now?" She lifted her head and looked at me, grinning.

"I think this would be the *last* place you'd want her right now." She raised an eyebrow.

That made me smile. "True. If she ever put her hands on you again…"

"Aww, my big, brave girlfriend is going to protect me. My big, brave girlfriend who hid behind the grocery cart from the big, bad police officer." She reached up and patted my cheek.

"How cute is that?"

I took her hand and kissed it. "God, you are *such* a brat."

She climbed on top of me, and my arms encircled her, holding her in place. "You know, though, if you think about it, what are the odds that we would both lose our virginity to the same woman?"

"Well, with the way Jennifer worked, I'd say the odds were pretty damned good."

She lightly kissed my face all over until her lips were hovering over mine. "I don't want to talk about her anymore."

"What do you want to talk about?"

"I don't want to talk at all," she said, ensnaring me with a tender yet passionate kiss that eventually led to some very sweet, slow-paced lovemaking that lasted long into the night.

The next morning, something happened that I really didn't like.

Lisa had to leave our warm bed to go to her house and get ready for work. No matter how much I begged, she was relentlessly responsible.

How was I going to leave her to go back to California when I couldn't even bear her leaving me to go to work? What was she doing to me? I was not like this; this was not me. I'd had prior relationships, but none had ever reached this level of commitment and had definitely not developed this quickly. It made me wonder if we would burn out as quickly as we caught fire, something that had often happened in my past. A woman would ignite my desire, and we would start hot and heavy. When the flame guttered out soon after, it was obvious there had really been nothing between us but sexual attraction.

My longest relationship had lasted just under a year, and it was turbulent from the beginning. The tempestuous undercurrent that brought us together was ultimately what tore us apart. The constant head-butting of two strong women who never really had much in common except their gladiatorial natures was doomed to fail, despite how intensely stimulating the sex was. She was someone I still occasionally connected with when neither of us was specifically dating anyone and we felt the need for some sexual companionship.

We discovered we were much better at being fuck buddies than we were at being lovers. She was the last woman I had been with before Lisa.

Something about what was happening between Lisa and me was very different from anything I had ever experienced with anyone. The completeness that washed over me in her presence was only matched by the emptiness that weighed me down during her absence. I almost felt a little lost now when she wasn't with me. I didn't want to go so far as to say that I was in love with her, because the concept of falling in love with someone in four days just wasn't realistic to me. But reality aside, as much as I tried to analyze and downplay my feelings for her, it always circled back to the "in love" issue. In the past that would have frightened the hell out of me, but now, with this particular woman, I welcomed it. I adored everything about Lisa Riordan. I wanted her in my life 24/7, and I knew she felt the same. But could we come to an agreement on how we were going to accomplish that?

As I showered, I stewed about Lisa's disclosure involving Jennifer Visson. If she lived closer, I would confront her. When she slept with me, Jennifer was four years younger than I was now, and only a year younger than I was now when she got Lisa. At my age, I could not fathom targeting an eighteen-year-old or younger, and I could only hope that Jennifer was not still luring young Sapphic virgins into her bed at age forty-six.

I had no doubt she was still beautiful, was probably one of those women who just got better looking with age, and I was sure she used that to her advantage when preying on her victims. But her misusing her position of authority and standing with a church to achieve some egotistically carnal goal was beyond appalling, it was reprehensible. Especially when she never stuck around long enough to deal with the consequences of her actions. Deviant behavior like hers gave lesbians a bad name.

I suddenly wondered if I could track her down using the Internet, or maybe start an online Jennifer Visson recovery group. I was becoming obsessed, and I had to stop.

After I fed Orion, I poured myself a cup of coffee from a

pot Lisa had brewed before she left. I retrieved the morning paper and glanced through all four, thin sections of *The Otter Falls Daily News*. I zeroed in on the list of open and closed court cases and then the obituaries to see if I recognized any names. My mother's services were listed, and I scanned for my name. "One daughter, S. Hunter Roberge from Glendale, California," I read aloud. "Sam must have given the information to the paper." I then found my horoscope, which advised me to look beneath the surface of the obvious, as not everything was what it appeared to be. And that differed from any other day of my life how?

Chapter 15

Before I returned to the house after delivering my mother's clothes to a very grateful shelter for battered women, I called my Aunt Cissy to see if I could stop by for a cup of coffee. She couldn't say yes fast enough.

I looked forward to seeing her, seeing how much she had changed. My aunt was a brave woman, and one of considerable emotional strength. I admired her greatly. She loved my Uncle David to excess, and losing him like she did and when she did was crippling, yet she never let it show, other than shedding a few tears behind the closed door of the bedroom they had shared for thirty-six years. They were raising four kids, and yet they took me in without hesitation. Even though I only stayed with them for two months, it was an unnecessary disruption to their lives, but she never once asked me why I was there or made me feel like I didn't belong. She opened her arms and her home to me, and I was ashamed that I hadn't kept in closer touch.

Aunt Cissy knew whatever had happened between my mother and me was a serious but painfully private issue. Whether she had guessed about me or not, I didn't know. There was never any indication that she had, and there were never any questions. My cousins also never implied that they had any inkling regarding my orientation. They were curious about what happened with my mother, but when I refused to talk about it, the inquiries immediately stopped. Maybe my aunt or uncle instructed them to leave it be; I never found out. Maybe my visit with her would give me more insight.

She was at the front door when I pulled into the driveway. I greeted her with a long, warm hug, and she linked my arm with hers and pulled me inside. In the last seven years, either I had grown taller or she had grown shorter. A few more wrinkles, a few more pounds, several more white hairs, but she was still my Aunt Cissy with the smiling eyes. She poured me a large mug of coffee and gestured me to the kitchen table, on which there was a big mixing bowl and all the ingredients for the makings of chocolate chip cookies.

I glanced around. The kitchen looked the same, save for a few more knickknacks, a different wall clock, and a new refrigerator loaded with photo magnets of what I assumed were her grandchildren. Before I sat down, I studied the pictures on the freezer door. "Wow. This one looks just like pictures of Uncle David when he was a teenager," I pointed out. "Is... Good Lord, is that Justin?"

She took a step closer and grinned proudly. "Yes. He's fourteen now."

"Wow. That's amazing." We took a seat at the kitchen table, opposite each other. Shauna, my oldest cousin, was the third to get married but the first to have kids. It seemed like once she started, her three siblings soon followed suit, and my Aunt Cissy now had fourteen grandchildren. Justin was seven the last time I saw him and pretty devastated that his grandpa was gone. Through talking with my aunt on the phone occasionally, I had kept up with the lowdown on all my cousins and their spouses, and which children were whose.

"Shauna gets home from work about two, then she has to be at a school conference by three-thirty. She'd like you to stop by, if you can spare the time."

"Yeah, I'd like that."

"Remember that I told you that Courtney works her accounting business out of her house? She would also like you to drop by there, since she can't get to Shauna's before three."

"Uh-huh." This was going to turn into an all-day venture. My other two cousins, Jeremy and Nicole, wanted to see me, too, but they also had things going on and would be home at different times, so even though they lived in separate sides of the same duplex, they probably wouldn't be able to see me at the same time.

As much as I loved Sam, I wouldn't want him living right

next door to me. Their family was very close, not just in their feelings for each other but also in proximity. They all lived within eight blocks of each other. I was going to tell Aunt Cissy that I didn't have time to stop and see them all in one day, but it looked as if she had already made the arrangements. Fortunately, I didn't have anything else going on until Lisa got out of work, and who knew what the immediate future might hold, so it made sense to visit with everyone today if I could.

We exchanged pleasantries and then by my third swallow of coffee, Aunt Cissy got right down to business. "Now, Hunter, you don't need to tell me, you know that, but did your mother kick you out all those years ago because you're a lesbian?"

My eyes snapped open, and I set the coffee mug down. "You guessed that about me, huh?"

"Honestly, no. I had no clue. Shauna's daughter, Lara, babysits for Lesley and Wally Melendy. Lara came home on Friday night very upset because Mrs. Melendy was saying terrible things about you. Called you a pervert and unnatural, said all kinds of disturbing things."

"Lesley knows who Lara is, then?" I was beginning to struggle with who I disliked more—Lesley or Dane.

"Oh, yes. You may remember that Shauna worked for Doug Riordan for two years before she got married. This is Otter Falls, Hunter. Everybody knows everybody else and everybody else's business. That has never changed. The only exception I can ever remember is what happened between you and your mother."

"Yes, Aunt Cissy. My mother threw me out because she found out I was a lesbian."

"That was it?" It was not a question of suspicion, as though I were holding out on her, it was more a statement of incredulity. She really didn't need to know the details; they didn't matter at this point.

"That was it." I bowed my head. Even after all these years, it still hurt. She reached over and gently put her hand on the back of mine.

"Oh, sweetie. Your mother..." She shook her head. "You know your mom and I got along like oil and water, which is

Cheyne Curry

why we only tolerated each other at Christmas and weddings. I never told you the reason for that, but it was because of the way she treated you."

That startled me. I had always assumed it was because Uncle David was my father's brother and she didn't want anything to do with that side of the family. "Really?"

"Yes. Really. I cannot tell you the fights your mother and I used to get into about you. You don't know how many times she told me to mind my own business. She never wanted to let you be who you were, never wanted you to develop your own personality.

She didn't even want you to be a mini version of her. It was impossible to know *what* she wanted from you, but if I couldn't figure it out, and I was an adult, there was no chance for you to figure it out."

"She didn't want me to be anything like my father."

"It would have been so much simpler if that had been it. But she didn't toss your father out until you were six. Her unreasonably harsh discipline of you started from the second you could understand the word 'no.' She always acted as if she was angry with you."

"It wasn't an act, Aunt Cissy, she always *was* angry with me. I could never do anything right in her eyes. She would ask me to do something, and I would do it, and even though I had never done it before, she would go around right behind me, berating me every step of the way for doing it wrong. She used to say, 'can't you do *anything* right?' or 'if you aren't going to do it right the first time, why do it at all?' I eventually got to a point where I just agreed with her and told her fine, I wouldn't do it then. But that, of course, got me into trouble, too. You know, just a little praise for trying would have been nice."

"Hunter, I don't know what motivated your mother as far as her treatment of you was concerned, but I think blaming your father was just a convenient excuse."

"So, you think she always hated me?" I looked up into sympathetic gray eyes, hoping she would say "no." It seemed okay for me to think it myself, but if my aunt confirmed that she did, indeed, think my mother *actually* hated me, that would instill a bitterness and a sadness in me that I didn't think I could ever overcome. Or forgive.

"No, sweetie, I think she hated herself. For some reason, you were her outlet."

"Why would she hate herself? My mother was beautiful and seemingly very popular. She was a good mother and very well regarded in the community." Had I just said she was a good mother?

Well, despite her treatment of me, my two brothers and I did grow up to be productive adults. I was an exemplary employee, quickly rising to the top of my field, keeping Bambi, Thumper, and all their little friends safe. Sam was managing his father-in-law's prospering construction business, making a name for himself in the entire state, not just regionally. And Dane... well, Dane, even though he seemed to live by his own set of rules, had made a name for himself in local politics and was a big deal at Mom's church. So in that respect, she was a good mother, instilling core work values that stayed with us.

"Hunter, I knew your mother before she married your dad. You know that she lived the typical young girl's dream of being her junior and senior prom and homecoming queen, Miss Otter Falls, and second runner up in the Miss Vermont pageant."

"Yeah. I never heard the end of that."

"Nobody else did either. And do you know why? Because it's all she had to hang on to. It was the last time in her life that she was her own person, that she was in control of her life. When your father came along, this handsome man just out of the Navy, he looked like a good catch and she thought she was going to live the American dream with him."

"Instead, she lived the American nightmare," I said.

She smiled, patiently and stood up. "Not quite." She went to the sink, filled a measuring cup with water, and returned to the table. Adding brown sugar, then white sugar to the big bowl, she said, "To my knowledge, your father never raised a hand to your mother, did he?"

"If he did, I didn't know about it. And believe me, if he had, I'm sure *that* would have been thrown in my face, too."

"Then it wasn't quite the American nightmare." She looked

up and saw me watching her prepare the dough. "They'll be done before you leave. I'll make sure you have some."

"Thanks, Aunt Cissy." I grinned happily, feeling like a little kid again. "Can I maybe have some dough before you use it all?" She looked at me, waiting. Then I remembered. "Please?" Jesus, I *was* a little kid again.

She laughed. "Courtney is always saying to me, 'Mom, I don't care how old I get, I come back into this house and I feel ten years old again.' I guess we parents always have a way of doing that, huh?" She returned to the subject of my mother. "Some of us tried to tell Sarah that she was making a mistake by marrying your dad, but she wouldn't listen. She was stuck on the fact that, together, she and your father were the perfect couple. I mean, yes, they looked fabulous together, like right out of a movie magazine, but he played her from the beginning. Your Uncle David talked to your father the night before the wedding, begged him to call it off. But, without going into details, your father wasn't about to give up your mother at that point."

"So you're saying it really was my father's fault my mother was the way she was?"

"Not at all. It was both their faults. Your father should have left her alone. Period. Devastatingly handsome though he was, he was a scoundrel from the word go, and your mother deserved better. So did you kids." She added the chocolate chips to her dough and continued to stir. "On the other hand, your mother should have been less focused on what other people thought or how it looked for her to be with anyone who had less than matinee idol looks. Appearances were everything with her, and she tried to maintain them. Especially after your father left."

"And I never fit in with what she thought was acceptable. I never heard the end of her disapproval that I didn't want her life. A date every weekend, or a steady boyfriend, or any of that stuff that was of no interest to me. There was never any let up of that *tone*, you know? The one that always said, 'What's wrong with you? You're not good enough, you'll never measure up.' She ridiculed everything I did. Whatever it was, it was never right." The old frustration boiled in my voice.

"Just because you didn't do something her way, didn't mean it wasn't right," Aunt Cissy stated gently. "You were always a very pretty girl, and you've grown into a stunning woman. You seem like a beautiful soul, too, sweetie. Why your mother never chose to recognize that, I'll never know. Why she chose to take her own personal failings out on you is also something I'll never understand. Your brothers could get away with murder, but you caught hell for every little thing."

As a gesture of consolation, she handed me a soup spoon full of cookie dough loaded with dark chocolate chips. She dropped the first batch on a cookie sheet, popped them into the oven, and brought the coffeepot over to refill our mugs. "Your mother should never have disowned you because you happen to like women rather than men. We have no control over that kind of thing. Why, hell, if it was acceptable to be angry at my kids because of who they fell in love with, I wouldn't be speaking to three of them. If your grandmother followed that philosophy, she would have disowned your mother. I'm sure no woman you brought home to your mother would have been any worse than her bringing your father home to your grandmother."

She wasn't telling me anything I didn't already know, but it was nice to hear that someone else had noticed it, too. It validated my belief that I really wasn't a bad daughter. We spoke frankly about my mother and my father, and I was given little tidbits of information that helped me put together a clearer picture of why my childhood had been so miserable.

Then she brought up a subject that had us all perplexed. "So, when your mother left you that house, that just shocked us all."

"I can honestly tell you that it shocked me the most. I don't know why she did it. No one else seems to know either, and I don't know if I'll ever find out."

"Do you think she left you the house as an apology, maybe?"

We both contemplated that idea for a moment and both shook our heads at the same time. "Nah, me either. I guess the only one who knows the answer to that is her."

After four cups of coffee, a half-dozen hot cookies, and two hours of "catch up" conversation, it was time for me to go. I wanted to go home and take a nap, but there was no way I could fit that into my immediate schedule. Aunt Cissy filled a bag with a dozen more cookies and set it on the table for me. I was just rinsing my coffee cup in the sink when the doorbell rang.

"Hunter, sweetie, would you get that? I need to get this batch of cookies out of the oven."

"Sure." I grabbed another fresh, warm cookie off the cooling rack and went to the door. I opened it and found a middle-aged woman standing on the stoop, holding a clipboard and a fistful of leaflets. She was a few inches shorter than I was, full-figured, nicely dressed in a red pantsuit, but a little haggard-looking. She had shiny red hair pulled away from her face by a barrette, dark eyes, rosy red lips, rosy cheeks, and an odd, yellowish-colored nose. She reminded me of a life-sized Tickle Me Elmo. "Yes?"

"Hi, I'm Vicky Stancliff, and I'm here to remind you to get out and vote next month. When you do, your vote for Dane Roberge for Congress would be appreciated." She was about to hand me something with a photo of my brother's smug face on it when I leaned back away from the doorway.

"Are you going to vote for Dane next month?" I hollered to my aunt.

"Hell, no. The little turd doesn't deserve it," she called back.

I returned my attention to Vicky, who was looking a little uncomfortable. "Sorry. Not interested."

Before I could close the door, she said, "Maybe that's because you really don't know him."

I raised an eyebrow and looked at her pointedly. "And how well do you know him, Vicky?"

"My husband has worked with him for the last two years. We think he's just what this town needs in a representative."

"Well, that woman in there? She's his aunt, and she's known him for the last thirty-one years, and she thinks if he gets elected, this town will be in deep bat guano. And her opinion is good enough for me."

She looked as though she was about to say something, but

I said, "Have a nice day," and closed the door on her. I went into the kitchen and kissed my aunt's cheek. "I won't be a stranger," I promised. I took my bag of cookies and went to reconnect with my cousins, Shauna, then Nicole and Jeremy, then Courtney. Then home to get ready to meet Lisa.

My cousins, and what I met of their families, were very glad to see me, and the only time the issue of my orientation came up was when Shauna and I discussed the incident that prompted Lesley to vent her prejudice on Shauna's daughter. Shauna told me that her daughter, Lara, was no longer allowed to babysit for the Melendy's two boys. She looked up at me from her height of all of five foot, three inches and promised she would kick my butt if I left again and didn't keep in touch.

As I was about to leave Shauna's house, her doorbell rang.

"I'm on my way out. Would you like me to get it?" She nodded, so I went to the front door and opened it. There was Tickle-Me-Vicky with her clipboard and leaflets.

She blinked at me. "Are you the lady of the house?"

"I am not," I told her. I turned and hollered, "Shauna, are you going to vote for Dane?"

"That lying little son of a bitch? If he was the only candidate running, I wouldn't even vote!"

Vicky's eyebrows shot up, and I smiled at her. "Guess you got your answer. And I saved you some time, to boot."

"But..."

"That woman in there? Well, she's his older cousin, and she's known him his whole life. If she finds him too dishonest to vote for, that's good enough for me."

"That's no reason not to vote for him. All politicians are dishonest—"

"Listen, she wouldn't believe anything Dane Roberge said, *including* if he said he was lying." It took her a moment to consider a response, and during her hesitation, I said cheerfully, "Have a good day," and I shut the door. I went back inside, bade Shauna goodbye, and went out to my car.

I stopped at Jeremy's first. He was putting the finishing touches on a deck he had been working on for a couple of weeks. He had changed over the past seven years, in that he stopped looking so much like his mother and started resembling his father, which meant he physically favored me more than my own two brothers did. I felt an instant warmth from Jeremy that I'd never felt from Dane, and it suddenly made me wonder when and why things had gone so wrong between my little brother and me.

And then I remembered.

"Mommy! Hunner hit me!"

I stared at Dane, shocked. I wasn't anywhere near him.

"What? Shut up, you little freakazoid."

"Mommy! Hunner hit me again, and she's calling me bad names." There was an evil grin on his Howdy Doody face.

"Hunter!" My mother's voice held a clear warning. "Get in here, right now."

"You're such a little weasel, you pain," I whispered harshly. "Now I'm in trouble, and I didn't even do anything."

"But Mommy will believe me, and I don't like you today, so I want to see you get a spanking," my demon spawn, four-year-old brother said.

"Sarah Hunter, get in this house. I will not tell you again."

Uh-oh. When she used both names, it was always a very bad sign. I had been helping Dane build a fort for his Army men in the sandbox, when he suddenly decided to turn on me. "I didn't do anything," I told her.

"Dane wouldn't say you hit him if you didn't. One…"

Now I was mad and upset. I didn't want to give in, but I knew I would be in for severe punishment if I was not standing in front of her by the count of three. I stubbornly crossed my arms, glaring at Dane who was still smirking at me triumphantly. He looked at me and yelled, "Mommy, Hunner just called you a bad name."

My sharp intake of breath was drowned out by my mother bellowing, "Two!"

I knew I was in big trouble anyway, so I stood up and stomped the beautiful fort we had just made. Now he had something to whine about, the little creep.

"Mawwwmeee! She just kicked my fort down," he wailed.

"Three!" My mother was right behind me. She yanked me out of the sandbox, and I felt the force of her hand on my butt seven times, one swat for each year of my life. She didn't hold back, and it smarted, but it hurt my heart more. I refused to cry, and I think that always made her angrier.

She pulled me into the house and up to my room. When she turned me to face her, I wouldn't look at her. "I didn't do anything," I repeated defiantly. Tears were stinging my eyes. Though they threatened to fall, they did not.

"You didn't do anything? You didn't just destroy his fort?"

"He's lying, Mom!"

She slapped my butt again, the force of it knocking my body sideways. "You're lying, Hunter. I saw you kick over the sand and ruin his fort. Why are you so mean to Dane? He's smaller than you. He's—"

"I'm not mean to him. He's mean to me. I didn't hit him or call him names. I didn't call you names."

"Then why would he say it? He's four years old, and if he's lying, then he learned how to lie from you. I don't know what to do with you, Hunter. You are such a difficult child. You are not the daughter I thought I would have. Why you couldn't be more like me instead of like your father, I'll never know. Now you will stay in your room until it's time to get up and go to school tomorrow. No supper for you, young lady." She released me, stood up, and left my room.

"I'm gonna run away to Aunt Cissy and Uncle David's!" I shouted to the closing door.

"They don't want a naughty girl, either, so you're stuck here."

Her voice faded as she returned to the kitchen. I could smell dinner.

Mom had been baking macaroni and cheese, one of my favorites.

It was only then, in the privacy of my room, I let go and cried.

Five minutes later, there was a soft knock on my door. Before I could say anything, I heard my mom's voice from the kitchen.

"Sam, leave your sister alone. She needs to think about what she's done. Go out and get Dane and start getting him washed up. We're almost ready for dinner."

"Okay, Mom," I heard him say.

I didn't see Sam until the next morning, when we were getting ready to catch the school bus. Mom picked out our clothes, helped us get ready, fed us breakfast, and sent us off into our day with no mention of the night before. That was okay by me. I just wanted it all to be okay until the next time. And I had no doubt there would be a next time .

That was only one memory of how Dane had always played my mother against me. Jeremy would never have thought of trying that with his sisters.

I was introduced to Jeremy's wife when she brought us each a beer, and we sat on the soon-to-be-completed deck and caught up.

They were fascinated with my career as a park ranger, and Jeremy's wife said, "Maybe you could come back to talk to our nine-year-old daughter, who is obsessed with the environment and cop shows on TV. Perhaps your job would be a natural path for her."

"Maybe before I leave, we can all spend an afternoon at Evergreen Ridge, and I can explain to her exactly what it is that I do and see if it interests her." She was, after all, only nine. By age ten, she might decide she'd rather be a professional wrestler.

I glanced at my watch. The day was flying by.

My cousin Nicole appeared at her back door in the other half of the duplex and called out, "Hey, Hunter, I'm home. Come on over whenever you're ready."

I hugged Jeremy and his wife. "Give me a call me on my cell. Your mom has the number, and we'll set up a date for that walk in the park."

Just then, we heard a voice behind me say, "Hi. I knocked and rang the bell out front, but you must not have heard me."

Turning around, I came face-to-face with Tickle-Me-

Vicky.

She stopped dead when she saw me. I just grinned at her.

"Let me guess… these are his cousins, too."

"As a matter of fact, yes." I looked at Jeremy and his wife. "This is Vicky. She's campaigning for Dane."

Jeremy grimaced. "Agh. I think not. Thanks, but no thanks. It's bad enough he's in the family."

Vicky's perky expression fell, and she didn't persist. "Thank you for your time." She disappeared back around the corner of the house.

I reiterated quick good-byes to Jeremy and his wife and rushed into Nicole's half of the condo through the back patio door. I got to her front door just as the doorbell rang. "May I?" I asked my cousin, who was clearly wondering what possessed me. When she shrugged and nodded, I opened the door. "Well, hi, there."

"*Another* cousin?" she asked, her tone more annoyed than defeated.

"Uh-huh." I stepped aside, allowing her access to Nicole, who stepped up next to me in the doorway.

Vicky ignored me and put on her best smile for Nicole. "Hello.

My name is Vicky Stancliff, and I'm—"

"Are those leaflets promoting Dane Roberge's campaign?" Nicole interrupted, seeing the contents of Vicky's hand.

"Um… yes."

"You're wasting your time here, lady," Nicole told her. "If this were *Survivor*, he would have been the first one voted off the island."

Vicky glared at me as though I was the cause of Dane being so hated. She thanked Nicole and left.

"Poor thing," I said as Nicole shut the door. "I wonder if she's met anyone who actually wants to support Dane."

"My guess would be only the bartenders at the Moose Club."

I gave my youngest cousin a hug, and we went back outside and spent another hour with Jeremy and his wife.

Poor Vicky must have thought the Fates had it in for her.

When I was about to leave my cousin Courtney's house after a lovely visit, I opened the door and ran right into Tickle-Me-Vicky, just as she was about to ring the doorbell. She looked at me, then at Courtney, just growled at me and left without a word.

An hour later, I was back home when Lisa arrived to pick me up to go to her house for dinner and to spend the night. I was feeding Orion when the doorbell rang, so I asked Lisa to get the door. A minute later, she shouted in to me, "Hey, you want to sign a petition to support Dane in the election?"

I shot up from the cat's food dish. It couldn't be. I practically sprinted to the door, appearing behind Lisa with a shit-eating grin on my face. "Vicky! Long time, no see."

The woman dropped her clipboard and just stared at me. "Who *are* you?"

"I'm Dane's sister."

"And you don't like him either, do you?"

"Not so much."

Tickle-Me-Vicky shook her head. "That's it. I quit. I'm going to go work for Bill DeMartino's campaign. Everybody seems to like him."

Chapter 16

Lisa had planned to cook dinner for me, but I talked her into letting me show her my grilling skills instead. After I impressed her with my salmon marinated with sesame, ginger, and lemon, we sat on her patio long into the night with Oz and Deke napping contentedly at our feet. We went to bed close to midnight and made passionate love for nearly two hours before we settled in to sleep.

When I closed my eyes, she was securely in my arms, her back tight against my chest, and when I awoke the next morning, she was spooning me.

Everywhere our bodies touched, my skin was on fire. I couldn't believe the overwhelming sensations this woman stirred up in me. I never wanted her to let me go. I was becoming less terrified that I would never live up to her expectations, to the fantasy of me she had hung on to for all those years. Clearly, either what we had together was exactly what she had anticipated, or her expectations hadn't been that high.

She dropped me off at home, leaving me with a kiss and a smile. I loved that it was the last memory I had of her to get me through the day until I saw her again. I was shocked at how much in love with this woman I felt, and I was grateful to her for showing me that I had the capacity to feel love like this.

I made myself another cup of coffee and finished reading the paper. Then I looked up the realtor my mother's will had stipulated, and I dialed the office number. The agent who answered was a very nice gentleman named Todd Jardine.

"Ah, yes, Ms. Roberge. I've been expecting your call."

"Good. Then I assume that you're familiar with my

mother's house. I'd like to set up a meeting with you so we can go over how I should proceed."

There was a brief moment of silence on the line, then Mr. Jardine cleared his throat and said, "Um, well, there is an impediment to our moving forward in any manner."

I had a pretty good idea what the "impediment" was, but I wasn't going to make things easy for the realtor. "And what might the problem be?"

He became quite nonplussed, hemming and hawing until he finally blurted, "I just received the legal notice this morning. The validity of the will is being contested by your brother, Dane. He is citing 'Undue Influence.' Sorry, Ms. Roberge, but until the inheritor is confirmed, all business dealings must be put on hold."

"I understand," I told him through clenched teeth. It wasn't his fault my brother was an asshole, and I wasn't about to take it out on him. "Thank you, Mr. Jardine. I'll be in touch." I placed the receiver in the cradle. "That little son of a bitch." I picked up the phone to call Sam at work.

After I told Sam that Dane was contesting Mom's will, I called Lisa and told her what was going on.

"Who's the lawyer?" she asked.

"Ray Palmisano."

I heard her shuffling papers, and then she said to someone there in her office, "Those need to go out in the mail today." I assumed she was speaking to her secretary. "Sorry, Hunter, just cleaning up some paperwork. Palmisano, huh?"

"Yeah. You know him?"

"Sure. Otter Falls, remember? We all know each other."

"What's he like, this Palmisano guy?"

"He's an experienced probate attorney with a decent reputation. He's getting tired, though, and can be lazy if he's not made to toe the line. I've heard rumors he's been going to retire, but it hasn't happened yet."

"How long has he been in business?"

"He's been practicing here for forty years."

"One of the town dinosaurs, eh? Would he be Florian Palmisano's dad?"

"No, he's Florian's uncle. Ray doesn't have any kids. Ray is also Kim Fredette's uncle on the other side of the family."

"Sheesh. Talk about a town with six degrees of separation."

"Six?" She laughed. "You'd be lucky if you can find four."

Within an hour, Sam and I were sitting in an office with my mother's attorney. Ray Palmisano was a short, sturdy man who looked to be in his mid-sixties, with a full head of more salt than pepper hair and a nose pink and bulbous from many years of hard drinking. His office was messy, cluttered with law books, files, and stray papers; it reflected his appearance. His shirt was only half tucked in, and his tie was still knotted but pulled down to accommodate the open first two buttons of his shirt. My initial impression of him was not a favorable one. He left us with the feeling that we were *bothering* him.

His secretary brought all three of us coffee, and Palmisano laid out the appropriate documentation on his desk in front of him, then looked up at me.

"So you're the mysterious daughter. I've wondered about you for a long time."

Sam and I exchanged glances, and I looked at Palmisano.

"Wondered what?"

"Just... wondered." He didn't elaborate. "Okay, here's the deal. Your brother Dane is alleging Undue Influence. What that means is he feels that somebody influenced your mother by excessive insistence, that she was improperly pressured to leave the house to you, Sarah, and as a result of that pressure, she was unable to refuse."

"Hunter," I said.

He looked back at me. "Excuse me?"

"It's Hunter. No one's called me Sarah since I was born." I half-smiled at him, hoping that might help ease the tension in the room. It didn't. When the attorney turned his gaze to the file on his desk, Sam reached over and patted my arm.

"Just exactly what does this mean, Mr. Palmisano?" Sam asked. "There's really no basis for Dane's accusations. You know Hunter had no influence over my mother. They weren't even speaking, and you and I worked directly with my mother on the preparation of this entire will."

"This is going to be more of a nuisance than anything else. Think of it like playing poker. You have an unbeatable hand, and you know your opponent is bluffing, but he still wants to play it out until the end. Because he can." He sighed and rubbed his bloodshot eyes. "As you have already encountered, Hunter," he said and put extra emphasis on my name, "the distribution process is temporarily suspended when a will is contested. I think I can prevent this from getting dirty and, hopefully, from getting too expensive, and I will do my best to keep it out of the courtroom. But if there's anything that might give validity to his claim, I need to know it right now."

His eyes bored into me accusingly. I didn't like his implication, and I'd had more than enough of his attitude.

"I have had no contact with my mother for sixteen years, and as Sam will tell you, I didn't want the damned house to begin with."

"Hunter." Sam firmly placed his hand on my forearm.

"I would appreciate you not cursing in my office," Palmisano said.

"Well, I haven't done anything to warrant Dane's challenge, and neither has Sam," I said hotly. "Does Dane claim that Sam unduly influenced our mother to leave me a house I didn't want? That doesn't make sense."

Palmisano shrugged. "No, it doesn't. Honestly, though, neither does her leaving you the house, especially with the two of you being estranged for so long."

"But you sat right here when she adamantly insisted that the house and everything in it, including the cat, go to Hunter," Sam reminded Palmisano.

"Indeed I did."

"Okay, so all accusations aside, what happens now?" I asked.

"While the claim of invalidity is investigated, the probate process will stop. Even though we're sure that Dane has no legal grounds to support his position, the resolution can take up a great deal of time and money and throw the will proceedings completely off schedule."

He focused on me. "If you had any specific date by which you have to return to the West Coast, you might want to make arrangements to extend it."

"Great," I said flatly, trying to tamp down my frustration.

"Look, I've dealt with your brother before, and I understand he can try one's patience," Palmisano said, in a transparent attempt at appeasement.

"Try one's patience? Mother Teresa would have smacked him by now." I crossed my arms.

"What's our next move?" Sam asked.

"We wait," he stated simply.

"I knew he was being too quiet," I said to Sam, outside Palmisano's office building. "Not seeing or hearing from him in any manner after that night at the house was too out of character for him."

"He doesn't have a legal leg to stand on," Sam said. "He can scream 'Undue Influence' all he wants, but that will is ironclad."

"Nothing is ironclad these days. Regardless, you and I know it's not about that. Dane may be a buffoon, but he's shifty. He knows that will is solid. He just wants to cause trouble for me. He knows that putting everything on hold is going to cost me money I don't have and time I can't take away from my job."

"He's always been a sneaky little prick, Hunter."

"Yeah, but something else is going on. He knows I know about his hushed-up DUI arrests. He also knows that if I come out publicly while I'm here, I could turn his political aspirations upside down by showing him up for the hypocrite he is. And still he's willing to take the risk that I'll run him into the ground with the local press. Why?"

"Maybe figuring you don't have the time or the money to fight him, Dane thinks you'll just give in and give him the house."

"He should realize by now that I never give up as far as he's concerned. It's got to be something else. He wants the house. Badly. Why?" I looked at Sam. "It's not about me. I'm just a pawn. It's about that house. What's in that house that has him so determined to get it, something that he'd be willing to give up his political future for?"

Sam mulled over what I had said and nodded slowly. "I can't answer your question, but something happened between Mom and Dane about three months ago, something neither of them shared with me, or with anyone else that I know of. Since then, things were prickly whenever they were around one another, even though they both tried to disguise it."

"Jeez, Sam, you never mentioned that."

He shrugged. "There was no need. When you and I talk on the phone, we don't usually mention Mom or Dane. And, honestly, I never thought much about it. If anything, I was surprised Mom hadn't become fed up with Dane's obnoxious antics a lot sooner."

Without knowing the cause of the rift, I couldn't discern any way to connect this new information to Dane's apparent obsession to come into possession of the house, unless Mom had given it to me to spite Dane. "To your knowledge, has Dane spent any length of time alone in the house since Mom died?"

"I don't know for sure, but I doubt it. Mom succumbed to a massive stroke on Tuesday morning, and he and I were busy making arrangements and just coping. Pretty much all of Dane's time is accounted for between Tuesday and the time you arrived on Thursday night." He tilted his head, as if he was searching his memory for anything else that had seemed out of the ordinary. "The night you arrived, after you left the get-together, Dane did say he hadn't expected you to come so quickly, if you came at all."

"Hmmm. Maybe that explains why he felt he could take his time about getting into the house." I shook my head in frustration. "It always comes back to the house. *Why* did she leave it to me? It just doesn't add up. You knew her better than I did. Why would she do that?"

He leaned against the Jeep. "Actually, nothing against you, but I thought that was strange, too. I was pretty sure she was going to leave the house to Dane because he always acted as if he were almost indentured to her, especially the last few years, up until that recent falling out. I thought that if, for some reason, she didn't want to leave the house to Dane, then it would definitely come to me. But then she pulls this one-eighty and is unyielding about leaving it to you. No explanation, just 'I want Hunter to have the house and everything in it, including Orion.'"

"I'm sure Orion was thrown in just for spite." Ideas were swirling around in my head, none of which made any sense.

"You and Orion making peace?"

"So far. Either she's calmed down, or she's making me think she has. She's been sleeping on the bed with us, down by our feet, and we actually have all our toes left. I'm still cautious but…" I shrugged.

"How's that going?" Sam raised an eyebrow and smirked. "You and Lisa."

"It's going really well, almost as though we've always been in a relationship. Honestly, nothing in my life has felt more right."

"And how does that figure into your going back out west?"

"She and I have got to talk about that. Soon."

"Well, thanks to Dane, it looks like you'll have a little more time to do that."

Sam and I said goodbye, and I called Lisa to brief her on what I had learned in Palmisano's office. She agreed to meet me for lunch.

There was a big part of me that wanted to drive to Dane's and ask him outright what he was up to, or pound him into the ground.

There was something more behind what he was doing than him feeling slighted; I could feel it. Was there something about the house I should know about? Was there something *inside* the house Dane didn't want me to know about? Was there something in that house my mother didn't want Dane or Sam to have? What had started out as an annoying inheritance was turning into an annoying riddle, one to which I was determined to find the answer.

I pulled into a parking space in front of Lisa's office and

was about to shut the Jeep off and go inside, when I saw her walk out her door and down the steps toward me. I hadn't realized I was so keyed up about what Dane might be up to until I saw Lisa's smiling face and suddenly my tension melted away. My relief didn't last long.

Lisa climbed into the Jeep and placed a kiss on my cheek. "I've taken the afternoon off. After I talked to you, I got to thinking about something that I know was also bugging you. I called Sam and asked him if he had put all your trophies and memorabilia on display in your old room. He said that the last time he saw your stuff was years ago. Your mother had packed most of your belongings into boxes, and there was nothing on your walls, vanity, or bureau. I think we need to go back to the house and check out your room."

I put the Jeep in gear and sped off. What the fuck was going on?

Chapter 17

We stopped by Lisa's place first, so she could change her clothes and look in on the dogs. When we got back to my mother's, Sam was waiting for us. When we converged on my old room, I suddenly felt like I was in the middle of a Nancy Drew mystery, with Bess and George by my side.

Lisa pulled clothes and boxes out of the closet, I rummaged through drawers, and Sam gathered pictures, posters, paintings, and articles off the walls and from around the room.

"What's with Palmisano?" I asked Sam as we sorted through our individual tasks. "Why his attitude toward me? I've never even met the guy."

"He's a fundamentalist Christian," Lisa said. "I would guess he knows you're gay and is only being civil to you because of his long-standing acquaintance with your mother."

"But how would he know I'm a lesbian? I'm pretty sure it's not something my mother would tell him, and I would say his gaydar is probably worse than Liza Minnelli's."

"Well, I certainly didn't tell him," Sam volunteered, leafing through a carton containing magazine memorabilia of Linda Hamilton from *Terminator 2: Judgment Day*.

"Ray goes to the same church as Lesley's husband, Wally. I assume that's how Ray found out. I bet you were the topic of conversation of choice, especially after we dropped Lesley off on Saturday."

"That makes sense." I rifled through a drawer of rolled-up socks. I picked up a handful and pitched them onto the bed. I could always use socks.

Lisa smiled as she held up my letter jacket. "I always wanted to be the one you chose to wear this." She carefully laid it on the bed.

"Just what are we looking for?" Sam asked, sounding frustrated.

"I don't know. Mom hated me, Sam, no matter what you say. Her leaving me this house just doesn't make sense. Leaving this room like this, especially if she didn't turn it into a shrine, doesn't make sense either. She's trying to tell me something, or make some point. Just exactly when she turned into Miss Marple, I don't know. As to what we're looking for? I hope I'll know it when I see it."

For two hours we turned that room upside down and found nothing out of the ordinary. The room went from being an orderly sanctum to looking more like it had when I occupied it: as if a bomb had gone off. The three of us started in different sections of the room and ended up sitting on the floor facing each other amid piles of clothes, books, pictures, and... stuff. I hadn't realized I had collected so much junk. Or that my mother had actually kept it all. I could hear her as if it were yesterday...

"Hunter, this room is a disgrace." My mother leaned against the doorway and surveyed the interior of my bedroom. She was right. Sam was the only one who voluntarily kept his room neat during the school week.

"I'm going to clean it up later, I just want to finish this article."

I was leafing through a science fiction magazine and had just found an interview with the cast of *Terminator 2*.

Saturdays always started out with a hearty breakfast, and the rest of the morning was spent cleaning our rooms and doing whatever other chores needed to be done. Unless something was specifically planned, my brothers and I weren't allowed to participate in any outside activities until all of our assigned tasks were completed.

"I want you to clean it up now, please."

I looked up at her. "Mom, it's the weekend. We're not expecting company. What difference does it make if I clean it up right now, or wait until I finish what I'm reading and clean it up ten minutes from now?"

"It makes a difference to me." She wasn't raising her voice.

She didn't have to. She was in one of her "absolute power" moods.

She had to prove that she was in uncontested control, and I never did know why. I guess on some days more than others she just needed to make a point to herself: No one would ever challenge her command in her house. Except me. And I always lost.

I knew she was probably deliberately goading me, and I knew I should not rise to the bait. But it pissed me off that she felt the need to exercise her authority just because she could. It made no sense.

As if she was reading my mind, she said, "Now, Hunter."

I slammed the magazine onto the bed, stood up, and kicked a few paperback books out of my way. "This is so lame!"

"And for that little display of temper, you just lost your TV privileges for the day."

That was fine with me. There was nothing I wanted to watch anyway. Saturday nights sucked, as far as viewing fare went.

"Whatever." I meant to say that under my breath. When I felt the sting of a hard slap on my bare arm, I silently cursed myself for not being able to keep my mouth shut.

"For sassing me, you're grounded for the weekend."

"What? Mom, you can't!" A palm print reddened my arm.

"Lesley's party is tomorrow afternoon."

My mother already knew that, and suddenly my being grounded smacked of premeditation. Lesley's parents were throwing a huge birthday party for her in their back yard. It had been planned for weeks, and my mother had been grumbling about it for just as long. She thought Lesley was a bad influence on me, and in my mother's eyes, the last thing I needed was encouragement in a negative direction.

Having fun with Lesley was not the real reason I was so eager to go. Tara Haberlin, one of the junior varsity cheerleaders, was going to be there, and I'd had a secret crush on her for a year. I was pretty sure she was straight, and even if she wasn't, I would have been too chicken shit to do anything about it. Still, I was counting the hours until I could hang out with her a little while at Lesley's party, just to be around her in an environment other than a school-related event.

"You should have thought of that before you mouthed off to me."

"I... I didn't mouth off. All I said was 'whatever.' I was accepting the TV restriction."

"With a disrespectful attitude."

"But... but... I'm fifteen," I wheedled, as though that should have been enough reason for a pardon.

"Just barely, Hunter, and at fifteen, you need to start acting more responsible and more mature." Except for slapping me, she still hadn't lost her temper. "There are consequences to your actions. From now on, you're going to start thinking about what you say and how you say it. That attitude has got to go. And don't test me, either. You know how I can get." She pushed off the door and turned to walk away.

"That's for sure," I mumbled.

She stopped. "What was that?"

"I said my arm is sore," I said louder, hoping she would buy it.

"From that little whack? You need to toughen up, young lady. You'll never have my threshold for pain. You're too much of a baby."

I ignored her remark. I was used to her calling me a baby and a weakling. "Mom, please don't ground me from Lesley's party. I'm picking up my room like you asked me to, and I'm sorry I answered you in a disrespectful tone."

She spun on her heel and returned to my door. Now she was angry. "It's too late. You're sorry now because you're being punished. If I had let your behavior slide, you wouldn't be sorry at all, and you would have continued with the sass and attitude. By grounding you and forbidding you from doing something you really want to do, maybe I'll convince you to remember this the next time you feel like being insolent." Her eyes swept my room one last time as I started putting books in piles. "I can't believe you can live like this. You're a lazy lout, Hunter. All you're concerned about is having fun with your friends. Life is more than that, and you'd best learn that now.

You keep on this path, and you'll never amount to anything."

I mouthed her final words with her as she said them: "Just like your father."

The three of us had been working in my old room for several hours. Glancing out the window, I could tell by the angle of the sunlight hitting the panes that it was late afternoon. Sam rubbed his stiffening lower back just as Lisa's stomach let loose a thunderous growl. She blushed and focused on the pile in front of her. "Must be getting close to supper time," she said.

I looked at Lisa, then Sam, and gestured at the disorder in the room. "Well, it seemed like a good idea at the time."

"Yes, it did." Sam looked around. "Are you going to pick up this mess, or just throw everything in boxes and bags and haul it away?"

"I might look through it again. There are some things I forgot I had that I might not throw away after all."

Lisa dug through the heap on my bed and fished out my letterman jacket. "I call dibs on this." She put it on and pushed the sleeves up onto her forearms. It was about four sizes too big for her, but it looked so cute on her that even Sam couldn't stop from grinning.

"Aw, isn't that sweet? Next thing I know, you two will be pinned," he teased.

"Pinned? They haven't done that since the sixties, have they?" Lisa asked.

"Unless he meant this." I tackled her, straddled her, and held her wrists to the floor with my hands.

She laughed, looking deeply into my eyes. "Oooh. Lisa likes."

"Sam likes, too," my brother said, standing up. "But that would put me into areas my shrink wouldn't be able to help me through for years, so on that note, I'm out of here."

"Sorry that we didn't find anything, Sam." I should walk him to the door, but I really didn't want to move.

"Don't worry about it." He glanced at his watch. "I can probably get an hour in at work before quitting time, so I'm going to get back to that. Call me if you do find something." He smirked at us. "It's okay, I can show myself out."

"Good. Make sure the door's locked behind you," I called after him as he descended the stairs. I looked at Lisa hungrily. "I don't want any surprise interruptions," I murmured and lowered my face to hers.

"Finally," Lisa said in mock exasperation, "I get to have sex with you in your bedroom. Another fantasy fulfilled."

"Yeah? Well, a fantasy of mine right now would be to have you in nothing but my jacket."

She sighed in restrained excitement, her breath ragged, her eyes sparkling up at me in anticipation. "Then make it so," she whispered.

It had been interesting making love to Lisa in my old bed and having her attired in nothing but my vintage maroon and silver high school jacket, while I kept all my clothes on. What made the experience even more satisfying was exorcising the memory of the only other woman who had ever been in that bed with me.

After a particularly satiating round of lovemaking, we cuddled.

I pondered whether I was turning into a sex addict. While Lisa dozed in my arms, my mind was working triple time. I couldn't kick the feeling that my mother was trying to tell me something. Why transform my bedroom if there was nothing to find? Had Sam been wrong? Had Dane been in the house without his knowledge? It was possible. But then, if Dane had already found whatever might have been hidden in this room, why would he go ahead with contesting the will? Unless it was just to be a bastard. If there was even anything to find in this room. Or in the house.

Preoccupied with the house issue, I softly, absentmindedly stroked under the jacket, up and down Lisa's backbone. Lisa stirred and nestled up against my side. We had been keeping some pretty late hours with our marathon sexcapades, so it was understandable that she was tired. I must have fallen asleep beside her, because I was startled awake by Orion pacing around on the bed. She appeared agitated and was meowing to the point of almost a howl.

"Shhh, you'll wake Lisa," I whispered. Orion jumped around the foot of the bed, then padded over Lisa to stand on my chest, where she proceeded to turn in circles, meowing incessantly. "What is it, Lassie? Did Timmy fall down the well?" I joked, keeping my voice low.

It was then I smelled the smoke. Paralyzed, I stopped all movement. I took a few measured breaths to make sure I hadn't imagined it. Nope. It was getting thicker, starting to burn the back of my throat. I grabbed Orion and shook Lisa frantically.

"Lisa! Come on, baby, we've got to get out of the house! Let's go!" I bolted out of bed and pulled her to her feet. At first groggy and dazed, she woke up quickly when I blurted, "I think the house is on fire. Put these on." I tossed her a pair of sweatpants and while she slid those on, I grabbed a T-shirt and handed it to her as I grasped her wrist and yanked her out into the hallway.

There was smoke ominously rolling up near the ceiling in the upstairs, but it didn't seem excessive. Something was on fire, but I wasn't so sure it was the house. Lisa pulled the T-shirt on as we raced downstairs and ran out the front door. Crazily, she had put the jacket back on over her clothes. Adrenaline was surging through my system, and I didn't immediately realize that Orion was digging her back claws into my leg sharply enough to draw blood. She was no doubt as frightened as the rest of us, and as she undoubtedly had saved our lives, I could forgive her anything. All the past evils that cat had committed against me were absolved.

Out on the front lawn, my throat and nasal passages stung with ash and my heart pumped nearly through my chest. I spotted the source of the smoke. The garage was on fire. Flames were starting to lick the side of the house. "Lisa." I removed the embedded claws from my leg and handed Orion to her. "Hold her in your jacket." I ran to the Jeep, got in, put it in neutral, and rolled it down the driveway into the street, where I parked it. Lisa had snatched her cell phone on the way out and was calling 911 while I was able to get to the hose without getting burned. I dragged it out as far as its length allowed and began saturating the side of the house with water, hoping to discourage the flames from jumping the gap from the garage. If the fire department didn't get there soon, it was going to be a wasted effort, as the garage was becoming fully involved.

It was then I remembered that Mom's car was still inside, and, although it was disabled, it probably still had gas in it and there were, no doubt, other accelerants in the garage, as well. This was not good.

Lisa ran up to me, Orion still safely ensconced inside my jacket. "The fire department is already on its way. One of the neighbors called."

The wind was blowing the smoke right at us, and we were both coughing. "Lisa, you need to move back. I don't know what's in the garage that might be combustible and—"

"Then you get back, too!" she shouted.

"I will when the fire department gets here. I have to keep water on the side of the house."

"No! Saving this house isn't worth your life." Her tone was determined and pleading, and with her free hand, she was tugging on my arm.

Lisa was right. If there was a secret in that house, it would just die in the fire. I stopped squeezing the nozzle handle, dropped the hose, and moved back with her to the street where neighbors and onlookers had started to gather. Moments later, three trucks from the fire department and one paramedic unit sped in and set up. They hooked into the hydrant near the driveway and got to work immediately. The roar of their hoses coming to life and the rush of the water hitting the side of the garage like a monsoon nearly overpowered the crackling and hissing of the flames.

"What happened?"

The question came from a man I assumed was the captain. He stood in front of us as the paramedics attended to Lisa and me. One EMT was treating a cherry-colored mark on my palm where I had held the hot nozzle. It had already begun to blister. I hadn't noticed the pain until he began dressing the wound, and it suddenly felt like I was holding a hot coal impaled in my palm by a dagger. It was definitely a second-degree burn.

I watched as the powerful streams from the fire hoses made quick work of controlling the flames engulfing the garage. "I don't know. We were in my room, the cat came in acting crazy, and then I smelled smoke. When we got outside, we saw the garage was on fire."

"When was the last time you were in the garage?"

"Yesterday afternoon. Listen, there's a car in there and it may have gas in it, and there may be some other flammable..."

"Thanks, I'll tell my guys." As he rapidly walked toward his crew, I was approached by a uniformed police officer.

"Excuse me, Miss—"

"Roberge."

"I'm going to need to get some information from you. Are you okay to talk to me now?"

"Yeah, I'm fine." And I was, even though my throat, nose, and eyes still burned. I answered his general questions, which included giving him all my contact information, whether I owned, rented, or was just visiting the house, and what I was doing when the fire broke out. After I gave him all the details he requested, I asked, "Any indications that this fire was set?"

The policeman seemed surprised. "Are you suggesting this may have been arson?"

"What I'm saying is that I don't think the fire set itself."

Chapter 18

The garage and everything in it was a total loss. Fortunately, the side of the house was only lightly charred and the interior smoke damage was minor. I made the decision to stay there as opposed to temporarily moving in with Lisa. Now more than ever, I was convinced there was something in the house that Dane didn't want me to find and my mother did.

My hand was loosely bandaged with gauze, and even though I still had stinging in my lungs and the back of my throat continued to burn a little, I refused further medical attention, as did Lisa. Once the fire was out, questions were asked and re-asked, and the investigation to determine the cause was underway. Lisa and I went back inside. I was just about to call Sam when he and Trina came racing through the front door, alarmed and upset.

"Jesus, Hunter, what happened?" Sam asked, as he and his wife followed us into the kitchen.

I took four bottles of beer out of the refrigerator, passed three around and kept one for myself. "Did you see the garage?" I took a long swallow, wincing as the carbonation scratched my already irritated throat all the way down into my stomach.

"Yes," Trina said. "What's left of it." She spied my bandaged hand. "Did you get burned?"

"The fire made the hose nozzle pretty hot," I told her. Quietly drinking her beer, Lisa leaned against me, and my free arm automatically went around her shoulder and pulled her close. She turned her body into my side and held on. She had released Orion as soon as we got back inside, and she was still wearing my jacket. She looked as unnerved as my brother and sister-in-law. I just felt numb, detached, as I explained waking up to the smell of smoke and what had happened right up until they arrived at the house.

As we were talking, Lisa's cell phone rang and she excused herself, moving away from me and stepping into the hallway. "Yes, Mom, I'm fine," I heard her say. "No, no one was seriously hurt.

Hunter's hand got burned while trying to put the fire out, but..."

She disappeared into the other room.

"She seems stressed," Sam said.

"What do you expect? Had it not been for the damned cat, we both could have very easily been crispy critters." The voicing of that possibility made me drain the contents of my bottle in three long swallows.

"What are you thinking, Hunter?" Sam asked cautiously.

"Dane?"

"I don't want to. I really don't. Regardless of how he feels about me, I don't want to think that my own brother would be so soulless and cold-blooded that he could murder two people by burning them alive. I don't want to believe I'm related to that kind of a monster. But to me, the question isn't *if* he set the fire, but *why?*"

"No! You don't think Dane set that fire, do you?" Trina's tone was incredulous. She looked back and forth between Sam and me.

When neither of us answered her right away, she said, "I know he can be the biggest asshole on the eastern seaboard, but do you really think he's capable of murder?"

Lisa rejoined us just as the fire captain knocked on the kitchen door. He was still wearing his insulated structural turnout pants, his navy blue logoed T-shirt under his suspenders, and his hood pulled off his head and slouched around his neck. His red helmet, denoting his status as captain, was tucked under his left arm. His weathered bronzed face was dusted with black-and-white ash, and his full head of black hair lay plastered to his head with sweat. I opened the door for him, and he took a step inside. I tried to place him as someone I might have known in my younger days, but there was no sense of familiarity there. His eyes alighted on my sister-in-law in recognition. "Hey, Trina."

"Hi, Chuck." She gestured loosely to everyone else in the room. "You remember my husband, Sam. This is his sister, Hunter, and—"

"Lisa Riordan," he said. "I've testified for her a couple times."

He reached over and shook Lisa's hand. "How are you?"

"I've had better days, obviously," Lisa responded, still shaky.

He looked back at me. "And this is your house?"

"It is now. I inherited it when my mother died a couple of weeks ago."

Captain Chuck walked over to the counter and leaned on it. He moved like a man with an abundance of confidence and inner strength and, despite his weary, haggard appearance, a man who took a lot of pride in himself and in his job. The look on his face was grim. "I've already put in a call to the county fire marshal. From what I can see—and this is just preliminary—the burn patterns are consistent with arson."

"So, you think the fire was intentionally set," I paraphrased, looking pointedly at Trina. I closed my eyes and pinched the bridge of my nose, hoping to thwart the headache of migraine proportions I knew was inevitable as I tried to organize my thoughts before speaking. I glanced back at our guest. "I have a suspect for you."

"Hunter..." The hesitant, cautioning voice belonged to Trina, who was obviously not pleased that I was making any accusations without actual evidence. "Think about this, Hunter."

"Why? Because he's family?" I certainly felt no blood loyalty to someone who just tried to kill me.

"No," she said defensively. "Because if you're wrong, we all—including you—will suffer the consequences from the inevitable publicity. If you're right, they'll crucify Dane. Maybe he deserves that if he just tried to set the house on fire with you and Lisa in it, but if you're wrong, our entire family will be picked apart on the Channel Five news and in the papers. This is the kind of story CNN would zero in on."

"She's got a point, Hunter," Sam said. "If he didn't do it, everyone is going to want to know why he was accused by his own sister. In this town, that would be a big enough story by itself, but since he's running for Congress, it would be *the* story. It would probably cost him the election and cost the rest of us any privacy we could ever hope to have for the rest of our lives if we stay in Otter Falls." He looked at Lisa. "That would include you."

Although it was a mildly compelling argument, it didn't persuade me not to follow my hunch. The events were too coincidental for my brother not to be responsible. Before I could speak up, Captain Chuck gave voice to my thoughts.

"If he's innocent, we can prove it. If he's not, we need to get to him while we can preserve any evidence he may still have on him and confiscate any clothes and shoes he may have been wearing before he has the chance to destroy anything." He looked at Trina.

"I'm assuming you're all talking about Alderman Roberge?"

Nodding reluctantly, Trina folded her arms. "Yes."

"Don't worry. I'll call Jimmy and ask him to pick up your brother-in-law for questioning. I'll ask him to be discreet, as this may just be a family feud."

"Family feud?" I bristled. "This is not—" A firm hand curled around my forearm, and Lisa deliberately leaned into me. Her intervention worked, and I immediately changed course. "Who's Jimmy?"

"Lieutenant James Macri," Lisa said. "He's in charge of the OFPD detective bureau. Dane and Lieutenant Macri are professional colleagues. Dane leaving work to meet with the lieutenant on some issue wouldn't raise any suspicion or curiosity."

"Are they friends? I can't foresee anything but a cover-up if they're friends," I told them, getting riled again.

Captain Chuck smiled patiently at me as he took out his

cell phone. "Ms. Roberge, off the record, I'm not a big fan of your brother's. He has caused my department some major problems, just because he seems to like stirring the pot. He has been even less accommodating to the OFPD. Unfortunately, for some reason, the mayor thinks your brother walks on water and indulges his every whim." He pushed a button on his phone and held it to his ear with a smirk. "Believe me when I tell you that, although Jimmy will be publicly prudent, the last thing he'll do is go easy on your brother."

Turning away, he spoke into the phone. "Hi, Patty, it's Chuck Sawtelle. Is Jimmy in? ... Yeah, I'll hold. Thanks." He went to the door, and as he stepped outside, I heard him say, "Jiminator! Do me a favor..."

After he closed the door behind them, there was an uncomfortable silence in the room. Sam was the first one to speak.

"Anyone want another beer?"

"I'd love one," Lisa said.

Sam collected our empties, set them on the counter, and pulled four bottles out of the refrigerator. He twisted the caps off before handing one to each of us. Trina and I were trying not to glare at each other. What she was saying wasn't for Dane or against me, she was just trying to give me time to not react so emotionally, to consider the impact of pointing a finger at my brother. However, she wasn't the one who was nearly incinerated by the bastard either.

"Hunter." Trina broke the silence, her voice coolly even, "I'm not trying to minimize what happened here, but I think you forget how small this town is, and you don't have to stay here."

"And that's supposed to make me keep my mouth shut about my little brother trying to kill me?"

"You're jumping to conclusions because you hate him."

"I don't hate him, Trina, but I sure as hell don't like him. Put yourself in my shoes. Anyway, I agree with your friend." I nodded my head toward the door. "If Dane didn't do this, he should have no problem proving it. But I'm done playing nice."

Eventually the tension in the room eased. It coincided with the smell of smoke dissipating to the point of being barely noticeable, and Trina and I called a truce. Even though we were thinking in different directions, she and I ultimately respected each other enough to agree to disagree. I don't think she thought Dane was incapable of such an act; it was more that she didn't want to believe he would actually do such a thing. And, although Lisa never said so, I had an inkling she felt the same way.

Maybe it should have shocked me more that I thought my own brother was capable of trying to burn me out, but it didn't, and it didn't seem to surprise Sam either. When Trina and Lisa went out to take another look at the garage, I said to Sam, "I sure would like to be a fly on the wall when 'The Jiminator' picks Dane up and starts questioning him about the fire."

"I'm sure he'll deny everything," Sam said. "And even if they pin him down and force him to admit it, somehow it won't be his fault. Nothing is ever Dane's fault." He puffed his cheeks out in contemplation and blew out air slowly. "Hunter, what if Dane didn't do it?"

"Do you really think there's a chance of that?" My tone made it clear that I didn't think there was the slightest possibility that Dane could be innocent.

"There's always a chance, regardless of how small, and it's my job to play devil's advocate."

That was true. Sam would always take the opposing side to whatever was firing me up, whether or not he believed in his position. It had always been infuriating. It was no less so now, but I found a grin for him. "Well, if it wasn't Dane, then the fire was unbelievably coincidental. This house has been here how many years? And some unknown party decides to set it on fire now? Come on, Sam, I haven't been in town long enough to piss anyone off that bad. Except maybe Lisa's sister." The visual in my mind of Lesley, three sheets to the wind and trying to set the garage on fire made me smile wider. If she were as drunk as she was the last time I had seen her, she would have been lucky not to breathe on the match and self-combust before the flame ever got to the garage.

"What's got you smiling?" Lisa asked as she and Trina returned to the kitchen.

She took up a place beside me as I reached under the microwave stand for the Yellow Pages and placed the book on the counter. "Other than you? Just Sam being Sam." I looked at Trina's unusually pale complexion. "You okay?"

"Yes, it's just... God, if that cat hadn't woken you up..."

"I'd rather not think about that." Putting that particular eventuality out of my mind was the only thing keeping me sane at the moment. "Why don't we order in and hang out here for a bit until we hear from Lieutenant Macri? Anyone up for Chinese?" I leafed through the restaurant section.

"Only if we order from Ling Chow Gardens," Sam said. "Last time we got food from that other place, I regretted it for three days."

"That's because you wouldn't believe me when I told you they spiced their General Tso chicken with a chi-chien pepper." Trina poked him. "Fire shot out of his ass for nearly a week."

I laughed. "I thought it was my *other* brother who was the flaming asshole."

The room got very quiet when we suddenly realized we were making fire jokes.

Lisa squeezed my forearm. "I'm going to go wash up. I'm also voting for Ling Chow, but whatever you all decide on, I'd like some hot and sour soup, two shrimp eggrolls, sesame chicken, brown rice, and a dozen crab rangoon."

"Got it," I said, finding the phone number for Ling Chow's. I looked up at my brother and sister-in-law to see what they wanted to order. They were both wide-eyed, watching Lisa's exit.

"She sure eats a lot for someone so tiny," Trina finally said.

"Yeah." I smirked, "She stores it up now, so that she has energy to burn later." Sam and Trina quickly glanced at each other, then at the floor, and then at me, sheepishly. "Orders, please."

We had just started in on our take-out orders when the front door splintered open in the face of an unseen force, and there was Dane, his eyes crazed, holding a .38 Ruger. Nobody moved. Dane's body twitched, probably with adrenaline, and his face was beaded with sweat. He took in the scene, scrutinizing each of us separately, though I doubt he saw anyone but me.

I put my hands up, level with my shoulders, palms out, and slowly started to rise. "Dane…" My voice was firm but calm. "Put the gun down. You don't want to do anything else you'll regret—"

"Anything *else*?" He sounded like he was on the verge of either laughing or crying. "I haven't done anything. I didn't set that fire. I wasn't anywhere near here. This morning from seven to nine-thirty, I was at a business breakfast at the Holiday Inn with two campaign contributors and at least a dozen witnesses. Then I went directly to my office, where I was in a committee meeting with six other people from noon right up until Macri pulled me out of it." He was waving the gun around wildly.

That stopped me dead. If Dane wasn't anywhere near the house all day, then who set the fire? I studied my younger brother who, despite all his nasty bravado, appeared very vulnerable at the moment. Had I made a terrible mistake that might cost someone in this room their life?

"Okay, Dane." My voice was as calm and as soothing as I could manage. "Let Lisa, Trina, and Sam go. It's me you want, me you're pissed at. Let them go, and you and I can talk about this."

This time he did laugh as he focused on me. "You? I don't want you, Hunter. The house, I wanted, but not you. No, I'm not here for you." He aimed the gun at Sam. "I'm here for *you*."

Everyone's head, including mine, swiveled toward Sam, who looked stunned. I turned back to Dane. "*Sam?* What did Sam do?"

He never took his eyes off our older brother. "What did Sam do?" he repeated sarcastically. "That's right. Sam would never do anything. Sam's perfect. Sam's the golden boy. Right, Hunter? Isn't that what we always used to call him?"

I was beyond confused. Why was Dane talking to me as though he and I were old buds, and why was he going after Sam?

"Sam, what's he talking about?" Trina was obviously just

as perplexed as the rest of us.

Before Sam could answer, Dane jumped in. "Yeah, Sam, what's he talking about? Tell them, Sam."

Appearing as puzzled as we were, Sam shrugged. "I don't know what you mean, Dane."

"Tell them, Sam, or I will." The danger in Dane's voice sent a shiver down my spine. But Sam's tone, when he responded, chilled me to the bone. It was a snarl, guttural, and if I hadn't been looking right at him and seen his lips move, I never would have believed it was Sam speaking. Lisa's and Trina's shocked expressions reflected the same incredulity.

"Shut the fuck up, Dane. Just shut up before you ruin everything," he hissed through gritted teeth.

His words struck me like a punch to the gut. *Before you ruin everything?* My eyes flashed to Lisa, who had also picked up on the phrase. Her brow furrowed, and she cocked her head as though she hadn't heard him correctly. Trina just kept blinking, dumbfounded.

Watching the scene playing out in front of us, the three of us were struck mute.

Dane didn't seem fazed by Sam's abrupt metamorphosis into someone so uncharacteristically sinister. "You're not running the show anymore, Sam. I'm done. It's bad enough I have to live with the things I've done, but I am not going to go down for the things that you've done."

Sam remained seated, but his posture was relaxed. Apparently he wasn't afraid of Dane. "Be careful what you say," he warned, his voice still threatening. "Don't forget there's a lawyer in the room."

The focus turned to Lisa, whose eyes were as wide as Trina's and mine. She waved off Sam's implication. "This is between you two... whatever this is."

I wasn't able to speak. I was usually never at a loss for words, but it felt like these two men, the two men I had shared parents and a childhood with, were total strangers. I would have normally jumped in and sided with Sam against Dane, but I was unable to do anything but listen.

"Why would you let Macri pull me out of a meeting and

question me about something you know I didn't do?" Dane was speaking to Sam as though the rest of us weren't present. "Why would you let Chuck Sawtelle leave here thinking I set that fire?

Putting suspicion on me for that wasn't *on course!*"

"Shut up *now*, Dane!"

"Or what?"

"Or I'll bury you."

"Yeah, you're good at burying things, aren't you, Sam?" Dane began to pace. He wiped the sweat off his forehead with the hand that wasn't gesticulating with the gun.

"Think about your career, Dane. Look at what you're throwing away," Sam said.

"What *I'm* throwing away?" Dane thundered. "Too late. You just did that for me."

"I didn't sic Macri on you, Hunter did." Sam's finger pointed toward me.

Barely glancing my way, Dane balled up his free hand and through clenched teeth, he said to our older brother, "And you did nothing to stop her, did you? I'm tired of it, Sam. Macri knows everything now."

"Everything? I doubt that, or he never would have let you go."

"He let me go home to get my affairs in order, and then I'm supposed to turn myself in. But he and his boys are on their way *here* to get you, Sam."

Sam's demeanor turned menacing as he slowly rose out of his chair. "What did you tell him?"

"Sam, what the hell is going on?" Trina's tone was frightened, yet determined. Her words expressed my sentiments exactly.

"Shut up, Trina," Sam hissed. *"What did you tell him, Dane?"*

I wanted to know what the hell was going on, and, more specifically, what Dane had confessed to Macri that had caused Sam to be acting so threatening. I looked at Trina, who was stunned into silence by her husband's words. I then looked at Lisa, who was transfixed by the interaction between my brothers.

"I told him you set the fire, Sam. And then I told him why."

I stared at Sam in utter disbelief. "*You* started the fire?"

Glaring at Dane, Sam said, "You've never believed Dane, Hunter. Why would you start now?"

"Because your behavior is freaking me out here, Sam. And if Dane has a solid alibi, where were you?"

Trina jumped into the conversation. "Hunter, Jesus, it was bad enough thinking Dane would do such a thing, but you know Sam would never—"

"See, that's the problem." Spit sprayed from Dane's lips. "He's got you all brainwashed into thinking that he's the good guy and I'm the bad guy. I'll be the first to admit that I'm not perfect, but *I'm* not a murderer."

"*What?* " Trina, Lisa, and I chorused.

"Dane! Shut up *now!* " Sam bellowed.

"No, Dane, don't shut up," I said. Sam was obviously hiding something that Dane knew about; and whether or not Sam was guilty of starting the garage fire, I wanted to know why he was trying to keep Dane from talking. "Stop being so damned cryptic, and tell us what the hell is going on. Say what it is you're here for."

My brothers were glaring at each other, until finally Dane turned to me. "Sam set the garage on fire, hoping to make it look like an accident, didn't you, Sam? Hoping the house would catch fire and burn to the ground, didn't you, Sam? Taking our sister and all the cremated evidence with it. Isn't that right, Sam? Except Chuck Sawtelle told me that the fire wouldn't have been hot enough to destroy the skeleton, and the secret would have been out, anyway. Didn't think of that, did you, Sam?"

I was finding it hard to breathe. There was no reason I should believe Dane, but something about the bearing of both my brothers in the last few minutes convinced me Dane was actually telling the truth. Before I could respond, Trina was on her feet.

"Shut up, Dane. What's wrong with you? Sam isn't capable of that kind of evil. This is ridiculous. Sam would never do such a thing. Put the gun away, and we'll try to help you with your problems," Trina told him, unrealistic as that offer was. If the situation hadn't been so grave, I would have rolled my eyes.

Dane wasn't as diplomatic. He did roll his eyes. "*My* problems? My problems begin and end with your husband." He aimed the gun at Sam.

Sam flinched; Trina and I shouted, "No!" Lisa stayed quietly alert on the couch, perched on the edge, gripping the armrest.

I tried to reason with him. "Jesus, Dane, you're scaring the shit out of everybody here. If Macri is coming here to arrest Sam, there's no reason to keep waving that gun around."

"Sure there is. I don't know what Sam might do. Besides, when Macri gets here, I want to make sure Sammy confesses."

"Confesses to what?" I asked, a second before Trina.

Sam slowly stood. "You are such a fucking idiot. We were almost there. All you had to do was tell Macri you didn't do it, prove you had an alibi, and let me do the rest."

"Murder our sister? And one of the town's most prominent citizens? I don't want any part of that."

"You hate Hunter, Dane! And you're not a big fan of Lisa's, either."

"I don't like them, but I don't want them dead. You should have just let me contest the will. I would have gotten the house, and it would have been done."

"What is in this house!" I demanded.

"Remains," Dane answered. "Heather Cushing's remains."

Lisa gasped and Trina sucked in a shocked breath. I looked at them in bewilderment. "What the holy *fuck* is going on here?"

Then all hell broke loose. The sound of several vehicles squealing to a stop outside and multiple voices shouting was overpowered by Sam screaming. He had just rushed past me when Dane aimed the Ruger directly at him, cocking the hammer back.

Before I could react, Sam grabbed me and swung me around in front of him, just as the gun went off.

There's an old joke that said, "If you heard the shot, it missed you." This was not true in my case. As if in slow motion, only a split second passed before I heard a sharp, high-pitched sound in my ears and felt the thump of the impact. The force of the bullet spun me around and knocked me to the ground as though I had been slammed by a Louisville Slugger. It felt like my upper body exploded. The bullet had entered the right side of my chest and exited through my back, just below my shoulder blade, feeling every bit like a hot ice pick going in and staying in. Then it really started to hurt.

It seemed like hours before I thought to take a breath. A continuous sensation like that of boiling water being poured into the bullet hole numbed my right arm, shoulder, and breast. I was nauseous and dizzy, and just before I passed out, I heard screaming and yelling, voices I recognized and some I didn't. The last thing I remembered was seeing Lisa's face. She was crying, and her expression showed she was terrified. Her lips were moving, but I couldn't hear her.

Then everything went black.

Chapter 19

I blinked into consciousness; it took a few minutes for the fuzziness to go away. My eyes slowly scanned my surroundings.

Everything looked white, smelled like antiseptic, and felt confusingly unfamiliar. When I made the mistake of trying to move, penetrating, pulsating pain shot from my back to my front, up my shoulder, into my neck, and down my right arm. It felt like I had been branded. From my waist to the top of my head, everything on my right side throbbed.

As what had happened started to come back to me, I knew that the excruciating pain was courtesy of a gunshot wound. My sharp intake of breath and involuntary groan brought about movement to my left.

"Hey, baby, you're finally awake."

My eyes zeroed in on a beautiful face and warm, caring, green eyes. "Hey," I croaked. My mouth and throat were as dry as cotton. My lips felt prickly, as though I had been sucking on a cactus.

"Where am I?"

Lisa gingerly sat on the side of my bed and kissed my forehead.

"Otter Falls Regional Medical Center. You were shot. You had to have surgery. You—"

The room spun wildly, and I could feel the bile rising in my throat. Panicky, I looked around for something to vomit into.

Unable to stop it, vomit spewed all over my precious girlfriend. If it hadn't been for the excruciating headache that accompanied my vomiting, I would have apologized. She now wore the contents of my stomach, which shouldn't have been very much but looked like a lot.

Lisa ignored the mess I had made on her and pressed the button for the nurse, then concentrated on me. She went into the bathroom and returned with a damp towel to clean me up.

"Oh, dear," the nurse murmured, as she entered the room and assessed the situation.

"Sorry." My head fell back on the pillow. "I'm really sorry." I always came out of anesthesia hard. I'd had a few minor operations where I'd been anaesthetized; coming to was never pleasant.

"Shhh." Lisa went back into the bathroom and returned with a wet washcloth. She lovingly wiped my face, then her lips pursed as she turned to the nurse. "I think she might have broken a stitch or two."

I looked down at the bandage covering my chest. I was definitely seeping blood; the gauze had blotches of bright red. The nurse smiled patiently at me and then looked at Lisa. "I was scheduled to come in to change the dressing anyway. I'll take a look at it." As she left the room to get supplies, Lisa started wiping the puke off her shirt with the washcloth.

"What happened?" I was finally able to ask. "I know Dane shot me but... what happened after that?"

Lisa studied me with concern. "Let the nurse change your bandage and get you stitched up if you need it." She must have recognized my agonized grimace. "And get you something for the pain."

"How long have I been in here?"

"Three days."

While I digested that, the nurse walked back into the room with whatever she needed, to do whatever it was she was going to do.

"Well, let's clean you up and see what we have here."

We had been alone for at least ten minutes before Lisa spoke again. She started to say something several times, but stopped, as if she was trying to find the right words to express her thoughts before she spoke. "Hunter, both of your brothers are in jail."

"Sam, too?"

"Especially Sam," she said bitterly. "He used you as a protective shield. And that's the second time he tried to kill you."

I looked away. Not Sam. But I knew it was true, because as Lisa reminded me of what had happened, my last conscious moments replayed in my head. I was still stunned at what I had heard in that living room, at how my life had changed dramatically even before the bullet hit me. The obscure exchange between Dane and Sam was enough for me to realize that the Sam I thought I knew was not the person he really was. The devastation of that truth was almost worse than the destruction of the bullet.

"Lisa, what the hell is going on with my family?" I was more resigned than angry. "And who is Heather Cushing?"

She poured me a cup of water, put a straw in it, and placed it on the tray by my bed. "You don't remember the Cushings? Mr. Cushing owns that big tire shop in West Otter Falls. It's been there for years."

"Nope. Doesn't ring a bell. Did I go to school with any Cushings?"

"Heather went to Otter Falls, but she was in my class. In our junior year, she disappeared. Nobody knew what happened to her.

At first, everybody thought she had run away, even though her parents insisted things were fine between them and there was no reason for her to leave home. The police started an investigation and search parties were organized, which your brothers both participated in, but there was no trace of Heather. It was as though she had disappeared off the planet. Now we know that one or both of your brothers murdered her."

I felt like Alice falling down the rabbit hole. "I just… can't believe this."

She took my hand and squeezed it compassionately. "I know, sweetheart. It's a lot to absorb. Do you want to talk about it later, when your head is a little clearer?"

"No, I want to know now."

"Okay. Sam and Dane are pointing the finger at each other,

each saying the other did it."

"But why? Why would either one of them murder someone?"

"That's the big mystery. Sam wisely lawyered up immediately when Macri arrested them, while Dane—who meant to shoot Sam and not you, believe it or not—sat there and poured his heart out until his lawyer arrived and told him to shut up. But your house is now a crime scene."

"Because I was shot?"

"And Heather Cushing's bones were found between two walls in the closet in your old room."

"Christ! How did they get there?"

"Dane told Macri she had been buried in the old woods behind Sparrow Pond. But when that area was selected as the location of the new recreation center, Sam went and dug up the remains before his company started digging the foundation. He hid them in a temporary location until your mother went on a three-week cruise with other members of her church, which Sam talked her into and which he and Dane helped pay for. Then Sam did a little reconstruction on your closet wall. He figured it was the perfect hiding place, since your mother never went in your room. Also, it seemed to be a given that the house would go to either him or Dane when she died, so it should have been a safe hiding place."

"But somehow my mother found out?"

"Apparently. About three months ago, she overheard Dane talking to someone on the phone, and she put two and two together about Heather. When she found out Dane was talking to Sam, she was devastated, but when she learned Heather's remains were in her house, it all became too much for her. The distress eventually resulted in her fatal stroke, but not before she had changed her will."

It felt surreal that she was talking about my family; it sounded more like the type of people who were immortalized on the Dr. Phil show. "Why didn't she just go to the police?"

"I don't know. Apparently she explained it all in a letter that accompanied your copy of the will."

A letter that was probably sitting in my post office box in

California. "So Heather's remains were what Dane was so crazy to get from the house."

"Yes. But Sam thought Dane was overreacting. Whether you kept the house or sold it, he was going to burn it down."

"With me in it?"

"Not at first. Remember that day we were in your room looking for something?"

"Yes."

"Well, Sam found it." She nodded at the widening of my eyes.

"Yeah, I know. Sneaky. It was a copy of the letter that's with your copy of the will. It was taped behind one of the sports awards hanging on your wall. I guess your mother figured that when you went to remove everything, you'd find it. It was written a week before she died. The letter said that she had instructed Palmisano to include a sealed copy of the letter with your copy of the will. When Sam found it, he knew that he and Dane would finally be caught. He couldn't have that, so he arranged for you to 'accidentally' die in a fire. And then the secret would still be between him and Dane. Funny, isn't it? Dane is the one who had the conscience in the end."

My head began to spin. Who was the horrible person that now inhabited my precious brother's body? If Heather Cushing disappeared in Lisa's junior year, Sam and Dane had been keeping their secret for about twelve years. That would have been when Sam was twenty-three and married to Trina for a year, and Dane was eighteen and still single. What had been their connection to that young girl? "Any guesses as to why my brothers might have killed Heather?"

"Sure. I have a lot of guesses at this point, but they're probably the same ones you have." She shrugged. "The frame of mind Dane was in, I really have no doubt that he will confess, and then everyone will know. As for Sam, at this point, what he will do is anybody's guess."

"Trina! God. How is she?"

"Understandably, she's a mess. I don't think she had a clue about any of this."

"I need to go see her when I get out of here."

"She's not seeing anybody. As soon as the police are finished with her, she's going to stay with her mother in St. Johnsbury. She needs time to sort things out. She knows that you aren't to blame for any of this, and yet, in some roundabout way, she does blame you. There's a part of her that feels if you hadn't come back, everything would have stayed like it was before."

"How do you know that?"

"That's what she said when Macri took Sam away. I'm sure it was just a knee-jerk reaction."

"Where's Orion?"

"I've got her. She's staying in my spare room so she and the boys don't kill each other. Well, I doubt they would kill her, but I'm not so sure she wouldn't make cat food out of them," she said with a chuckle.

"Wise decision." I tried to shift my body, but my shoulder protested. Lisa helped me move into a more comfortable position.

"When can I get out of here?"

"The doctor will be in to talk with you later; that's something you'll have to ask him. By the way, your Aunt Cissy is your next of kin since your brothers can't be here, and she's waiting to see you.

She graciously spoke with the staff about allowing me priority access to you. The hospital administrator is a friend of mine, anyway, so that also helped. I don't want to tax your strength, so I'll grab a cup of coffee and run some errands while Cissy visits. Don't worry, I'll be back." She gently kissed my dry, cracked lips. "I love you, Hunter."

"I love you, too, Lisa." It was no longer in question; it was a fact.

She kissed my cheek and left. I was dizzy, not from illness, pain, or medication, but from all the updated information Lisa had conveyed. Talk about a dysfunctional family. No wonder my mother had a stroke, discovering that her two perfect sons were murderers and her deviant daughter was her best child after all.

"Oh, Hunter, sweetie," Aunt Cissy wailed the second she

entered the room. She was crying and smiling at me sympathetically. She leaned over the bed to give me a careful hug, then sat down in the sole bedside chair. "How are you?"

Suddenly I was smiling. "You mean other than nearly being killed twice in one day by my brothers, finding out my family is crazier than bedbugs, and that there really *is* a skeleton in my closet? Ignoring all of that, I'm fine."

Lt. Macri made a courtesy visit to the hospital, but his inquiries were perfunctory, as Dane had admitted that I wasn't involved in any manner. However, the lieutenant did ask me to come to the station when I was out of the hospital to read and sign some statements.

My suitcases and other personal belongings weren't considered to be a part of the crime scene, so Lisa had picked them up and taken them to her house. Two days later, I was released from the hospital and was back at Lisa's. My arm was nestled in a sling, mainly to keep me from moving it too suddenly. Mobility was limited on my upper right side, and the pain was ever present but subsiding. Lisa wanted me to spend the day taking it easy and resting, but with the doorbell and phone ringing off the hook from reporters all wanting an exclusive, I couldn't relax. I had as many questions as the media did, and I wanted answers. I contacted Lt. Macri, and he made arrangements with the regional correctional facility for me to visit, if my brothers were willing.

Sam wasn't talking to anyone and was on a suicide watch in solitary confinement. Against his lawyer's advice, Dane agreed to see me. We were scheduled to meet alone in a private room set aside for attorney-client meetings or police interrogations.

The town's medium-security prison was a two-story, steel-and-concrete building that looked like it might be a school or an office building, except for the razor wire that enclosed the perimeter.

I entered the facility, passed through one metal detector, registered at the desk, and was met at the superintendent's office by the deputy warden and Lt. Macri.

"Your brother Sam isn't eating," the deputy warden said. "If he turns away one more meal, we're going to have to admit him to the hospital and provide nutrition through an IV."

"I know he's refused to see me, but could you please ask him one more time?"

The deputy warden, a bear of a man whose name was Corben, nodded. "I'll ask, but Sam has refused any visitors. He won't even talk to his own attorney, so I doubt that he'll see you." He picked up the walkie-talkie from the charger on his desk.

I cleared my throat. "Tell him I'm not angry, and that I love him."

Both men looked at me as though I was as nuts as the rest of my family. "After what he did to you?" Corben said, aghast.

"Just tell him, would you please?" I snapped. I couldn't honestly have said whether my irritation was at them or myself. I suppose it did sound insane for me to still love Sam after he first tried to burn me to death and then got me shot. I hoped that maybe, if he thought I would forgive him, he might talk to me.

Corben keyed his mic. "William Two to Sam Three."

I guessed that the William Two designation referred to his status as deputy warden, and the Sam Three designation was for the sergeant who was either third in command, or in charge of Section Three, or something along that line. It was a pretty universal code, except William usually referred to Watch Commander.

"Mr. Corben," I said. "Could you deliver the message yourself? I think that might make a difference."

For a second time, he looked at me as though I had lost my mind completely. "Ms. Roberge." His tone was patronizing. "I can't possibly deliver a personal message to a prisoner. If I agreed to a special favor every time someone asked, I wouldn't have time to do my actual job."

Macri rolled his eyes. "Get over yourself, Pete. At this point, we should try anything that might make this guy talk. The Cushings need some closure. It might help if they knew why their daughter died."

"Then break the other brother. He's been singing like a

bitch in heat since he came in here."

"But other than to say that he didn't kill her, Sam did, Dane hasn't said anything about what actually happened the night Heather Cushing died."

"But, Jim." He was almost whining. "That would set a bad precedent."

I placed my good arm over my sling to make it appear as though I was crossing my arms. I pinned him with a glare, conveying what a big baby *and* putz I thought he was. I shot a glance over at Macri, who was giving Corben the same look.

"All right!" Exasperated, Corben left.

"Was he born an asshole, or was it something he has perfected along the way?" I asked Macri.

"Nah. It's a gift. Warden Vandine is on vacation, and being in charge has gone to Pete's head." He lightly tapped my shoulder.

"How are you doing?"

"I'll be fine. Thank you for asking."

"I know this has got to be tough on you. Well, on everyone involved, I'm sure." His compassion seemed sincere.

"Have you heard from my sister-in-law? I'm worried about her, but she's gone into seclusion."

"She's been very cooperative, but we've only communicated with her through her attorney. She hasn't come to see your brother, if that's what you're asking."

"I was wondering about that. Maybe a visit from her would help bring Sam around."

"In my book, he's damned lucky to be offered a visit with you. I don't think I'd be able to do it."

"Honestly? I don't know why I'm here."

A surprised deputy warden returned to his office with the news that Sam would see me. I secured all my belongings in a locker, passed through another metal detector, and was momentarily locked in a sally port with Corben. He escorted me to the high-security area where I signed in at another desk, walked through two more electronically secured doors, and was set up in a private office with a heavy wooden table and four plastic chairs.

"An officer will be in the room with you, just in case."

"I don't want anyone else in there. I'm sure I won't be able to get him to talk to me if anyone else is present."

"I can't guarantee your safety if—"

"Your officer can stand right outside the door."

"Ms. Roberge—"

"Mr. Corben, if you want to hear what my brother has to say about this, you'll let me see him alone. If not, we're just wasting our time here." I realized he had regulations to enforce, but I knew Sam would ask to go right back to his cell if we didn't have privacy.

"I'm sorry, I just can't allow that." He gestured me into the room.

"How about this—leave the door open and have your officer stand right outside." I looked at him expectantly.

"Ms. Roberge, I would think that the fact that your brother tried to kill you in two different ways in one afternoon would be sufficient to discourage you from being alone with him."

"I won't be alone with him. Your guard will be three steps away from us." Before he could respond, I heard the clanking of the iron-barred gates rolling back, and I saw Sam shuffling toward me, his wrists handcuffed to a waist belt and his ankles shackled. He wore an orange jumpsuit and was flanked by two correctional officers, who looked more nervous about approaching Corben than they were about escorting an alleged murderer and arsonist. Sam was motioned into the room, and one of his escorts was about to accompany him when Corben's hand shot out and stopped the guard at the door.

"Wait out here," he said. "But make sure that the door stays open."

I nodded my thanks to the deputy warden and focused my gaze on the hollow, sunken eyes of the older brother I had loved.

Chapter 20

"Hi, Sam." My voice broke at the sight of him, and at the loss of our relationship.

He sat down in one of the once-white chairs; I sat opposite him.

Finally he looked up at me. "Can you ask them to close the door?"

"I already did. This is the best I could do." I sighed and glanced around the room. "It doesn't matter. I think we both know this room is most likely wired."

He focused on his bound hands, which were folded on the table. "You want to know why." It wasn't a question.

"Among other things, yes." I couldn't help it. I wanted to reach over and pull him into a hug, grasp his hands, do *something*, but I knew any kind of contact was prohibited and more than likely would end our meeting.

I realized that I hadn't just loved Sam, I had worshiped him, and as I studied him across the table, the disappointment and betrayal hit me hard. I didn't want to believe this was the same person who had tried to end my life just a few days earlier. Without warning, the tears started streaming down my face.

Sam heard my snuffling and looked up, his face contorted with despair. "No, Hunter, don't cry. Please…" As he slid his cuffed hands across the table, the guard stepped into the room.

"Roberge." With a sharp flick of his wrist, the officer motioned for Sam to move his hands away from mine. When Sam slowly complied, the officer assessed the safety of the situation and stepped back outside the door.

My attention was completely focused on my brother. He was crying, too, which pushed me into sobbing. "Christ, Sam, what's going on?"

"Hunter, I am so sorry. *So* sorry. I never meant to—"

"Don't you dare say you never meant to hurt me. You tried to kill me, Sam. Twice. That kind of puts the lie to you saying you didn't intend to hurt me."

"I was desperate, out of my head. When you became an obstacle, it was like you weren't even a real person anymore." The look on my face must have told him that I wasn't seeing his explanation as reasonable. "You have no idea what it was like having to be the man of the house since I was seven years old, what it's like having to be perfect all the time—the perfect son, the perfect husband, the perfect father, the perfect brother, the perfect employee. You have no idea what I had to deal with after you left.

You thought Mom was impossible before? She was unbearable after you were gone. I didn't know what you had done, but I knew whatever it was, she treated it as though she had spawned Satan's child. She was so adamant about maintaining our family reputation and an air of flawlessness that—"

"Wait, are you blaming your actions on me?"

He stared at me blankly, then said, "No, of course not. I'm blaming Mom."

I wiped the tears from my eyes. "Sam, there comes a time in our lives when we have to stop blaming our childhood for the choices we make as adults. If I had used Mom's treatment of me as the foundation of my adult behavior, I would probably be on the FBI's Ten Most Wanted list. I made a conscious decision to not believe her characterization of me as a worthless degenerate, and I turned my life into something positive, despite her. Or maybe even because of her."

"Well, bully for you," he said sourly. "You didn't have to stay around here and deal with her shit. If she hadn't kicked you out and disowned you, maybe you would have turned out a lot differently."

"Maybe. But the fact remains, if we accept your excuse, if any of the three of us should have turned out to be the criminal, it should have been me. All I'm saying, Sam, is that there are consequences to the choices we make, and at some point, we have to take responsibility for them."

He pushed his chair back, as though he was going to leave. "If that's how you think, I guess listening to what I have to say won't mean anything, so I might as well go back to my cell."

"Please don't. I want to hear what you have to say. I want to know, Sam. I have to know. Please."

He sighed and shook his unwashed hair away from his face.

His several days' growth of beard displayed a few random whiskers that were actually gray. He scratched the side of his chin against his shoulder, making a slight scraping noise. His eyes were tormented, apparently haunted either by the memory of murdering Heather Cushing, or by the existence he was now facing for the rest of his life.

"Honestly, I don't know what it was like for you growing up, Sam. I was pretty overwhelmed by having to deal with my own issues with her. I thought it was okay for you, for the most part. She seemed to put you on a pedestal, and you were the ideal I was supposed to live up to. I thought, compared to me, you had it pretty good. And I thought we were good with each other about it. I thought that Dane was our common nemesis."

"Dane was a little shit, but I kept thinking I could control him."

I was getting impatient, although I tried not to let it show.

"Dane was always *out* of control, Sam. Maybe you could control him, but he was smart enough not to go after you. I never had that luxury. I had to get back at him when I could, which wasn't that often."

He adjusted his position and stretched his legs out. "I soon discovered I couldn't control him. It seems I was always getting him out of trouble. A majority of stuff, you have no idea about. One stupid scrape after another. I'd clean up one of his messes, and there'd be another, each one escalating into a bigger fucking mess.

Mom was always warning us to keep our lives above reproach. That suck-ass little brother of ours would play up to her and then turn right around and get into some shit again."

"Big shit or little shit?"

"What difference does it make? Either way, it smells bad, and Mom didn't want any stink at all. You know how she was when she didn't get her way about something— *everybody* suffered for it. Forever."

I rested my chin on my folded hands. "Sam... what happened to Heather Cushing?"

He hesitated. "My attorney advised me not to talk about that."

I was disappointed and I couldn't disguise it no matter how I tried. "I understand."

"No, you don't. And you couldn't possibly... because... I don't." His voice was threaded with what sounded like remorse.

"I'll never understand how everything spiraled so out of control that night."

There was a delicate silence between us. I ran my hand over the bandaging around my chest, an action he didn't miss. "You mean, like the afternoon I was shot?" I asked quietly. "What happened to you, Sam? The person you were that afternoon wasn't you."

"I don't know." He sounded distant, detached. "It's like when my nice, orderly little world gets threatened, something snaps in me and I can't rein it in. I feel like I'm in another person's body. I know that sounds trite, but it's real."

"When did that start? Because I never remember you being like that when we were kids." And I didn't. Sam was always the diplomat, the negotiator, the peacemaker. Dane could cause him to lose his temper but not to the extent I had witnessed the day of the fire.

"The first time I noticed it was that time when we were in church and they were passing the collection plate. Dane palmed money instead of putting his dollar in. Mom saw it and, as usual, instead of disciplining Dane herself, told me to handle it. I remembered the previous time she told me to handle something he did, and I didn't handle it right, or at least not to the extent where she felt Dane wouldn't do it again. All I heard for the next week was how I had to set an example for Dane and if I didn't, however he behaved was on me."

I hadn't realized the negative impact my mother had

actually had on all of us. How foolish and selfish to think she had just singled me out.

"So the fact that the little fucker had just done something to make my life a living hell again pushed me to a breaking point. I hardly remembered thumping him." He drew in a deep breath and then sighed.

"I wasn't there when it happened," I said, "but I remember that night at supper, Dane showed up at the table looking like he had been run over by a truck, sporting some nasty scrapes and bruises.

You told Mom that Dane pulled away from you when you tried to talk to him, and he lost his balance and fell down the hill behind the church into the scrap heap. Mom bought it, or pretended to, and she chewed Dane out for exaggerating."

"That's the time, yeah."

"So when Dane whined to Mom that you almost killed him, he wasn't lying."

"No. And if Jackie Riffey hadn't come out back to look for me, I might have killed him. I remember being really angry, but it was like I was watching the whole thing from above my body."

"Wasn't Jackie afraid of you or what you were doing?" Jackie Riffey was the Reverend Riffey's youngest daughter, the same age as Sam. She had a huge crush on him all through junior high school.

"Hell, no, she wanted to help me. That was the week after he ran to her mother at the youth fellowship meeting and told her that Jackie and I had been making out in back of the pipe organ. But the sound of her voice brought me back to my senses that day. It just got worse from there. I should have gotten counseling, I should have seen somebody about the anger. I knew it was abnormal. I brought it up to Mom once, and she told me that only crazy people see psychiatrists. She said going to a psychiatrist would send out the wrong idea about our family, and she wouldn't hear of it. She said there was nothing wrong with me."

"Jesus. Her whole family was insane. Talk about denial."

My grandparents died before I was born so I never got to

know them, but I'd heard plenty of whispering about them from the men who had been married to my mother's sisters. According to my mother, her parents were eccentric saints, but in the opinions of my uncles, my grandparents were fucking nuts, which was probably why we weren't allowed to see or associate with my mother's brothers-in-law after her sisters died.

My mother had three sisters, two of whom committed suicide—one by overdosing on sleeping pills, and the other from carbon monoxide poisoning. She had locked herself in her garage, in her car with the motor running. In her suicide note, she said it was what the little people who lived in her light fixtures had told her to do. The third sister passed away after a brief, undisclosed illness. We were always told it was cancer that took her, but I never bought it.

They all lived a substantial distance from Otter Falls, so the whispers that were spread about them were pure conjecture. The only person really in a position to deny or confirm the rumors and gossip about them was my mother, and she remained silent on the subject. Now the third generation was suffering.

"Didn't you think about getting counseling on your own, when you became an adult?"

He lowered his gaze. "By that time, I had adopted Mom's philosophy. I believed if I pretended that everything was okay in my head, it would be."

"Was Heather Cushing a casualty of believing everything would be okay in your head?" I asked gently.

"God. She didn't deserve what we did to her." His voice was anguished.

"What happened?"

He lifted his hands to push his hair back, and his handcuffs clanked and jangled. It was a harsh reminder of our surroundings.

He placed his hands back in his lap. "It was Dane again. He fucked up. One more in a succession of many. He had been trying for months to get Heather to go out with him. She was always busy or dating someone else. She had just broken up with some guy from the community college, so Dane asked her to the senior prom. She said yes, because it was only a week away, and I guess being with Dane was better than not going. Once she got him there, she ignored him."

I grimaced. "Dane or not, that wasn't a nice thing for her to do."

"I agree. But he just should have left it alone. Three nights later, he came over to the house and talked me into going with him to Heather's so he could talk to her. He said he needed to tell her off, and he needed me there for moral support. I remember telling him to be a man and go alone, but he was very upset, so I said okay."

"Where was Trina?"

"She and Eric had gone to her mother's in St. Johnsbury for the week. Her mom was recovering from some kind of surgery or something, and Trina went up there to help out." He sniffed and shook his head, blinking his thoughts and recollection into focus.

"Anyway, we got to Heather's, and she told him he couldn't come in because her parents weren't home. He asked if he could talk to her about prom night, and she told him there was nothing to talk about, that she never promised him anything more than that she would go to the prom with him. She said that's exactly what she did, then told him he was lucky he got that far with her. Then she saw me waiting in his car, and that's when the trouble started."

Sam looked out at the officer standing just outside the door. He raised his voice just loud enough for the guard to hear. "Do you think we might be able to get some water or something in here?"

The officer glanced at Corben, who nodded, and the guard said something into his radio and no more than a minute later, two large bottles of water were brought in. I opened one for Sam, who took a very long drink.

"Where was I?"

"Heather saw you waiting in Dane's car."

"Right, right. She pushed by Dane and walked up to the car and leaned in the passenger side and started flirting with me.

Right in front of Dane. Now, I didn't like the little puke, but that just wasn't right. And I could see Dane was just devastated. I was polite to her, but she was pissing me off because she kept trying to get closer to me and touch me, and I finally told her to knock it off and apologize to my brother. She got this really funny look on her face and said she'd only apologize to Dane if I took her for a ride in the car, and then she winked at me. I told her I was a married man, and I wasn't going anywhere with her, then I told Dane he was an idiot to have the hots for such a slut. I said that we needed to go, that he was wasting his time. So then she turned to Dane and told him that she'd give him a blow job if he took us all for a ride. He looked at me like a whipped puppy, but I said absolutely not. Told him I didn't want any part of it. Then she said if he didn't take us all for a ride, she would start yelling 'rape,' and I'm thinking, 'what kind of wingnut is this?' so I told Dane she was bluffing and we needed to leave, and damn if she didn't start screaming. Dane tackled her and put his hand over her mouth to shut her up. If anyone heard her, they never said anything about it." He took another drink from the bottle.

Was *everybody* in this town—with a few exceptions— certifiably loopy? I was beginning to thank the entity I didn't believe in that my mother had kicked me out and that I'd had the presence of mind to leave Otter Falls, as opposed to staying and trying to prove something to her. The more I thought about it, the more I was grateful that Lisa had turned out so well-adjusted, unless she, too, was hiding an alternate personality from me. I couldn't fathom that, so I returned my attention to Sam.

"When Dane took his hand away from Heather's mouth, she told him that unless we took her for a drive, she'd start screaming again. I was out of the car by this time, and I told him to let her scream and let's go. But she reached down and started rubbing Dane's crotch and gave him this kiss that almost got me hard just watching them. I tried to yank him off her, but he started dry-humping her right there. I told him that was it, I was walking home.

Then she said she would only let him continue in the car,

and only if I drove them around."

"And you went along with it?"

"I refused at first, but horny little Dane begged me. He wanted her bad, and it was obvious that he was ready. I don't know why I went along with it. I guess I didn't want her to give either of us any trouble. If driving them around until they got off would do it, then I was all for it. I figured that she was a spoiled brat and they were horny kids, and I thought I had made myself clear about not being interested in what she was offering me. I know I should have left, or insisted Dane leave, but I remembered what it was like to be that horny and that hot for someone and having the opportunity to go for it."

"Trina wasn't your first?"

He glared at me. "You're kidding, right?"

Actually, I hadn't been. I truly thought that he was a virgin when he met and fell head over heels in love with Trina. He always struck me as being too shy to be any kind of ladies man. However, I realized that I had been mistaken about so many other things, it only made sense I would be wrong about this, too.

"Jackie Riffey was my first, if you must know," he said. I looked up at the ceiling, wondering where the microphones were planted. Now the whole town would know. "I was sixteen."

"Sixteen? You lost your virginity with the minister's daughter when I still lived at home and you never told me?"

"Well, *you* lost your virginity with the minister's *wife* when I still lived at home, and you never told *me*."

Point taken. I imagined the listeners in the main control room would have a field day with this. I glanced out the door at the wide-eyed deputy warden and then looked back at my brother, who had a raised eyebrow and a familiar smirk. For that moment, he was once again the brother I knew and adored. It made me want to burst into tears again.

"I think we should move away from that subject and get back to the other," I suggested.

"Yeah. That. So I gave in and agreed to drive them around while they did their thing in the backseat. Do me a favor... if you do get to talk to that little bastard, call him 'minuteman' and watch him go ballistic."

"Too much information," I told him, smiling. Poor Dane. He was apparently a failure at pretty much everything. "Let me guess—that wasn't enough for her."

"Don't think it was enough for him, either, but she was finished with him. She said she wanted a man, not a boy, one who knew how to satisfy a woman. She climbed into the front seat and started kissing on me. I told her to knock it off, but she didn't. She grabbed me and started stroking me."

This girl sounded like she was as much a piece of work as my brothers were. "What was Dane doing?"

"Recovering." Sam looked at the ceiling, randomly studying the soundproof tiles, taking a few measured breaths before looking back at me. "I kept trying to push her away from me with one hand, push her back to the passenger side, but she wasn't having any of that. She held on to my johnson like her hand was Super Glued to it.

I had to pull the car over before she caused an accident. Things just went crazy from there."

"Sounds like they were already crazy."

He buried his face in his hands. "I've relived this every day since then, but this is the first time I've talked about it since that night." When he dropped his hands back onto the table, his face was red and his eyes were misty. "She thought I was pulling over to fuck her, so she crawled onto my lap... and despite myself I got an erection. She unzipped me and, God help me, she almost had me in her when I just... lost it. I love Trina. I didn't want my marriage ruined by some slutty, insatiable teenage girl who meant absolutely nothing to me. So, I threw her off me. It took all my strength to do it, so when she landed against the door, she hit pretty hard and it knocked the wind out of her. It also split her lip and put a gash in her cheek, and when she got her breath back and realized she was bleeding, she came unhinged. She attacked me, screaming that I had ruined her face. She said she was going to go to the police and tell them that Dane and I had ganged her. She wouldn't stop pounding on me and screaming accusations."

"And what was Dane doing all this time?"

"Nothing. He just sat there in the backseat, too afraid to do anything." He took another sip of water. "I ended up having to drag her out of the car. I could tell you it was to calm things down, but that would be a lie. I was too far gone by that point. I don't really remember exactly what I did to her. The next thing I remember, Dane was shaking me violently and bawling like a baby, and yelling over and over, 'Sam, what did you do?' I looked down at Heather Cushing's body, and I knew she was dead."

By this time, he was crying, and my heart was breaking for him. I didn't condone his actions, but I could certainly understand how the situation had mushroomed into the tragedy it had become.

"Are you sure Dane didn't kill her during the time period you don't recall?"

"The blood was on my hands. Literally and figuratively."

"And obviously you didn't go to the police yourself."

"And tell them what? That I drove a minor around isolated areas of town so that she could have sex in the backseat with my brother, and when the oversexed little lust bucket turned her voracious appetite on me, I killed her? Yeah... you tell them that and see how it works out for you"

"What happened next?"

"We put her into the car and drove to the west side of Sparrow Pond, you know, the marshy, deserted side. And we buried her there. It took us all night to dig a hole deep enough with a crowbar, a window scraper, and our hands, but we did, and no one ever found her. I burned her clothes. Maybe I should have burned her body, as well. When it was announced that a new recreation center was going to go up in that area and they were going to dredge out the marshy area to extend the pond, we knew we had to get the body out of there. I didn't know what to do. That's how the skeletal remains ended up in the house. I thought for sure the house would go to Dane or me when Mom passed away. But Mom overheard Dane, drunk, on the phone to me one day, and she confronted him. He told her what had happened and where Heather's remains were. She told him he was never to speak of it again. If anyone ever found out, it would have been the ultimate scandal, you know? But I think that's what led to her stroke. We didn't know until the week before she died that she was leaving the house to you. I really think she got some satisfaction out of having me right there when she told Palmisano she was changing her will."

The thought of broaching this part of the discussion made my head begin to pound. I didn't really want to rehash the idea of my brother wanting me to burn alive, but I had to know— when he had other choices, why he made that one. "Why didn't you set the house on fire before I got here?"

"I thought you'd sell the house, and when you went back to California, I would burn it down. But you started figuring out that Mom was trying to tell you something, and that she had set your old room up the way she did, hoping you would discover what it was.

That concerned me. Then finding her letter and reading what she wrote to you, seeing that she sent a copy to you in California... I... I wasn't thinking. I was acting purely on instinct. I was protecting my secret any way I could. I... I panicked."

"Sam, what did Mom's letter say?"

Chapter 21

I knew my mother didn't like me, but it really hurt to learn that she had stopped loving me, if she ever had. Through the years, I tried to believe that her dislike for me was just a surface thing, that in the depths of her heart, she forgave me for not being the daughter she wanted. Yet instead of the years softening her, she became hardened and contemptuous regarding anything to do with me.

When I did finally get to see Trina, our meeting bore no resemblance to the joyous family reunion we'd had when I first got back. I was surprised to get Trina's call, especially since Lisa had been under the impression that she wouldn't see anyone. The warm, beautiful house Trina owned with Sam, that had seemed so welcoming the night I arrived back in Otter Falls, now came across as cold and uninviting. There were several moving and packing boxes scattered throughout the residence, and the interior was in a state of general disarray.

Trina looked as though she had passed through six levels of Hell; her demeanor reminded me of an Undead in a zombie horror film. Her once vibrant, laughing eyes were now lifeless, and she looked as though she had aged ten years in just the last few weeks.

I was cautious because her expression told me she was about to bite my head off. "How are you doing, Trina?"

"How do you think I'm doing?" she snapped at me. "How would you feel, finding out you've been married to a murderer for over a decade?"

"I can only tell you how I feel knowing that my brothers are murderers," I yelled back. I knew she was hurting and that she felt betrayed, but no more than I. Our eyes met in a silent impasse, and she blew out a long breath.

"I just needed you to know this isn't easy for me, either," she said, her tone a bit more conciliatory than defensive.

"I never doubted that this situation would be anything other than a heartbreak and a major breach of trust for you, along with so much else," I told her. My timbre matched hers. I didn't want to fight with Trina. I had no reason to be angry with her.

Unfortunately, she didn't feel the same about me.

"You know, I just can't stop thinking, if you hadn't come back…" Her words drifted off, but her meaning was clear.

"If I hadn't come back, this horrible secret would never have come out."

She nodded, as if ashamed and indignant at the same time. "Yes."

"And you would have lived the rest of your life with a lying murderer."

"But if it had never come out, we… we would have lived the rest of our lives just as before."

"Until when? Until Sam decided to murder again? How do we know Heather Cushing was his only victim?"

Her slap struck me unexpectedly. It was quick and retaliatory, and it was the only way she could respond to my accusation. She pulled back her hand and appeared to be surprised by her own action. My left eye teared above the red mark that formed on my cheek. I didn't strike her back. She had been hurt enough already.

"I don't want to prolong this meeting, Hunter. I found this letter crumpled among Sam's clothes, and I thought you should have it." She handed me a wrinkled piece of paper.

I took it from her and noted it was a typewritten message, but before I could actually read it, Trina cleared her throat to get my attention.

"I would prefer you look it over on your own time. I have things that need to get done."

"Is this the letter Sam found in my room?"

"Yes."

"Why call me over here at all, especially for this?" I looked up at her. "I have a copy waiting for me when I get back to

California."

"Because I don't want it in this house. And it is addressed to you."

"Did you read it?"

"Yes." She had the decency to look somewhat apologetic. "It's pretty harsh."

"No big surprise there. Why did you and Sam try to make me think Mom felt something positive toward me?"

"Sam…" It clearly distressed her just to say his name. "We didn't think you needed to know the extent of the hatred your mother felt for you."

"Extent? You mean it was even worse than I figured?"

"Your mother would go into a fit of rage at just the mention of your name. And that would be the highlight of any conversation regarding you."

I gripped the letter tightly, not sure how to respond. Finally, I said, "Trina, I'm sorry, sorry you ever married into this family. You and Eric deserved so much better."

She bit back a sob. "Please go. You know the way out."

If I had any deep-seated fantasy that there would be a fairy tale ending to the saga of my mother and me, that she would admit that she had overreacted and profess her undying love for me, such a hope was vanquished forever by the contents of the letter.

The tone of the missive was cold and blameworthy. She could very easily have written it to a total stranger, except the stranger's version probably would have contained more compassion. When I got back to Lisa's, I immediately handed it to her.

She accepted the paper from me. "What's this? What happened with Trina?"

"Trina is bitter and a tad hostile. Not that I blame her." I went to her refrigerator and took out a beer. Lisa followed me into the kitchen, removed the beer from my hand, and put it back in the fridge.

"You're on a heavy dosage of painkillers."

"I don't care," I said, reaching for the beer.

"I do." Lisa gently pushed my hand away and shut the refrigerator door. She tapped the paper I had given her and repeated,

"And this?"

"It's what Sam found in my room—a copy of the letter from my mother, telling me about the house."

"What does it say?"

"Read it," I told her, desperately wanting that beer.

Lisa smoothed it out and began reading aloud.

Hunter,

If you are receiving this letter, it means I have gone Home to my Heavenly Father. I would have said 'our' Heavenly Father but I can't imagine you have changed your ways from those of the Godless deviant who left this house at 18.

It is the house that is the subject of this letter. It appears that both of your brothers were involved in an incident that resulted in a death. I have not bothered asking for the details, because I'm sure it was the little whore who was at fault.

I have left the house to you in my will. It is a legal document that binds you to the structure and property.

Please do not be under the impression that this is a gift. I was recently made aware that the bones of the deceased have been hidden between the walls of the closet in your room. This knowledge leaves you with a decision. If you turn your brothers in and ruin their lives and the family name, it will be on your shoulders. If you spare them, it will be on your conscience.

"So," I interrupted. "She knew somebody would suffer, but she tried to set it up so that, either way, I would be the bad guy."

"This is unbelievable," Lisa muttered, shaking her head in disgust. "Are you sure you want—"

"Please finish."

We reap what we sow, and your unnatural, unforgivable sins have brought you to this pivotal point in your life. I believe your evil must have rubbed off on your brothers for them to have committed such an act. Your moral sense, if you have any, will be sorely tested by this decision.

Sarah Joelle Hunter Roberge

Lisa handed the letter back to me, stunned. "Wow. Nothing to even indicate she was your mom."

"I know."

"Amazing that your mother opted to stand by her sons, not caring about the circumstances that led to them committing a murder and then covering it up, while she disowned her daughter, whose only crime was loving someone of the same sex."

"I didn't love Jennifer," I said mildly.

"Your mother didn't know that. And obviously, she didn't care." Lisa was clearly aggrieved on my behalf. "How does that make sense? How could she perceive being gay as being worse than taking a life? How could she die feeling sanctified? How could she still think this made her more righteous or superior? She professed to be so obedient to the teachings of the Bible, yet she makes no judgment on them for committing murder."

"If I remember my commandments correctly, my brothers' transgression ranks number six, whereas my so-called sin never made it into the top ten."

Lisa's outrage was not dampened one iota. "How could she know her sons were harboring this terrible secret, help them keep it, continue to protect them, and then place the responsibility of their disposition on you?"

"Because she hated me. I was her easy out. I could have been as perfect as a child could possibly be, lived an exemplary life as an adult, and she still would have favored her sons over me."

"Why?"

"Because I wasn't her."

It took me days to recover from the import of what were, in essence, my mother's dying words to me. Though nothing she said was really much different than the negativity she had showered on me all my life, my need to hear something more positive from her, my longing for her approval and acceptance were embedded more deeply in my heart than I would have expected them to be.

When I heard there was a letter to me from my mother, deep down inside I wanted it to be an apology, a proclamation of tolerance, and an admission of guilt at how wrong her treatment of me had been. I would have settled for a simple, "I love you." Those three little words wouldn't have changed anything about my past with her, but they would have meant so much. The letter was her incontrovertible last word that my hope of being morally exonerated in her eyes was never going to come true.

I realized now she was the last person who should have judged anyone on their morals, and my wish that she absolve me for my "corrupted principles" was a foolish one. I was better than the needy little girl who had been emotionally starved by my mother's disinterest. I would have to find a way to deal with us never having been able to forgive each other face-to-face, as I guess I had always hoped. The impact of that reality hit me harder than I ever imagined it would.

Lisa continued to be my rock throughout the ordeal. While remaining upbeat and sensitive, she became my personal sentry. She not only kept a tight rein on who was allowed access to me, but she also continued to monitor my emotional state, ensuring I wouldn't sink too deeply into the abyss of self-pity. She unquestioningly understood when I needed to be alone to absorb all that had taken place and the implications of what it all meant. She held me at night and let me cry out of frustration or sadness or silently shake with anger, and she never once told me what I should be thinking or saying or doing.

She offered her opinion and her advice and her support, even when she didn't agree with me. She was there when I needed her and not there when she knew I needed to figure things out for myself. Had Fate somehow not brought this wonderful woman back into my life, I had serious doubts that I would have survived this living nightmare and the discovery that my immediate family was as unbalanced and disturbed as the generation before us and the one before that.

Lisa was seated across the table from me, having just poured me a cup of coffee. "Do you think I'm as deranged as the rest of my family? I mean the Roberge-Hunter family, not my Aunt Cissy or my Roberge cousins."

"No," she said, almost sounding defensive of me, then she softened her tone. "No, absolutely not. Do you?"

"I hope not. I'm... concerned... that I have that same mental illness gene, and it's lying dormant, but its eventual emergence is inevitable."

"Oh, Hunter, I would think it would have come to the surface long before now. You would have had some indication that it was there," Lisa said in a reassuring tone.

"But how would I know? I can hardly be objective. And, as many years as you've known me, you really don't know me as an adult. All you know about me, after I left here at 18 years old, is what I've told you."

"Have you lied to me about anything? Hidden anything from me that you thought might turn me against you?"

"No. But how do you know I'm not lying now?"

Lisa reached over and entwined her fingers with mine. "I don't. All I have is my gut, and that tells me you're nothing like them. As I recollect, you were never like the rest of your family. Your mother was too rigid, Sam was too accommodating, and Dane was too manipulative. I never met your father. All I know about him is what you've told me, and if you turn out to be anything like him, trust me, I won't tolerate it like your mother did. Your mother was a martyr, I'm not."

I squeezed her fingers. "As far as I'm concerned, I learned a hard lesson about cheating and abandonment from him. I don't ever want anyone in my life to have to learn that from me. I guess I get scared that mental illness is so prevalent in my lineage, I don't see how it could skip me."

"It hasn't shown up yet. Maybe if it's even in there, you have the tools to keep it tamped down. I think you're over-thinking the possibilities, but I'm not against a preemptive strike. If you like, I can recommend a couple of local therapists who, if you choose one, can do an initial intake workup and give you a pretty good idea of your mental or psychological standing."

"How do you know them? Do you trust them?"

"I know one through work and one from school, and yes, I think they're both competent and definitely respected. Just say the word, and I'll arrange an appointment."

I studied her. "You're amazing. Your family has threatened to disown you if you continue this 'scandalous' allegiance to me, you've lost friends and business associates because of your connection to me, and you're under the glare of a most unflattering spotlight because of me, yet you stay. Why?"

"Where else would I be? Was I supposed to turn my back on you because something reprehensible happened when you didn't even live here? Because your brothers committed a monstrous crime, was I supposed to level blame at you, too? Did you expect me to run away because of something you had nothing to do with? Guilt by association?"

"Others would have," I said quietly.

She smiled patiently. "I'm not 'others,' am I?"

"Definitely not. Someone else would have crumbled under the pressure."

"If I got intimidated every time somebody said, wrote, or thought something improper or appalling about me, I would never have had the grit to become an environmental lawyer. Or the mettle to be so open and unapologetic about my orientation in such a conservative little town as Otter Falls."

When Dane found out I had seen and spoken with Sam, he refused to see me. I don't know why he chose to throw a tantrum about that. I wanted to hear Dane's side of the story, but then, when it came to my younger brother and his typically narcissistic logic, there usually was no other side to a story. My guess was Dane figured that after speaking with Sam, tradition and experience would prompt me to not believe Dane. He couldn't have been more wrong. I really wanted to hear how closely Dane's description aligned with Sam's. Unfortunately, all I heard from Dane was what his attorney said at the press conferences: "The truth will come out at trial."

As much as I didn't want to be the focus of attention, I was caught in the media storm, especially since no one from the press was allowed access to either of my brothers. The local press stalked me everywhere. They doggedly asked me questions, and I had no answers that would ease anybody's conscience, so my response was always the same—silence. When I first got out of the hospital, the reporters were like a school of piranha, looking for flesh to rip into.

When they realized they would get no inside information from me, they moved on to another story or backed off until they uncovered a tidbit they could get their sharp little teeth into. Each press conference with the attorneys set off a feeding frenzy. Sometimes it was extremely hard to ignore the media, as their behavior and questions were often offensive and vicious in addition to being intrusive.

My aunt and my cousins, the *other* Roberges, were stunned by Sam's involvement, and despite Dane's frequent out-of-bounds behavior, they were still shocked at his participation. They knew I was an innocent bystander, and they rallied around me, my Aunt Cissy like a mother bear protecting her cub whenever anyone spoke ill of me around her. She, her children, and her grandchildren risked ostracism, but they remained loyal, doing their best to maintain my honor. When my fellow Otter Fallsians exhausted their tirades about my brothers without getting a rise out of me, then they would start insulting my sexual orientation. How my aunt and cousins didn't end up in jail on assault charges is something I will never know.

The day I returned to the outpatient clinic to have my stitches removed, I noticed a woman seated several chairs away from me who looked vaguely familiar. She was about my age, and I briefly wondered whether we had gone to high school together, as she was staring at me. By then it was difficult to differentiate whether a person was from Otter Falls or one of the pack of journalists I had seen around town.

I stopped thinking about the other woman in the waiting room when I was called into the sterile office. My stitches were quickly removed, and I made a follow-up appointment to have a recheck the next week. Before I left the building, I decided to use the restroom. I had just locked the door in one of the two stalls and unzipped my jeans when the bathroom door squeaked open. In the stall next to mine, the door opened, then closed and locked, and I saw a pair of expensive sneakers planted on the floor.

"Hunter? Hunter Roberge?"

"You've got to be kidding me," I snapped.

"Hunter, it's me, Davia. Davia Brownlow. From high school."

"Who?" I would have thought I would remember a name like Davia, even if it had been sixteen years.

"Day-vee-ya, from high school," she repeated, slowly and loudly, as if I were hearing-impaired and English wasn't my first language.

"I heard what you said. I don't remember you."

"Oh, Hunter, that hurts my feelings." You could tell she was speaking through a pout. It reminded me of Shirley Temple singing *On The Good Ship Lollipop*.

"Pardon me for questioning your timing, Dayveeya from high school, but what is it you want?"

"I was wondering if you would give me a statement for the local paper. You know, for old-times' sake."

"You work for the *Herald?*" *Oh my God, these people are shameless.* I decided I didn't need to use the facilities after all and zipped up.

"Yes. You may remember that I worked for the *Patriot* in school."

Suddenly it hit me. "Wait, didn't you have a nickname in high school? Dodo or something?"

"It was Dodi, but yes!" She seemed thrilled that I had remembered. "Sophomore year, I asked everyone to start calling me Dodi, based on my middle name, Delores. I began using my first name again when I began working for the *Herald* because it was more eye-catching."

"Well, Dodo," I said purposely, "you hated my guts in high school, so I don't see where I owe you anything for old times' sake." I pushed out of the stall. "I have no comment. I will never have a comment, at least not one that is fit for your readers' eyes."

"Oh, Hunter, don't be like that. That was so long ago."

"Okay, then, how's this for a statement?" Before she could exit her stall, I grabbed a heavy chair from the lounge area of the bathroom and pushed it up against her door, jamming it under the door lever, trapping her inside. I was going to pile the coffee table on top of that, but I didn't want to run the risk of reinjuring the area that was still healing. The door handle jiggled.

"Hunter?" The lever wiggled again. "Not funny, Hunter."

"No, it isn't, is it? You have a nice day, Dodo. For old times' sake."

As I left, she was slapping the door, and shaking it. "Let me out of here, Roberge!" She didn't sound so congenial anymore. She wasn't as slender as she had been in high school, l so I knew it would take her awhile to climb under the door to get out. In the meantime, I was going to make it as adventurous as I could for her.

When I left the restroom, I went to the desk. "Excuse me, but do you have an 'Out of Order' sign? It seems as if both toilets have a plumbing issue."

The busy receptionist hurriedly whipped out her black marker and wrote **Out of Order, Use Other Bathroom By Entrance** on a sheet of white paper. She handed me the paper and a roll of tape.

"Would you mind terribly sticking it on the door for me?"

Before I could answer, she picked up another ringing phone. "Hold a moment, please," she said to the caller. She smiled hopefully at me as she held up a heavy keychain. "Could you please lock the door so that no one ignores the sign and makes a mess in there?"

"Sure. No problem at all." I took the key and turned toward the bathroom.

"Make sure the room is empty before you lock it up," she called after me and turned back to the phone call.

Neither the dodo nor her newspaper bothered me after that.

I had stopped watching the news or reading the paper. I'd had my fill of reporters taking little tidbits of truth and distorting them beyond recognition. They had taken to interviewing my brothers' neighbors and co-workers, who knew nothing about anything.

Speculation became gospel, and anyone with the last name of Roberge got dragged through the mud by association.

Strangely, I found comfort in Orion, spending hours just stroking her mink-like fur while she curled up on my lap and tolerated my attentions. Why Mother had insisted on the cat being bequeathed to me was still a mystery. My best guess was that she remembered that the cat viewed me as a clawing post and an object on which to sharpen her teeth, so she tossed Orion into my inheritance to add insult to injury. If she could have guessed the cat would save my life, and the life of my very female lover, I have no doubt she would have made different arrangements for the sly Abyssinian's care after her death.

If I had been told a month earlier that I would ever be grateful to own this cat, I would have laughed myself sick. If I had been told a month earlier that both my brothers would be in jail awaiting trial for a twelve-year-old homicide they had covered up, that my mother had kept that secret from the moment she discovered it, and that I would meet my soul mate during the time that I spent in Otter Falls, I would have told the prognosticator that they were more insane than my loony relatives.

I sat on the back deck, using my good arm to toss a ball to Oz and Deke. The screen door slid open, and Lisa stepped outside and shut the door behind her. She had the phone tight to her ear, concentrating on the call. The dogs ran to her, circling her and yipping as though she had been gone for weeks instead of hours.

She sat down and petted the dogs, giving them each equal attention while she listened to the person on the other end of the line.

Finally she said, "Yes. ... Yeah, I'll tell her. ... You bet. Thanks, Ross." She pressed a button to end the call and set her phone on the patio table, then looked at the dogs. "Good boys. Go play now. Go on." Her tone was firm. Deke ran back to the ball in the yard, and Oz curled up by Lisa's feet. Lisa leaned over and gave me a quick kiss.

"Hi. What'll you tell me?"

She reached over and took my hand in hers. "Sam pled out."

Apparently Sam had changed his mind about talking to his lawyer. "What? When?"

"About an hour ago."

"Won't that screw up the immunity Dane was bartering for his testimony against Sam?"

"Yes."

"What, exactly, did Sam plead to?" Deke brought the slobbery ball to me. I threw it back out into the yard and wiped my hand on my pant leg.

"Voluntary manslaughter. Ross Franke, your brother's lawyer, reached out to the Cushings' attorney, and that was the deal they made."

"What are the terms?"

"Well… what he pled to was that Heather's actions provoked him, and he acted impulsively and without reflection in the heat of passion. He has to allocute to the court and to the family, pay restitution—"

"How much?"

"I don't know if the amount has been decided yet."

"Jail time?"

"He will be sentenced to twenty years at a maximum security facility in Virginia. He'll be eligible for parole in fifteen years."

"And the Cushings are okay with that?"

"They must be. They agreed to it. They probably didn't want to take the chance of Sam getting off on some technicality relative to Dane's confession. Our police department doesn't exactly have the best reputation for doing things by the book. The Cushings want to make sure Sam can never return to Vermont when he's released, but that condition is still under review. Also, he still will be tried for arson and attempted murder."

I was quiet as I tossed Deke's ball across the yard.

"Dane still insists on a court appearance, but his attorney advised him that now that Sam has made a deal, criminal proceedings would be a mistake and finding an impartial jury for a fair trial anywhere near Otter Falls would be damned near impossible. His attorney knows that abetting in a felony usually carries the same penalty as the felony itself. Voluntary manslaughter is a first-degree offense. Dane should start looking for a deal, too, because if he risks a trial, he might be facing life in prison."

"Dane is awfully pigheaded," I said.

"I know. He's in a lose-lose situation though."

"Think I should try again to talk to him?"

Lisa's gaze captured mine. "That's got to be your decision, baby. I know how dealing with Dane gets to you. My concern is that a meeting with Dane will set back your recovery."

I loved the intensity with which she looked at me. "I hope that doesn't happen. I wish this were all over, but honestly, I don't know if it will ever be over. As much as Dane irritates the shit out of me, it wouldn't be right if he's sentenced to more time than Sam. I'm not absolving him of his responsibility in the crime but..."

"I understand."

I wanted some kind of closure with Dane. "I'll call in the morning and find out whether he'll see me."

The metal detector at the correctional facility was silent as I passed through the frame. I took two steps forward and stuck my arms out to my sides, my body forming a T while an officer ran a wand over me as insurance that I was weapons-free. I could only partially lift my injured arm, but the officers accommodated that restriction.

After I had cleared security, I was escorted to a room similar to the one I had been in with Sam. I sat in another uncomfortable plastic chair and waited for Dane to be brought in. This time I didn't request that the officer stay outside. I didn't want to press my luck.

The noise of the electronic lock sliding back on the door to the jail side of the visiting room sounded incredibly loud in the quiet room. The door opened, and Dane shuffled in, accompanied by an officer twice his size.

Dane looked disheveled and exhausted, but most of all, he looked haunted. I doubted that he had ever thought he would get caught, much less spend any time behind bars. We stared at each other as he sat down opposite me. I was about to address him when the guard spoke.

"Hunter, how're you doing?"

I looked up at the massively muscled man, studied him curiously, and then squinted at his nametag. Machain. Then it hit me. Ryan Machain was the guy Lesley had the hots for in high school. "Ryan! Hi. Wow. You look… great." I wanted to say he looked steroidal, but I decided against it. No sense in being locked in a room with two hostile people.

"You look great, too. Well, considering everything that's been going on."

"Thanks, Ryan."

"Far be it from me to interrupt your happy little reunion," Dane snarled, "but I believe this is *my* visit, and Machain, you are barking up the wrong tree if you're looking to get hooked up. She only goes for indoor plumbing."

Ryan glared at Dane as he stepped back against the wall to assume his official position. "Watch your attitude, Roberge," he said, his demeanor now professional. "Good to see you, Hunter, regardless of the circumstances."

"You too, Ryan." I turned to my younger brother. "Hey," I said, "how are you doing?"

"How do you think I'm doing?" he snapped.

"Dane, why are you angry at me? I'm not the one who committed a crime."

"You were the one who got the ball rolling."

"Seriously? You're blaming me because you got caught? You're not taking any responsibility for your own actions?" I tried not to be annoyed with him, but he was making it difficult. "Is that why you agreed to see me? So you could blame me?"

"You've always had it in for me." He pouted like a child.

I drew a deep breath. "You never got in trouble because of me, Dane. Not ever. Name one time I caused you to be punished by our mother."

He was silent while he thought back on our childhood. Finally he said, "That doesn't matter, you still always hated me."

"I never hated you. I rarely liked you, but I never hated you. You're still my brother, and I love you."

My words must have caught him totally by surprise, because tears suddenly appeared in his eyes. "Bullshit," he said without any vehemence.

"Dane, you never gave me a chance to get close to you. I would've loved to have had you as an ally when we were growing up. You always played me against Mom. Even when you knew how hard things were for me, you always did your damnedest to make them worse."

"Because you always sided with Sam."

"No, usually Sam sided with me, and usually it had to do with something you instigated. I never had to side with Sam, because Sam never got in trouble. I refused to side with you because you never did anything to earn my allegiance." I tried to control the volume of my voice. "Face it, Dane, you were a pampered little shit growing up. You reveled in anyone else—mostly me—taking the brunt of punishment that should have been yours. It's the story of your life, and you're still doing it. You don't want to take any responsibility for me getting shot or for what happened to Heather Cushing."

"If Sam hadn't—"

"What? If Sam hadn't pulled me in front of him? If Sam hadn't tried to do you a favor by driving your horny little ass around the night Heather Cushing died?"

"Is that what he told you? That it was me who was doing her?"

His genuine shock made me take notice.

"Sam said you went to Heather's house to confront her about the way she treated you at the prom, and everything spiraled out of control from there. He said you wouldn't listen to him when he told you to leave her alone."

Dane stared at me, mouth agape. "And you believed him."

"Yes, I believed him. He admitted he murdered her. I even gave him the chance to say that you might have done it during his blackout, but he was adamant that Heather died by his hand." I suddenly had a bad feeling.

Dane's expression was truculent as he shook his head. "You're as much of a fool as I am. Sam the great. Sam the perfect. Yes, I did go to the prom with Heather, but only because Sam had arranged it.

He didn't want anyone else to be around her. Sam was the one fucking Heather, not me. It was Sam's big secret, and he entrusted me with it. I thought it would be a bond between us."

My head was beginning to pound. "Sam was having an affair with a sixteen-year-old girl?" If that was true, it went contrary to everything I believed about my older brother's character. "That makes no sense, Dane. Sam was married, and very much in love with Trina. Why would he risk his marriage, his job, and his reputation by sleeping with a child?"

"Well, it's an interesting thing, Hunter. It wasn't just one other woman, it was several. Heather was the only minor I knew about, but that doesn't mean there weren't others. Sam was a chip off the old block."

His words made me nauseous. But could I believe him? He had always manipulated facts to his advantage. Then I remembered something Sam had told me. I looked Dane in the eye and said, "And what about you, Minuteman?"

"What?" Dane seemed confused.

"Minuteman. Sam said to call you Minuteman."

He looked even more bewildered. "Why?" There was no hint of anger or embarrassment in his expression, just puzzlement. And my little brother had been many things, but never a good actor.

Deflating quickly, I mumbled, "Something about your sexual performance in the backseat with Heather that night."

"What! I wasn't in the backseat with Heather. I was in the front seat, driving. Did he tell you Heather and I were having sex?"

"Yes."

"Jesus! I don't believe him." Dane was incredulous. "That son of a bitch."

"What happened that night?"

"He needed my car because Trina had theirs. He also needed me as an alibi. Like I said, I went along with it because I thought it might bring us closer, but I was stunned when I found out he was screwing Heather. I mean... she was about my age. I was more surprised that *she* was with him. He was married, and she just didn't seem like that kind of girl."

"Didn't either of you give any thought to Trina in any of this?"

"No. Trina always could fend for herself."

I stared him down, and he bowed his head. "No wonder you've been married three times." He glanced back up, about to protest, but I put up my hand to stop him. "About that night?" I prompted.

"I picked Sam up and drove him to Heather's. Her parents weren't home, but I think Sam already knew they would be out. She got into the car, and Sam told me to drive around so they could mess around in the backseat. But instead of having sex, Heather told him she was pregnant. Sam freaked, to the point where he was making me nervous, so I pulled in to a rest area. He and Heather got out of the car, but the windows were down and they didn't exactly speak quietly, not even when he told her he would pay for an abortion. She said she wanted to keep the baby, and he told her she couldn't. She said she didn't want anything from him, because she knew he was married and she didn't want to ruin that. She just wanted the baby.

He told her there was no way. She said he couldn't force her to have an abortion. It just got worse from there. Sam got so angry. I'd never seen him like that before. He kept hitting her, mostly punching her in the stomach. He pushed her to the ground and I thought he was going to rape her, but... he strangled her." Dane's words choked in his throat.

"Didn't you try to stop him?"

"When I realized what he was doing, I tried to tackle him off her. He shook me off like I was nothing. By the time I got back to my feet, I could see she was dead. I started screaming at him, 'Sam, what did you do?' and, it was like he wasn't affected at all by what he had done, he was only worried about getting caught. We put her back in the car and drove around until Sam got the idea of dumping her in Sparrow Pond. You probably know the rest."

I knew the rest. "Why stash the remains between the walls in my room? What made you decide to put them there?"

"Sam saw it in a movie. He thought that because you were out of the picture, it was the best option."

I rubbed my face in frustration, outraged at my brothers' lack of conscience.

"Time's almost up, Roberge. Sorry, Hunter," Ryan said to me with an apologetic smile.

"Dane, you've got to talk to your attorney. The D.A. has already agreed to Sam's plea deal, so your plan to testify against him won't get you anything. Lisa said you could get life if you go to trial. Please talk to your lawyer about making a deal. Please." I reached over to take his hand, but Ryan cleared his throat and shook his head to warn me off touching the prisoner.

"You mean you actually care about me now?" Dane asked.

"Yes. I don't think you should get the full punishment for Sam's crime. Dane... I didn't know. I had no idea."

"Of course not. You got out. You did the right thing, Hunter. You escaped, just like Dad did. You wonder why he never looked back after he left? Probably the same reason as you. Your life changes when you're not constantly under a microscope. But living in Otter Falls is like being in a huge glass house. The stone throwing here just depends on who has the biggest rock. If you stay here, the only way to survive is to pretend everything is perfect."

"God, Dane, *nothing* is ever perfect. Especially life. You should have learned that from Mom."

Chapter 22

As was common with the Otter Falls grapevine, when Lisa got home from work the next day, she had all the details of the plea bargain Dane had worked out. After Oz and Deke settled at her feet by the couch, she reached over and covered my hand with hers.

"Dane's lawyer didn't waste any time after your brother called him. I think you seeing Dane was beneficial."

"Beneficial for whom?" Not me, I wanted to say. I was exhausted from all the emotional upheaval.

"Beneficial for everybody involved, as it turned out. Dane decided to plead to accessory, conspiracy, and impeding an investigation. He will receive fifteen years at Newport, a medium security farm facility near the Canadian border."

"Any chance of parole?"

"No. The Cushings wouldn't agree to parole being on the table, with only fifteen years on the books."

"Still, fifteen years is a pittance compared to the lifetime sentence he and Sam gave the Cushings."

"He also agreed to establish a Heather Cushing Memorial Scholarship, which would be presented to an Otter Falls high school senior each year to help out with their first year of college."

"Wow," I said, unenthusiastically. "I didn't know Dane had that kind of money."

"He'll have help. He'll initiate the fund with fifty thousand dollars. The Cushings are going to organize a celebration of life ceremony for Heather at their church and make the announcement that in lieu of flowers, they would prefer and appreciate donations to the fund. A separate bank account will be set up so that every year, near the anniversary of Heather's death, there will be an all-day fundraiser showcasing local musicians and entertainers. All proceeds will go into the memorial fund. Any expenses incurred by the fundraiser will be taken out of the separate account that Dane pays for."

"That was a lot to be arranged in one afternoon."

"Yes and no. Heather's family never did believe that she had just run away, as the police insisted. They had a lot of years to think about how they would like to honor her life if it was ever discovered for certain that she had been murdered. I think the surprise was that Dane and Sam agreed to their conditions so quickly."

"Why? They're guilty."

"There was always the chance one or both of your brothers would insist on going to trial to try for a not guilty verdict, even if it was a long shot."

"Well, good for my brothers. Somehow, I doubt either will ever grow a conscience, regardless of what they think they are 'giving back.'"

Lisa squeezed my hand. "Do you really think the impact of this hasn't affected your brothers' sense of right and wrong?"

"Right and wrong? My brothers are clearly sociopaths. Just look at their behavior. The only remorse they show is for getting caught."

"Being a sociopath usually means being antisocial," she said.

"Your brothers certainly have never outwardly exhibited antisocial behavior."

"Maybe they're like functioning alcoholics in that respect—they perform very well in societal situations, sometimes even being the consummate worker, spouse, or neighbor. In all other respects, they're normal. Deep down, they know something isn't right, but they're in denial until something else brings it to light."

"Hunter... you are not them."

Her gentle, comforting tone affected me, penetrating my wall of righteous indignation. I could feel the lump forming in my throat and that restricting sensation in my nose that instantly caused tears to sting my eyes. "Even Trina blames me instead of the two who committed the crime."

"No, she doesn't. Not really."

"Sure she does. She told me as much. I don't understand why there's no empathy. Can't Trina put herself in Heather's parents' shoes? What if it was Eric who went missing and the horrible truth came out a decade later? And where was my mother's empathy? She called Heather 'the little whore,' when it was her precious Sam who was really the little whore."

"Sweetheart, you've already admitted the psychiatric issues that plague your family. Their behavior goes beyond rational interpretation."

I couldn't stop the tears from escaping. "That doesn't make it any easier to deal with."

She pulled me into her arms and held me while I sobbed. "I know, baby. I know," she said.

I cried myself out, and she handed me a few tissues to blow my nose. "I feel so... betrayed and deceived and foolish."

"Foolish? Why?"

"Everyone in my immediate family is fucking pathological. I'm... frightened."

"The only way to combat your fear that you might carry the crazy gene is to start therapy as a preemptive strike. You've already agreed to do that."

"Yes. And to escape the embarrassment, I need to get the hell away from Otter Falls and never look back. It would help to not have to be confronted with the physical reminders every day. If I stay here, I will be painted with a stigma I don't deserve just because I share the same last name as murderers."

"Time will heal those wounds, and the stigma will fade."

"No. Not in Otter Falls." I knew she hadn't yet made a decision about whether she would go back to California with me or try to persuade me to stay in Otter Falls with her. If she really wanted to be with me, what I was saying would make the decision for her, one way or the other. "You know there are people in this town who live to make others miserable. My mother and her sisters were among them. I'd eventually relax, thinking the ordeal was finally in the past, and someone would start in on me again."

Lisa sighed. "Someone like Lesley."

"Yes."

Late the next morning, I left the County Clerk's office after making copies of the deed information on my mother's property. I dropped one copy off at the office of the Cushing's lawyer, and the other at the D.A.'s office. I suppose I should have been frustrated about what was going on with the disposition of my mother's house, but I wasn't. I was actually grateful all the decisions would be taken out of my hands.

Lisa had sent me a text message to call her when I left the attorney's office, so I dialed her number as I sat in the parking lot.

"That part's done," I told her tersely.

"Have you talked to Todd Jardine about it yet?"

"No. The office manager at the real estate firm had already informed me that Mr. Jardine will no longer be handling the sale of Mom's house. The contract was for three months, and he has chosen not to renew. There's too much notoriety and too many legal tangles."

"How does that affect the deal your brother made with the D.A., with the Cushings' blessing?"

"It really doesn't. The Cushing's lawyer—"

"Eli Lynch?"

"Lynch, right. Appropriate name for a lawyer," I mumbled.

"Better name for a judge."

"Anyway, he said that since the papers and the news programs have dwelled on the house being a secondary crime scene, morbid curiosity alone has stirred up a lot of interested buyers. Mostly from out of state."

"That, and the fact that the asking price has been lowered considerably."

"Yeah, well, that, too. Regardless, it's a hot property. Lynch told me that Jardine's participation is no longer necessary, and that the adjudicators will apply whatever the sale fetches against the total of whatever the Cushings' wrongful death suit is settled for. That includes the sale of the house and everything in it, minus their percentage, and whatever inheritance anyone was originally entitled to from my mother's modest estate."

"Are you okay with that?"

"Sure. I don't want anything of my mother's, and my brothers don't deserve anything. Besides, Lynch told me he was going to push for having my mother charged posthumously with being an accessory after the fact and obstructing justice for having failed to turn Sam and Dane in when she found out what they had done."

"Given the atrocious crime, I can't say as I blame Lynch for wanting to ensure that no one can come along and stake a claim on the assets." She suddenly seemed to remember she was talking about my mother and my brothers, as she added, "Sorry, Hunter."

"Don't be. Killing an underage girl because she inconveniently got knocked up with your baby after you've been having an affair with her behind your wife's back, and then being calculating about burying her? Yeah, that's pretty heinous. Just because my family was involved doesn't make it any less monstrous."

"Still—"

"It's okay. Really. I'd better let you get back to work. I'll see you at your place after I get a coffee."

We said our goodbyes and hung up.

As I walked the short distance to the corner entrance of The Coffee Break, a local breakfast and bakery establishment that was holding its own against big name rivals, I ran directly into my nephew.

"Aunt Hunter?"

A tall, towheaded young man with a few days' growth of ginger-colored beard stared at me, waiting for confirmation that his assumption was correct. "Um... I'm Hunter," I admitted hesitantly.

"It's me, Eric."

I took in the not-yet-filled-out form of the man-child. Since there was none of my family DNA in him, he didn't bear any family resemblance, yet there was a familiarity about him, and when he smiled, a deep dimple appeared on just one side of his face. It made his smile a little lopsided and was a telltale sign that this was indeed the mature version of the nine-year-old who was Trina's son.

"Eric! Good Lord, you've grown." I gathered him into a hug, pleased that he hugged me back without reservation.

"I hope so. I'm nineteen now. How big was I when you last saw me? Four feet tall?"

I released him and held him at arm's length. "Look at you. So handsome." I brushed my hand over his whiskers. "And this. Growing something, or too busy to shave?"

"I thought I'd try a goatee. Maybe. We'll see." He grinned then gestured at the café. "Were you going to get some coffee or something?"

"Yes, actually."

"Great. Me, too. Come on." He held the door open for me, and when I passed him, he said, "You're buying."

After we picked up our orders, we found a table in the corner that placed us away from the dwindling morning crowd.

"Jeez, Aunt Hunter, I don't know where to begin."

"I don't either, Eric." I rested my chin on my hand and studied him. Now that I got a good look at him, I could see that he was really starting to look like Trina. "I am so sorry all this happened. I'm assuming that's why you're home from school."

"No, I'm on break right now, but, yeah, it's… I'm shocked. If Dad hadn't confessed, I never would have believed it."

"Me, either, buddy." I lifted the coffee cup to my lips and blew on it before sipping. "How's your mom?"

"This really fu—" He glanced up at me, catching his near slip.

"It's screwed Mom up. She's a mess. At least we're finally almost done packing. She started divorce proceedings. She's going to court to take back her maiden name, and she wants me to legally change mine, too."

"I can't blame her." I set the cup down on the saucer.

"I know. Nothing personal, Aunt Hunter, but I'm not sure I'd want to keep the Roberge name even if Mom wasn't after me to change it."

"It is personal, Eric. Not to me, but to you and your mom, because you will be judged by your last name. There is so much access to information these days, if anyone Google's your last name, your dad's and uncle's crime will turn up as a matter of public record. Roberge isn't a common name. You don't want their mistakes following you around. Starting out in the working world is hard enough without having one or two strikes against you before you even begin. I have to agree with your mom."

"But I love my dad. Even with everything he's done. I was so happy and proud when he adopted me and gave me his last name."

"I love your dad, too, but I don't like him very much right now. And I'm pretty disappointed in him for the choices he made that cost an innocent girl her life. Her family didn't get the pleasure of living their daughter's milestones with her, and now you and your mom are being painted with his shame. You don't deserve that, and neither does your mom."

"Neither do you."

"No, but I can go back to my home, three thousand miles away, where l have a secure job and an established integrity."

"Is that what you're going to do?"

"I can't stay here."

"What about Ms. Riordan?" Eric grinned and blushed.

"You know about Lisa and me?"

His blush became deeper. "Mom told me."

I raised an eyebrow, and when he wouldn't look up from his coffee cup, I said, "Does that bother you?"

"No. No, Aunt Hunter, not at all. My roommate is gay. I think if Ms. Riordan makes you happy, then it's nobody's business but yours." I smiled at him, and he broke into a grin. "And she's kind of hot."

"I think so, too." We each sipped our respective beverages. "Is your mom still going to move back to St. Johnsbury?"

"Yeah. Grandma can't wait."

"When is she leaving?"

"As soon as her attorney has filed all the legal paperwork. I think she has a meeting with the bank tomorrow."

"I had to do the same thing. The paperwork is in progress. I just have to wait for the call to go back and sign and notarize."

"Are you going to be able to stop and see us before we leave?"

"Your mom and I said our goodbyes already. She doesn't want me to keep in touch," I said with no malice in my tone. "But, here."

I grabbed a clean, handy napkin out of the holder and took a pen out of my satchel. "Here's my number and address." I wrote them down and pushed the napkin across the table to him. "I'd love it if you'd keep in touch. Even better, you could come visit me sometime."

He perked up. "Seriously?" He folded the napkin and put it in his pocket. "I'd love to. Thanks, Aunt Hunter."

By the time I was physically healed and legally disentangled so that I could leave Otter Falls, I had been there for three months.

Fortunately, my boss had granted me leave under the Family Medical Leave Act clause that cited "not being able to work due to a serious health condition." I had knowingly accepted the possibility of getting shot while I was on the job, but never suspected that it could happen in Otter Falls, Vermont, while on bereavement leave.

Life in the fishbowl had actually started to settle down, when Lisa and I went and stirred it all up again.

"Lisa, listen." I had her attention, but I didn't know what to say next. I'd had this conversation in my head a hundred times. In every made-up chat, the outcome was always favorable for me. Now that the actuality of the discussion was upon us, I wasn't so confident.

"Yes? I'm listening."

"We haven't had *the* talk yet and—"

Laughter bubbled out of her, and she said, "Hunter, I had 'the talk' when I was twelve."

"Not that talk." I chuckled nervously. "We need to make a decision."

"About?"

"About whether you're staying here or coming to California with me."

Lisa cocked her head. "Sounds like your decision has already been made."

"I can't stay here." I didn't think this was an unexpected or grand declaration. If she had been paying attention, she already knew there was no other conclusion I could come to.

She folded her arms across her chest. "Let me ask—had this not happened with your brothers, was there ever a chance you would have considered moving back here?"

I considered carefully before I answered. "The idea of being without you is physically painful to me. Before all hell broke loose, I would have seriously looked into the possibility of staying, if it meant being with you."

"Really?" The single word held a hint of skepticism.

No flood of words would convince her if she didn't already know what was in my heart, so I didn't try to convince her.

"Really."

"Right answer," she said, stepping up to me and pulling me into an embrace.

It took me a minute to catch on to what she meant. "Wait... are you saying that you'd be willing to give up everything here to come with me?"

"I would. I mean, yes, I will."

"Just like that? No discussion, no debate?"

"There's been an internal debate, and I already weighed all the pros and cons because I knew you would ask me. At least, I was hoping you would ask."

I kissed her, a gesture of gratitude, which quickly turned into passion. She broke the kiss and tucked her head into the crook of my neck. "Boy," I said, "are my friends going to kid me about us being the epitome of the lesbian U-Haul joke."

She laughed. "You're tough. You can take it," she teased. "Be back in a minute." She left me and went into the kitchen. As I shared the big news with the dogs, who didn't seem to grasp the excitement of it, I heard a cork pop.

Lisa returned to the living room carrying a tray with an open bottle of wine and two glasses, which she set on the coffee table.

"Hunter…" she said hesitantly. "There's one more thing I would like to discuss with you." She sat next to me on the living room floor in front of her gas fireplace. She reached over and took my hand in hers, entwining our fingers, and passed me a glass with her free hand.

"Okay."

"I know this isn't the setting I wanted, but… oh well, here goes. Hunter Roberge…" She took a deep breath. "I've dreamed of this my whole life. Will you marry me?"

The look on her face reflected both her anticipation and her trepidation. Her proposal surprised me, but it shouldn't have; it was clear that we were heading in the direction of some form of commitment.

"Married. Wow. That's… that's a big step." I tried to keep my voice level so as to ensure that it didn't express any emotion other than contemplation. "You mean, get married before we leave Vermont?"

"Well, it's something we can't do in California. Yet." She sounded hopeful.

I set my glass on the coffee table, removed the glass from her hand, and set it next to mine. I took her hand. "Come here," I said, pulling her closer. "I would love to marry you." A delighted, relieved smile lit her face. "But…"

Her smile faded. "But? There's a 'but'?"

"A lot has happened in the last three months. You are certainly the best of it. In fact, you may be the best thing that's happened to me, ever."

"But?" She searched my face for rejection.

"But I don't want to screw it up." She drew a breath, and my fingers stilled her lips. "Please hear me out." She nodded and settled back, her hands in mine. "You have been my anchor throughout this whole stormy mess. You've seen the worst side of my family, the worst side of me, the worst of just about everything, and still you've been the one solid thing, other than Aunt Cissy and my cousins, that I have been able to hang onto. Nothing that has happened while we've been together has even come close to being normal."

Oz bounded into the room with Deke right behind him, followed in close pursuit by Orion. She had them running for cover.

"I'm surprised the old girl still has it in her. They must have stolen some of her Kibble," I said.

"I'm going to let the boys out to run off some of that energy."

Lisa pulled free of my hands. She stood up and went to the patio door, whistling for the dogs and letting them out back. She closed the door and returned to her spot on the floor. "Brrr." She folded her arms across her chest.

"Lisa, I love you. There isn't a single doubt in me that our feelings are true and deep. There's nothing that would make me feel more complete than marrying you."

"There's still a 'but' in there."

"I think we should wait. I want to make sure that when we say 'I do,' we're both certain of what we're getting ourselves into. I want us to have every chance at making it, and I'm not so sure it would be fair to either one of us to jump into marriage without first seeing if we can handle each other."

The smirk on her face was downright bawdy. "Oh, I think we've been handling each other just fine." Her voice was husky, suggestive.

I felt a blush crawl up my neck and into my cheeks. "Oh, we're fine in that area. Not that I don't want to continue working on perfecting anything that isn't."

Lisa grinned. "Practice makes perfect."

"Exactly." I waited while the pink left my cheeks. It was difficult to think about sex with Lisa and not feel the heat suffuse me inside and out. We were most definitely compatible in the bedroom; in fact, I had never met anyone in my life who was so in tune with my needs and desires. It was as though we instinctively knew how to satisfy each other. That had never happened with anyone before her.

"Hunter, I know we need more to build a life on than just a phenomenal sex life."

"We do. We—Wait... phenomenal? Really?" That kicked

my ego up a few notches.

Lisa laughed and swatted at me. "Like you didn't know."

"I knew we were good, but I like phenomenal much better." I cleared my throat, hoping to reset my brain on the train of thought I had been pursuing before the visual of our lovemaking had derailed it. "Lisa, you said you've been dreaming about this your whole life.

Before Fate drew me to the bar the night of your birthday, you were just Lesley's tagalong sister. I had no idea I was about to meet the love of my life. You've got to give me a chance to catch up. You've loved the idea of Hunter Roberge for a long time, and that's a lot for me to live up to. I don't want to be a figment of your dreams. By the time we marry, I want to be sure that we know we are in love with each other, not with what we've built each other up to be. I don't want to be an illusion. I want you to know who I really am, and I want you to want who I really am. I want to be your forever love, which is why I think we should wait."

There were tears brimming in her eyes. She was smiling when she leaned forward and kissed me. "You haven't disappointed me yet. A year won't make any difference. I can't see myself ever falling out of love with you."

"I hope not."

She kissed me again, lingering this time. When she broke the kiss, she cupped my face in her hands. "So, does this mean we're engaged?"

"I believe it does. Wedding date to be determined." I nodded toward the glasses of wine. "Shall we toast our engagement and your upcoming relocation?"

"Absolutely." She picked up the glasses and handed me mine.

"To us and to our future."

I raised my glass. "To the eventually-to-be Lisa and Hunter Riordan."

Stunned, she nearly dropped her glass. "You want to take *my* last name?"

"You don't think I want to keep mine, do you? Besides, I

can't think of a better *gift* for your sister." I arched my eyebrow.

She shook her head. "You're so bad. I love that about you." We clinked our glasses together and toasted our future.

I was deliriously happy with my brand new fiancée and our family of two middle-aged dogs and a cranky, elderly cat. We might be a little out of place in Otter Falls, but we would be right at home in Glendale. I already had a like-minded circle of friends there, and aside from missing all that was familiar to her, I knew Lisa would settle in, just like I had. The news that we were engaged and that I would take the Riordan last name nearly gave Lisa's mother and sister apoplexy. Life was good.

Her parents and sister didn't renounce her, as they had initially threatened, but things between them were somewhat thorny, especially when I was around. Lesley refused to speak to me or even look in my direction, which was fine with me. I had lived over half my life without her in it, I figured I could manage. I felt badly for Lisa, although she insisted it wasn't that big of a deal. She told me that if Lesley was going to behave like a horse's ass, then she could certainly be treated like one. Mr. and Mrs. Riordan promised Lisa that they would visit her, but I wasn't going to hold my breath, considering that Lisa and I were now a package deal.

Lisa and I worked with the district attorney's office to resolve the charges against my brothers for the attack on me. I didn't want to hang around any longer than I had to, and going forward with two trials for Sam and one for Dane would have wreaked more havoc on me in the long run. Sam pled to another deal that added five years to his original sentence. His lawyer requested that his sentences be served concurrently, but I was okay with the judge ordering Sam to serve it after he finished his present stretch. I was still quite angry with Sam for lying to me, especially during the opportunity he'd had to bare his soul. I would have preferred he told me nothing rather than inciting sympathy in me through a confession grounded in fiction. Dane, even though he was the one who shot me, was sentenced to two years of probation to be served after he had served his time for

Heather's murder. That meant, once I left Otter Falls, I was not legally obligated to return, and that was just fine with me.

I couldn't believe that once we made the decision to leave, everything seemed to fall into place. Lisa had arranged for reliable legal representation for her clients, closed her practice, and sold her house to a nice gay couple that moved to the state to get married and live peacefully. We were on our way to the closing on Lisa's house.

"I hope they know what they're getting into," I said, as we waited at a stoplight.

"Who?" Lisa asked.

"Charles and Wes, the guys who bought your house."

The light turned green and we began moving again. "They seemed really excited about living here. Come on, Hunter, this is a nice place."

"Aesthetically, it's gorgeous. Especially in autumn."

"Sweetie, I know you are so over Otter Falls right now, and you have every reason to be, but this could be a decent place for them to start a new life. They came here to get legally married."

I pressed my lips together to stop myself from telling her I thought she was clueless because she had lived here all her life.

"I'm not knocking Vermont's progress in that area. What I am saying is that the state may be accepting of their legal right to marry, but do you think they researched this area well enough to know that there are many more conservatives than liberals here? This isn't Burlington. Hanging rainbow flags and advertising their orientation is only going to bring out the radical fringe."

"I've always found this to be a 'live and let live' state."

"Sure. As long as you keep your differences to yourself."

"I haven't done too badly here."

"Yes, but you've never really lived anywhere else," I said finally. "Otter Falls is the type of city where if you're born here, grow up and go to school here, get married here, have children here, and either own your business or inherit your family business, you're golden. Even if you continue the family legacy by working in the same factory your parents and grandparents worked in, that's all that's expected of you."

"That's not entirely true," Lisa argued mildly.

"But it is." I was trying not to sound defensive. "The populace doesn't like change or progress unless it somehow puts money into the pocket of the city or town. And even then, if it isn't a conventional business, chances are it's likely to fail."

"What about Ira Portnoy? He owns the jewelry store on South Central Street. He's a success, and he's open about his sexuality and nobody cares."

"Yeah, they do. They're grateful that his business has boosted the downtown economy and tourist spending, but his 'lifestyle'—as they still call it—is the constant source of gossip and ridicule."

"This is Otter Falls. They do that to everybody."

"It's different when you're gay or lesbian, Lisa, and you know it. The message is very clear. The money we bring to town is welcome, we are not."

"Baby, please don't say anything to them about your misgivings. I know you won't be happy until we leave, and we aren't going to be able to sell to anyone local."

"My point exactly! Because of who you are and my family's notoriety."

"I've been as up front as I can be with Charles and Wes, and they seem to be okay with everything. Charles is from the mountains of Pennsylvania. He's the first one to say that's about as backwoods as you can get there. He knows firsthand that part of Pennsylvania is still fighting the Civil War, on the side of the South.

His contention is that if they can survive there, Vermont will be a breeze for them."

"True," I conceded. "Otter Falls definitely isn't *that* far behind the times." But it was close. "I think you'll be able to see what I mean once we get to California."

"So you're trying to tell me that California doesn't have homophobia?"

"Every place has homophobia to some extent. And yes, there are still hate-related crimes there. They just aren't as prevalent or swept under the rug as they are in more rural areas that rail against progress."

"But California is obstructionist in moving forward with legal rights. What about that constitutional amendment that was passed in 2008 that stated marriage is only legal between a man and a woman?"

Hunter grimaced. "We're working on that. Look, all I'm saying is that where I live, gays and lesbians aren't freaks. We aren't so in the minority. We're more accepted as mainstream. There are businesses, recreation, and churches that cater specifically to our community. And the weather is better," I threw in for good measure.

"I'm glad we're having this discussion now as opposed to in front of Charles and Wes. You might convince them to move to California instead of here."

I certainly didn't want that. I kept my mouth shut during the closing, right up until I offered my congratulations to the happy couple when Lisa handed over the keys.

We hired a moving company to transport the combined personal belongings we had agreed to keep, to be delivered to my storage area at my apartment complex. It would be a temporary arrangement until we found a house to buy. We purchased a previously-owned, forty-five-foot recreation vehicle, packed up Orion, Oz, and Deke, and began our journey to California, where we would embark on a new life together.

I still couldn't believe I was actually going to get married. That was certainly something I hadn't foreseen on my flight to Vermont three months earlier. There were so many things that wouldn't have happened at all, had my mother not died. I studied the rose-gold promise band on my left ring finger and thought about what it represented. When I looked at the matching ring on Lisa's finger, I couldn't stop grinning. When I left California, I was single, lonely, indifferent, and emotionally empty. I was returning with a fiancée who made me feel whole and respected and deeply loved.

I wasn't exactly sure what would happen once we reached

our destination, but I knew, if I chose to, I would finally be rid of any ghosts that haunted my past. I would be free to start a future with the extraordinary woman seated next to me, who, at my insistence, was highlighting tomorrow's route on the map. She just wanted to close her eyes, place her finger on the map, and chart a course from there. She wanted to go wherever the road would take us.

I think the willingness to go anywhere and try anything as long as we were together was going to be the template for our shared life.

Author Cheyne Curry
Photo by Lida Verner

About the Author

Cheyne Curry was born in Vermont, raised in New York and spent a majority of her adult life being bicoastal. She has lived in Monterey, Pebble Beach, Ventura, Hollywood, West Hollywood, Studio City and Palm Springs, California as well as spent time in Alabama, Minnesota, Pennsylvania, Massachusetts, Delaware and Italy.

Most of her work experience is law-enforcement related. She was a Military Police officer in the US Army, a civilian police officer, a federal police officer, a civilian correctional officer, a private investigator, a surveillance agent, and in entertainment security management.

Cheyne, a drummer and rhythm guitarist, currently spends her time writing books, sketching, composing music and writing screenplays for short films, some of which can be viewed at her website: www.cheynecurry.com

She now lives in the Midwest with her wife, Brenda, and their 3 fur kids, Liam, a shepherd-mix, Mesa, a black mouth cur and Belladonna Bossy Pants, a neurotic black cat who runs the house. All are rescues.

The Tropic of Hunter was a finalist for The Golden Crown Literary Society's Ann Bannon Popular Choice Award in 2014.

OTHER TITLES BY CHEYNE CURRY

PREVIOUSLY PUBLISHED

Clandestine Tia Ramone is a gritty, self-destructive, ex-CIA operative who seeks absolution in a bottle. Jody Montgomery is a naïve heiress to a vast fortune, married to a man she discovers she really doesn't know. Tia's and Jody's paths cross in a sinister plot they are forced to take part in. With both their lives at stake, can the clandestine meeting that brought them together ultimately be the bond that saves them?

Renegade What would you do if one minute you were in the 21st century and the next you were in the 19th? One day you're driving a Mustang and the next day you're riding one? Dirty cop Trace Sheridan faces this dilemma as she moves from a present day mob war to a range war over a hundred years in the past. The year is 1879, when cattle barons, crooked lawmen, saloons, painted ladies, cowboys and Indians ruled the Wild West, and laws were only as strong as the gunman who upheld them. In Sagebrush, the town and the sheriff belong to the Cranes, who take what they want or bad things happen. Trace finds this out firsthand when she ends up on the land of Rachel Young, a struggling ranch woman who won't give in to the merciless cattle baron and his obsessed son. For some unexplainable reason, Rachel trusts the enigmatic Trace who uses 21st century sensibilities to battle 19th century turmoil, while Trace is forced to keep the secret of her origin from the attractive and vulnerable Rachel. Renegade is a story of redemption in its purest form as Trace discovers what truly matters in life and how past really is prologue.

COMING SOON:

Permission To Recover   It's 1977 and Army CID agent, Lieutenant Dale Oakes is awaiting a medical discharge when she is reactivated by her former commanding officer and secret crush, Lieutenant-Colonel Anne Bishaye. Dale is planted into the first, experimental, co-ed OSUT (One Station Unit Training) company. Her assignment is to spend at least 16 weeks to expose who is setting up drill sergeants, giving the battalion a black eye. She and her undercover partner, Lt. Shannon Walker, get caught up in a whirlwind of unintentional intrigue while trying to keep their cover as new recruits and military law enforcement trainees. Dale discovers much more than is ever intended about the case and herself, as well. Can Dale and Shannon solve the mystery before time runs out?

www.ingramcontent.com/pod-product-compliance
Lightning Source LLC
Chambersburg PA
CBHW071136260626
47162CB00003B/811